Maybe Baby

a novel

Kim Golden

ECHO BOOKS
STOCKHOLM, SWEDEN

Published: Kim Golden/Echo Books
Cover design: Arijana K./Cover It! Designs
Cover image: Christopher Bernard/iStockphoto.com
Book Layout: ©2014 BookDesignTemplate.com
Publishing assisted by **Black Firefly**

(Shedding light on your self-publishing journey)

http://www.blackfirefly.com/

To my gorgeous, noisy muse.

You know who you are.

I love you always.

Contents

CHAPTER ONE

Things Better Left Unsaid

I want to have a baby."

The words flew out of my mouth before I even had a chance to properly register them. But saying them—sending them out into the orderly world that was my life with Niklas—felt good. Cathartic, even. I wanted to have a baby. It had been bouncing around in my head for months now, the invisible sleeping giant that shares our apartment and takes up a tad bit too much space.

Niklas stopped tapping a text message long enough to flash a slightly amused smile at me. He set his iPhone on the leather seat of the Lincoln Town Car cruising us towards Newark Liberty Airport and patted my thigh. "Since when?"

He didn't sound flummoxed or annoyed or encouraging. He was using that neutral-with-a-twist voice he reserved for his clients when they called at inopportune moments. I didn't want him to switch to that voice. I wanted him to sound like normal Niklas, not like Niklas the therapist who was going to try to get me to talk about my feelings and the triggers for why I had these feelings. He was probably already working out a way to explain this desire.

He waited for me to elaborate.

I didn't. Instead, I repeated my initial statement. "I want to have a baby."

"Yes, I heard you the first time. My question to you is why you have this sudden desire to have a baby."

"It's not sudden." I angled my legs away from his, dislodging his hand. He slid it back toward his phone. I knew what was happening now. He'd finish sending his text message. He was probably updating his kids or his ex-wife with our expected arrival time in Stockholm. We'd been in the US for five weeks, part of the deal that kept me afloat during the long winter months in Stockholm. Three weeks, every summer, in the US so I could get my much-needed dose of America, of sunshine and candy and proper bagels and shopping. It was a trip that usually filled me up until at least the end of January. Then two more weeks someplace warm like Thailand or Bali to escape the winter darkness for a while. I squeezed the hell out of memories of digging my toes in sand that warm, not chillingly cold like at our summerhouse in southern Sweden. I went crazy ordering too many deliveries of Vietnamese food to the various apartments we borrowed from friends and family, because I wouldn't have this luxury in Stockholm. Swedes didn't "do" home delivery of food. It was one of the many things I learned to accept since I moved to Sweden.

"Well, you've never expressed any interest before in children." Niklas sent his text, and then inserted his iPhone in his leather duffle bag. "You barely even get along with my kids."

"Your kids are teenagers. And I do like them. They just don't like me."

"Laney, come on." He smiled indulgently at me.

"You know it's true. Siri has never liked me, and Jesper... I don't even know what he thinks."

"Jesper likes you, trust me."

"As long as Siri isn't around—"

"Is that why you want to have a baby?"

"What? No, don't be an idiot, Niklas. I want to have a baby because I love you—and we've been together five years—and I always assumed we'd start a family of our own."

"We have a family together—we've got Siri and Jesper."

"Siri and Jesper are your kids with your ex-wife." I stared at the back of our driver's head and wondered what he made of our conversation. He'd probably heard it all before. "They're not my kids."

"Semantics, Laney. You and I are a couple, so my kids are your de facto kids."

"I don't think they see it that way," I reminded him. He knew his daughter was only civil to me when he was around. His kids didn't really like me in his life. And while I tried to ingratiate myself to them, tried to put on a front of family unity because I didn't want to rock the boat too much—I had to admit that I was not always too fond of them, either.

Siri, who was eighteen, behaved as though our apartment in the Vasastan section of Stockholm was a flophouse. She showed up at all hours of the night, with whichever boy she picked up at the multitude of bars and clubs she frequented, and had ear-shattering sex in the bedroom that was hers whenever she chose to visit. Niklas pretended not to hear her nighttime antics. He said she was an adult, and it was not his job to keep track of whomever she chose to sleep with.

Jesper, his son, was not as vile. In fact, when Siri was not around, he was quite sweet. He helped around the house, asked for my advice about the girls he was interested in, even asked if I'd help him with homework he didn't understand. But the moment Siri appeared, he turned sullen and incommunicative. And he became a willing participant of any nasty prank she concocted.

Niklas thought this was a phase his children were going through—a very long phase of adjusting to the "new" woman in their father's life. He said we needed to meet it with patience and understanding. Lots and lots of patience and understanding. And I was trying, believe me. I'd known his kids since they were ten and thirteen, but five years was a long time to wait for them to become accustomed to me. And, really... they were nearly adults now. How much more of this should I have to take? Even in the name of love?

Neither of us spoke again until the familiar sights of Manhattan faded and we edged closer to New Jersey and the airport. Niklas tried to lighten the mood by stroking my hand and saying, "You know, we can't take a baby back to Bloomingdale's if we don't like it."

There was a gentle teasing to his voice. I knew he wanted to smooth away any conflict before we boarded the plane and returned to Sweden. Conflict was not his forte. Even with his being a therapist. Any argument brought his insecurities about our relationship to the surface. He tried to joke these away.

But I was not in a joking mood. "I'm not Siri," I retorted, knowing I sounded petulant. "I am well aware you can't buy babies at a store. I don't think it's unreasonable to want to start a family if we love each other."

"Laney, I'm sorry, I don't mean to tease you." He kissed my cheek. Not even breathing in the clean scent of his skin knocked away my annoyance. "But... baby, you know I had a vasectomy. I had it after Jesper was born."

Another pregnant pause. I didn't even know how to respond to that. I wouldn't have forgotten he'd had a vasectomy. Had he ever even told me? Or was this like so many things he'd neglected to tell me that he sprang on me with a "But you know this..." or "I told you about this already..." I didn't think I knew this when we decided to get together. I would have remembered.

"You never told me you'd had a vasectomy."

"I did, Lanes. Back when we first moved in together, I told you about it."

"Vasectomies can be reversed."

"I don't want to reverse it."

"So you love me enough to get me to stay in Sweden, live there with you, and help you raise another woman's kids... but not enough to have a child with me."

"Now you are putting words in my mouth, Laney, and that isn't fair at all."

"Life isn't fair," I quipped. "Isn't that what you're always telling me and your patients?"

"And you're being childish."

"Don't you think you're being selfish?"

"I don't want to have any more children. That's why I had a vasectomy. After two rounds of sleepless nights and potty-training and the terrible twos and threes... even with how great it was watching my kids grow up, I don't want to deal with that again."

"I always thought we would have a family."

"We do have a family," he said for the third time. He looked flummoxed. He wasn't used to me standing my ground. This was my fault. I usually gave in to whatever he decided. Not all the time. But often enough that it put us off balance. "We have Siri and Jesper."

"Siri and Jesper aren't my kids! They're Karolina's children." Karolina was the one who ruined Niklas for other women, or at least she liked to tease him with this on those occasions when we are all together. Which was often. They'd remained friends despite the divorce. He called her for advice. They spoke on the phone nearly every day. In too many ways, it felt like they were still married, even with our five years together.

"You and me, Laney, we're a family, we always have been."

"We're a couple."

"We're more than a couple. After five years together, we've earned the title 'family.'"

"But..."

"Baby, we can talk about this later. It's not really the sort of conversation I want to have in front of a stranger."

I glanced at the back of the driver's head. I acquiesced too easily. It wasn't until we'd checked in, gone through the security check and were safely ensconced in the business class lounge that it occurred to me our driver wouldn't have understood a word we were saying. He didn't even react. Of course he didn't.

We were speaking Swedish the entire time.

CHAPTER TWO

The Best Decisions Are Made Over a Bloody Mary

It took several days before I even broached the baby subject again. I'd waited, swallowing my anger at his blatant avoidance of the issue. We slept in the same bed without touching one another. Now it was Sunday and we were reading the paper in our kitchen in Vasastan. Croissant crumbs and blobs of lemon marmalade dotted the tabletop, vying with the messy pile of Swedish and English-language newspapers. I pushed aside my *New York Times*. There was no way I could concentrate on any of the articles when all I could think of was how to bring Niklas around to the possibility of our having a baby.

We lived in a turn of the century building on Dalagatan with a view of Vasaparken and the Astrid Lindgren memorial. Our kitchen had none of the Art Nouveau charm of the rest of the building—it was sleek and modern, with polished concrete countertops and seamless cabinets that had no handles. The walls were painted a warm shade of white called "Stockholm White," the floor a slate so dark it looked black. Everything in this kitchen screamed "Modern." When we first moved into the apartment, it still had its original kitchen with cabinets from the early 1900s. The appliances had been updated in the 1990s, but otherwise the kitchen looked as one imagined it would have in the days when August Strindberg still reigned supreme in Stockholm. Then we moved in and Niklas, who'd loved the old kitchen when we bought the apartment, decided it was not functional enough for us and hired a contractor and an architect to completely revamp not just the kitchen, but also the entire apartment. The only thing left from the old days was the tiled stoves towering in corners of our living room and bedrooms. It was a showplace of an apartment. It was bigger than the row house I grew up in West Philadelphia, and its sheer size was overwhelming. I used to be so proud of it. It reminded me of something from a fairytale with its intricate crown molding, gracefully old-fashioned chandeliers and creaking parquet floors. Now it felt more like Niklas's place than our place. I missed the way it used to be.

"We could adopt a child," I said. "That could be a good option for us, couldn't it?"

"Maybe." Niklas didn't look up from the main section of Svenska Dagbladet. He coughed and reached for his glass of orange juice.

I'd tried not to think about babies since we arrived home from New York. Instead I'd focused on getting over my jet lag with Melatonin tablets and returning to work. But the thought of a baby—our baby—niggled at me. I spent more time Googling adoption processes than catching up on my new project at the agency.

"We could get help from Adoptionscentrum," I continued, hoping I could snatch his attention away from the woes of the western world. "We're in a perfect situation. We have a stable relationship, a good income... we're both healthy."

"I'm healthy," Niklas corrected. "You smoke."

"Not often."

"They won't care if it's once in a while or every day." Niklas finally lay the paper aside. "You smoke, so that's a strike against you."

"Niklas, be serious."

"I am being serious, my darling." But he was grinning at me, like he thought all of this was an amusing way to pass the time. "Besides, you know these adoptions take forever. You may as well adopt a rescue dog."

"I don't want a goddamn dog. I want us to start our own family. You and me, together."

He sighed. "You know, I was talking to Karolina about this..."

"You discussed this with Karolina?"

Niklas nodded. "It came up in conversation, yes."

"Why would you even discuss something so private with your ex?"

"Laney, calm down. I simply mentioned to her that you wanted to have a baby."

He was so matter of fact about it. God damn him!

"You know how much I hate it when the two of you discuss things about us that are private," I retorted, my voice escalating. I could already feel my skin growing hot. My throat went tight. "Our private life is not something you should be discussing with your ex!"

Niklas folded his hands in front of him. "I don't understand why you feel so threatened by Karolina."

"I think you know exactly why I don't want her to know, Niklas." I didn't even want to bring up his past transgression with her. We'd discussed it so often that it was more like a blister that never healed properly. "I don't feel threatened by her, Niklas. I just don't want you discussing anything that has to do with me, with us, with your ex. Talk to me instead."

"Laney, I don't feel comfortable with the conditions you're putting on me."

"Would you want me discussing our sex life with one of my exes? Shall I start asking Jens for advice during our coffee breaks?"

He tapped his index fingers on the tabletop. "You can discuss whatever you like with Jens." He smiled again but it was the bland smile I'd seen him use with annoying neighbors. He didn't like being reminded of Jens, or any other man who'd been in my life before him.

"So it's all right if I go to work tomorrow and dissect your predilections with my ex? Maybe I should ask him about using a vibrator on you, considering some of the other things we've done together."

"You've made your point, Laney."

"Good." I took advantage of the situation. "So, now... about adoption, I was thinking we could adopt a child from Africa. Initially, I considered the US, but there's just too much red tape."

"You know it's going to take at least a year," Niklas said.

"That's not so bad." It wasn't, not really. If I could wait nine months to have a baby the natural way, I could wait a year to meet my adopted child.

"It could take longer. I've heard of adoptions that take almost three years to finalize."

"Niklas, don't look for problems where there aren't any."

"I'm just trying to be realistic, Laney." He gives me a pragmatic look that I know is his way of saying *Come on...* But I didn't want to kill the dream before it had even begun.

I counted to ten in my head. It was a good way to stay calm when dealing with the Type-A side of Niklas's personality. He insisted on planning everything. He needed to know what to expect before taking a step into the unknown.

I was probably the only aspect of his life that wasn't planned well in advance.

We met, by chance, at the American Club's Third Thursday event. I usually never went to those mingle sessions the club, hosted at the Hilton Slussen. Mostly because the people who showed up were consultants looking to network, or divorcées looking for husband number two or three. I was blissfully single then. I wasn't looking for a relationship. I'd just started working for the Stockholm office of a UK-based branding agency as a copywriter. I was also sleeping with Jens, one of the art directors I worked with. He was Swedish. Younger than me by five years and good-looking enough that he made me weak at the knees, but he wasn't relationship material. He was too much of a player, and I wasn't interested in being his or anyone's girlfriend. We worked together. We fucked whenever one of us was in the mood. But we never spent the entire night together. I liked sleeping alone, and so did he. And we both were adamant we liked our no strings attached mode. We came and went as we pleased, and it worked for us.

But by the time I went to that fateful Third Thursday, our arrangement was becoming less satisfying. I was still convinced I didn't want a relationship, but whenever Jens and I hooked up, a little piece of me wondered why he never wanted more from me. The emptiness of it all ate away at me, even as I claimed I wanted to be free to sleep with whomever I wanted when I wanted, until I met someone who peaked my interest enough to believe in true love. And as I walked around the bar, occasionally chatting with people and wondering how much longer I should stay, Niklas appeared in the doorway. He wasn't even there for Third Thursday. He'd shown up looking for one of his colleagues. Instead, he found me. I won't say it was love at first sight. It wasn't really like that. He wasn't as slick as the men I was used to from my office. The men who wore skinny jeans and clunky boots with tight black T-shirts under even tighter jackets. He didn't look like an overgrown boy. He looked like a proper man, someone with experience and enough confidence that he didn't need to assume a facade of bravado.

Niklas wasn't blond like your stereotypical Swede. He had thick chestnut hair that he swept back from his face. He looked more French than Swedish, and later I found out his mother was from Normandy. When he approached me, he claimed he thought he recognized me from a conference he'd attended in Vienna. I knew it was a bullshit line, but I liked that he didn't do what most Swedish men did when they tried to pick me up. He didn't address my breasts, and he didn't think he had to sound tough just because he was talking to a black woman from the States. He bought me a drink and we ended up trading notes about our favorite places in Stockholm. I remember thinking I liked the faint lines of crow's feet around his eyes and the sharpness of his cheekbones. I liked his full lips, and the very masculine notes of the cologne he was wearing. Most of all, I liked the shape of his hands and I couldn't stop thinking about how they'd look cupping my breasts. I wanted to take him home after just a few minutes of listening to his voice.

As the bar filled, the crowd pressed us closer and closer together. I was practically in his lap thanks to being jostled around by people anxious to order drinks while the special American Club discount price was still available. My ass brushed Niklas's crotch and met the thick hardness of an erection.

"I think we should get a room," I suggested.

He looked a little surprised, but I could tell he was into it. He looked away, the tips of his ears burning red. I didn't move. I stayed there, wanting to tease his erection with a gentle sway, but I stopped myself. I wanted him, but I didn't want to come across like a sex-crazed teenager. But then he rested one hand on my hip and, turning to look at me again, said, "You've got to be the sexiest woman I've ever met."

"I think we should get a room," I said again.

And we did. We spent the night together, fucking in that frantic, almost crazed way that only happens with a stranger. When your senses are a little too heightened and it either works—and you keep coming and coming no matter what he does to you—or you don't come at all and you fake it because you're still having a good enough time that you want to keep him going. But I didn't have to fake it with Niklas. We were a good fit. Every time he touched me, he chipped away at the wall I'd built around me until all that was left was the part of me that wanted to feel safe, and he gave me that. The warmth of his skin, the way he whispered my name in that dimly lit hotel room. He felt so steady, so calm, even with the haze of arousal surrounding us. I didn't want to go home to my apartment. I wanted to stay in that bed with him. He was the first man I wanted to spend an entire night with. I liked how it felt to curl my body around his. I liked how it felt when he kissed my neck and held me close. I liked how his skin smelt after we'd fucked... sweet, almost like honey. He made me feel safe.

But now, as we sat in the kitchen and he began listing all the things that could go wrong with an adoption, I wondered where the old Niklas went; the one who made me feel safe and who made me feel like I was the sexiest woman on the planet. The one who cared about my hopes and dreams. There was a glimmer of him beneath the facade. In New York, he'd blossomed again, waking me up with morning sex, taking me on romantic walks in Central Park, kissing me deeply in doorways and subway trains... in backseats of cabs and in elevators. I was in a constant state of arousal. Maybe this was when the desire to have a baby, to have his baby and start a family of our own, anchored itself in my thoughts. He lit this longing inside of me with his kisses and his cock and those beautiful hands anxious to touch and explore every part of me. Then we returned to Sweden, and his reserve cloaked him again.

I wished the New York version of Niklas had come with us back home.

"Are you trying to talk me out of even considering adopting?" I asked carefully.

"No, no, no. Nothing like that. I'm simply weighing our options."

"Maybe we shouldn't discuss this anymore until you've finished analyzing the possibilities."

"Now you're just teasing me, Laney." He sounded exasperated even if he was trying to smile at me.

"No, I'm not. I just don't see the point of possibly getting into another argument, since you've obviously formed an opinion and you're trying to figure out how to back it up."

"Adopting is still an option for us."

"I hope so. The natural way obviously isn't."

"No, it's not. I'm not getting the vasectomy reversed. That's not an option."

"Yes, you made that clear a few days ago."

"Well, you asked and I just want to make sure you understand."

"You used to say you would do anything for me."

"This isn't about 'doing anything' for you, Laney," he said, sounding more and more exasperated. "Do you think it was easy for me to decide to get a vasectomy in the first place?"

I shook my head. I knew he thought I was being unreasonable. I just never thought this path would be closed off to us. I thought there would be a day when it would happen and we'd have a child who would be this perfect amalgamation of us both.

"Karolina was going through a hard time, and neither of the pregnancies was easy... and after four years of sleepless nights, watching my wife falling out of love with me and our marriage falling apart—I just didn't see any more kids in my future. And, let's face it, I don't want to go under the knife again... not in that area. Once was enough."

"Okay, okay." I waved my hand in defeat. There would be no swaying him.

And really... I guess if I had a penis, I wouldn't want to go through surgery in such a... vulnerable area just because my girlfriend who'd always said babies scared her suddenly announced she wanted to have one.

*　　*　　*

He tried to smooth things over with make-up sex, and while I felt loose and satisfied physically, I was still empty emotionally and mentally. So I got dressed and walked to Kungsholmen. It wasn't a long walk, but it gave me enough time to think about the last few days. Why was I so determined to get pregnant? I didn't even know if I actually liked children. It was like there was someone else controlling my thoughts.

Around me, Stockholmers rushed from one open house to another. It was Sunday afternoon, which meant every newly-minted couple who'd decided to make a go of it (and newly divorced ones as well) would be looking for the perfect apartment. I'd passed enough signs advertising "*till salu*" or "*visningar*" to know that there was a bumper crop of apartments on the market.

It reminded me of when Niklas and I were doing the very same thing. We planned each Sunday with the precision of a military campaign. Hit five open houses in one day, spend Sunday evening ruminating over which we'd bid on, get annoyed when someone outbid us. It wasn't a fun process. But there was something wonderful about our Saturday brunches, spent bent over the real estate section, the spreadsheet Niklas made so we could compare square meter prices, and the checklist of must-haves that helped determine if we'd bid.

Once we'd tortured ourselves with enough open houses, we'd retreat to our favorite Italian restaurant, tucked away on Tunnelgatan and discuss which apartments to continue considering over ample glasses of Chianti classico and plates of pappardelle with truffle oil or cacciatore, followed by cheese and dessert wine or tiramisu and coffee. By the time we waddled back to our old apartment—the one Niklas and Karolina had shared and which still felt very much like hers—we were too full and too exhausted for more than a cursory cuddle and vegetating on the sofa. But I remember thinking that we were so attuned to one another. I knew, without even having to ask, which apartments would immediately turn him off and vice versa. Somewhere along the line, we lost that. And I was trying to convince myself that this longing to have a baby wasn't some ridiculous attempt to resuscitate our relationship.

I didn't think it was. I still loved Niklas. There was no question of that.

So I kept walking, dodging the joggers who crossed Barnhus Bridge and later the gaggles of latte mammas with their designer baby carriages, and didn't stop until I was at Norrmälarstrand and looking across the dark waters of Lake Mälaren. My thighs were sore from the walk, even though it wasn't very far. I'd become lazy since moving to Vasatan. We so rarely went to other parts of the city—though exceptions were made for exhibits at Fotografiska Museet, brunch at Hotel Rival at Mariatorget and dinners at the Flying Elk or Oaxen. Almost everything we needed was in Vasastan. I was so lost in thought, staring at the Art Nouveau buildings looming above Södra Mälarstrand that it took a few seconds to notice my phone vibrating in my jacket pocket. When I pulled it out, Eddy's number flashed on the display. Eddy was my cousin and my closest friend here in Stockholm. We both moved here around the same time for the different reasons. Eddy and her Swedish boyfriend moved here because Andreas was homesick; I moved from London for a job and stayed for Niklas.

I pressed answer and, before I could even greet her, she said, "I'm at Orangeriet. Couldn't you sneak away from Niklas for awhile, cross the bridge for me and come keep me company?"

"You're in luck. I'm already across the bridge."

"Goody! So hurry up, I've got a great table, and I've already ordered a pitcher of Bloody Mary. And I've got some good dish for you."

I shoved my phone back in my pocket and then walked the three short blocks to the café, where Eddy was waiting for me. When I arrived, the place was already packed with the über-stylish and the moneyed masses that always crowded Melker Andersson's restaurants. They were all lean, blond, and too sleek for their own good. They didn't really eat. They picked at food and drank copious amounts of coffee before switching over to cocktails and imported bottled water. Eddy and I stuck out. We always did. More often than not, we were the only blacks at the mingles and dinners and events we were inevitably invited to. This never bothered me when I lived in the US. Every now and then it annoyed me in Stockholm. I hated how people reacted—like we were either intruding, or as if we were these little bits of exotica. Usually, there was someone who assumed we were hired help or who felt the need to tell us how much they loved Spike Lee or hip-hop or Kanye West.

Eddy has chosen two of the best seats in this pseudo-greenhouse/conservatory—two shabby-chic leather armchairs positioned by the wall of windows looking out over Lake Mälaren, perfectly positioned to catch the mid-afternoon autumn sunlight. How many of the insect girls did she have to jostle to get that table? We air-kissed each other's cheeks. God, we'd been living in Europe too long. Then she dived into a story about her dishy Swede, Andreas, and how he was taking her to Paris in a few weeks. Her Swede used to be a male model, and he'd made a pretty good living at it. Now he had a shop in PUB Galleria that specialized in vintage menswear. Eddy worked with him, scouring consignment shops and estate sales for cool clothing for the hipsters of Stockholm. Sometimes I envied her, just a little. She and Andreas seemed to get on so well, to move through life without the problems the rest of us had. But I knew this wasn't true. I knew they argued about who was taking out the garbage, or picking up their miniature schnauzer from doggy-daycare, but most times she seemed so relaxed, so untouched by the sort of squabbles Niklas and I had on a daily basis.

"How was New York, by the way?" she asked as she refilled my glass. "Did my mom make you guys come over for dinner?"

"No, she was in Georgia with your grandmother," I said. "It was... nice. New York's always nice."

"Nice? Now, that's what I call an understatement. Nice, indeed. C'mon, spit it out. Did you two go ballistic there?"

"More like I had a mental breakdown on the way home."

"What? Why? What did he do?"

"It's more what he won't do."

And then I shared with my cousin the whole sordid tale of my sudden epiphany and Niklas's categorical refusal to reverse his vasectomy. She made all the right sympathetic sounds, but she seemed more amused by the story than anything else. I guess I would have been, too, in her shoes. After so many years of both of us saying we didn't want to have children, I'd suddenly listened to the blaring alarm of my biological clock.

"You know you're insane, right?" Eddy teased. "You know how much of a hassle it is with kids? You just finished helping him raise the brats he already has, and now you want to have your own?"

"I'm serious, Eddy."

"I know you are; that's why I can't understand the change of heart, Ever since you and Niklas moved in together, you've been dealing with how awful his kids have been to you."

"Jesper isn't as bad as..."

"As Siri, I know. But he's no angel, either, especially when his witch of a sister is around. I've been at your place often enough to see what Niklas lets his kids get away with."

"At least they're not with us as often anymore."

"And you want to start all over again."

"It would be different this time. It would be my child, not Karolina's."

"And he never told you about the... snip?"

"No. I thought he was joking at first."

Eddy shook her head. "If Andreas ever pulled anything like that..."

"I don't even know if he pulled anything. Maybe I forgot." But, of course, I knew I hadn't.

"But you really want to have a baby?"

I nodded.

"So get a sperm donor. If Niklas's little buddies aren't swimming, you can always find some that will." Eddy refilled our glasses again and then winked at me.

"I'm not going to trawl a bar looking for a guy to get me pregnant, Eddy. That's just so wrong."

"Who said anything about bar-hopping? I'm talking about going to a sperm bank and getting artificial insemination, you idiot."

"Oh." I wasn't expecting that suggestion. Somehow the idea of going to a sperm bank felt so... clinical.

"Talk to Niklas about it. Since he doesn't want to get snipped again, you two could go to the sperm bank together and pick out a donor who looks enough like Niklas—"

"Wait. I thought sperm donations were anonymous, and that all you got to know about them was background information."

"That's how it works here," Eddy said. "But there's a place in Copenhagen where you can even meet your potential sperm donor, and make sure you feel comfortable with him as the... well, biological father. I was going to say something else at first, but I figured it was too crass."

"How do you even know about this place?"

"Honey, Andreas has so many gay cousins, I know just about everything there is to know these days about how gay couples get married, have babies, adopt babies... you name it." Eddy winked at me and then drained her glass. "Now, what we need is a plan."

"A plan?"

"Yes, we need a game plan to get Niklas on board with the sperm donor idea, and hustling you over to Copenhagen so you can pick out the man whose jizz is going to get you preggers."

Only he would never be on board. "I still need to think about this."

"You've already thought about it. Enough that you and Niklas are fighting. This is the most obvious solution."

"Maybe you're right."

"I know I am. Now, come on, look at the menu and figure out what you want to eat. I am freaking starving here."

"Has one of Andreas' cousins already tried this sperm bank?" I didn't even think I knew anyone who'd ever been to a sperm bank. It was one of those things you saw on TV or in the movies, but you just brushed it aside and thought no one ever really used them.

Eddy nodded. "His cousin, Uma. She's used the same donor three times now." She waved at a waitress and then ordered for us.

"So she's a satisfied... customer, then?" How off-putting it was to think of obtaining ejaculation, sperm, jizz as a transaction. I tried to picture Uma—beautiful, blonde ice goddess Uma, who probably could have asked any man in the world for a quick lay just so she could get pregnant—browsing through a binder full of potential donors. What had her must-have conditions been?

"She must be. She went back three times." Eddy shrugged. "Whoever she picked must have been as gorgeous as she is. All three of the kids are beautiful."

By the time our food arrived, I'd allowed the idea of going to this sperm bank, or at least discussing it with Niklas, to germinate in my mind. Eddy had already changed the subject, bored with talking about possible babies and all the multitude of ways one could be acquired. We ordered another pitcher of Bloody Mary and, as my fourth of the day slid down my throat, I decided I could follow Uma's lead. If Niklas wouldn't give me a baby, I would go to Copenhagen and find someone who would.

CHAPTER THREE

A Happy Coincidence

The next morning, Eddy convinced me to go for a run along Nörr Mälarstrand. I stupidly agreed. We'd only run three kilometers and I was already worn out. Eddy was in much better shape and probably could have pushed on. I ran when I needed to clear my head or when my favorite jeans were a little too snug. Now, it was a combination of the two after the New York trip. As soon as we reached the bench, I slumped onto it and tried to catch my breath.

"Copenhagen Cryo."

"What?" Long lines of sweat trailed down my face and neck.

"The clinic Uma uses for super sperm." Eddy was still jogging in place, waiting for me to catch my breath.

"I wish you wouldn't call it that." I gasped and used my already damp sleeve to wipe my face.

Eddy bumped my sweaty shoulder with hers and grinned. "You have to admit—it must be pretty good sperm if she's gone back so many times."

"Yeah, well you've got a point there."

"Proof is in the pudding." She loosened her armband and slid her iPhone from the sleeve. She tapped the screen a few times and then handed her phone to me. "Check him out."

The face staring back at me was ruggedly handsome, with the square jaw and cheekbones of a young Viggo Mortensen. His lips were full and generous, curled into a knowing smile. He was looking directly into the camera, and there was something almost too candid in his pale blue eyes, like he knew what you were thinking and was game for whatever you suggested.

"Wow," was the only word I could breathe out. I swallowed hard and quickly handed Eddy's phone back to her.

"Wow, indeed," Eddy said and laughed lightly. "Uma says he's worth every penny she pays. Well, you've seen her kids. They're gorgeous."

"And she found him in Copenhagen?"

Eddy nodded. "He's one of the donors at Copenhagen Cryo."

I shook my head in wonder. No wonder Uma kept going back for more. Sure there was nothing sexual going on between them, but there must have been some spark that made her decide he was the right donor for her.

"I need to talk to Niklas," I said, still thinking about Uma's donor. Did they all look that good? I'd always thought sperm donors would be average, nothing special. "I can't just make a decision like this without him. I mean, I am going to raise the baby with him, so he should know if I am going to go through with it."

Telling him I wanted to go to Denmark to investigate sperm donors sounded... wrong. His reaction was anyone's guess. We'd barely spoken the last few days. I was back at work again, working on a project for the global launch of a new mascara that kept me in the office until nearly nine or ten in the every night. Niklas was leading group therapy sessions for overeaters. When I came home from the office, he was often bent over his computer reviewing notes for his next session, or he was still at his office, preparing for the next day's patients. We reached for one another in the middle of the night, pretended not to hear the carnal noises coming from Siri's room, and held onto one another as we drifted back to sleep. In the morning, he was still asleep when I dragged myself out of bed to go to the gym and torture my body for an hour before heading to work, and the whole process started all over again.

I told myself I wasn't keeping my decision about looking into the clinic from him. I really did want to discuss it with him. I thought I could tell him everything in small doses and omit the part about meeting the sperm donor.

I wasn't being dishonest. Was I?

*   *   *

I found the sperm bank's website pretty easily—all it took was Googling "Copenhagen Cryo" and the clinic's very impressive, very Danish modern page was on my screen. I was sitting at my desk in the open-plan office where I worked. Most of my colleagues had gone home already. Only Jens, who was now the creative director of the agency, was still around, and he was probably too busy on a transatlantic conference call to pay much attention to my computer screen.

The website looked credible enough. Very professional, without seeming too slick, it told me everything I needed to know about how to gain access to their register of Danish men interested in becoming sperm donors. I skimmed the first few pages until I found the tab for testimonials. Well, this was a first—none of the Swedish sites for artificial insemination and sperm banks had testimonials. Copenhagen Cryo had women from around the globe who'd used their services gushing about how professional it all was, how reassuring it was to get to know the person who'd share their child's DNA. How the openness of the entire process made it less daunting and not at all sordid. And then I found one that seemed to speak directly to me: "My biological clock was ticking, but my husband's had already stopped. I still longed for the family we'd always talked about having, but his sperm levels were too low. So apart from adoption, this was our only option. I'd heard too many horror stories about women going to sperm banks and getting their doctor's sperm, or getting sperm that was no good, so it was reassuring when I saw Copenhagen Cryo was certified by the Danish Ministry of Health as a quality provider, and that they could guarantee healthy sperm, as each donor was carefully screened before even being allowed to donate. I went to the information session and any misgivings that remained were put at ease. I met the man who would eventually become the biological father of my two children, and he was a perfect match. I don't know where I'd be without Copenhagen Cryo."

By the time I got to the end of her testimonial, I knew I was ready. I filled in the request form for more information. And then I began planning how I could get to Copenhagen without Niklas becoming too suspicious. Maybe I would have to ask Eddy for help. Or moral support.

*   *   *

The next morning, I was greeted with an email from Copenhagen Cryo, inviting me to come for an information session. Ida, the case consultant who'd sent the email, suggested several dates in the coming week and pointed out one date in particular when the clinic would have a meet-and-greet mingle for potential parents and donors.

God, this felt like it was happening too quickly. I wasn't even sure why I was doing this anymore. I kept trying to imagine telling Niklas I wanted to try artificial insemination. He wouldn't like it, but maybe he'd think it was a better option being pushed, so I checked the date against my iPhone calendar. I was due to go to Copenhagen next week for a meeting with our cosmetics client. That meeting was scheduled for Thursday and the mingle was on Friday. I could stay the weekend and kill two birds with one stone. Before I could talk myself out of it, I replied to Ida's email and said I would come on Friday, then I rebooked my airline ticket and hotel room to accommodate a weekend stay. I stared at the hotel confirmation on my computer screen. There was no going back now. Everything was booked and paid for. Do you know that feeling you get when you're about to do something insane? That scary feeling that makes you nervous and giddy? That was how I felt. And I liked it.

I glanced around my office. Jens was standing by the door to the conference room, where the rest of the team was waiting for me. He gestured for me to hurry up. I nodded and mouthed "okay" at him, as I gathered my laptop and cup of coffee. I rushed over to him, my heels barely making a sound on the carpeted floor. My heart was racing and it wasn't from excitement over whether our client liked our pitch. Jens grinned at me.

"You look happy," he said, and raised an eyebrow at me. "Is there something I should know?"

I shook my head. "Everything's fine." Then I ducked into the conference room and slid into my usual chair. Now all I had to do was figure out a good spin to put on this so Niklas wouldn't get the wrong idea.

*   *   *

I called Eddy while Niklas was in the shower. It was one of those rare mornings when we were both up at the same time and, despite the spaciousness of our apartment, we seemed to be under each other's feet all the time. Luckily, there was no sign of Siri or Jesper. I'd already checked their bedrooms and confirmed that it was just Niklas and I. When Eddy answered, I went into my walk-in closet and closed the door.

"I did it," I told her in a rushed voice. "I made an appointment with the sperm bank."

"So Niklas is on board with the idea then? Good for you!"

"I didn't tell him... yet."

"Honey, what are you doing?"

"I'm just going to get information. Besides, I have to go to Copenhagen anyway for a meeting. This is just so I know what to expect and how to explain everything to Niklas. You know I can't go to him with a half-baked idea."

"I guess you've got a point there. But you are going to tell him, aren't you?"

"Of course I am. It would be a bit weird if I suddenly turned up pregnant. I think he'd figure it out pretty quickly, or jump to the wrong conclusion."

"Just make sure you two sit down and have a good, long discussion when you come home. I don't want to see either of you get hurt."

"I promise, I will tell him everything when I come home on Sunday evening." And I would. It was the right thing to do.

Niklas didn't seem surprised or upset when I told him I would have to stay a day longer in Copenhagen. I was already packing when I sprang the news on him. He was reading in bed, engrossed in the last book of Stieg Larsson's Millennium trilogy. He nodded and then asked me if I was going to sneak in a visit to the Louisiana Museum of Art.

"Maybe," I said as I continued packing my suitcase. "It depends on how long the meetings run."

"You should try to see Anton and Ingrid while you're there," he said without looking up from his book.

Anton and Ingrid were two of my closest friends from my college days in the US. They'd moved back to Copenhagen after close to fifteen years in the States, when Ingrid became pregnant with their first child. Meeting them now... no, maybe it wasn't a good idea. I still hadn't told Niklas about the sperm bank and the idea of artificial insemination. Every time I thought about bringing it up, something held me back. Was it fear that he would say no? Or was it simply that I wanted to avoid his trying to talk me out of it?

"Maybe," I said again. "The schedule is pretty tight, but I might be able to meet them on Saturday."

"Do you have to work on Saturday as well?" he finally lowered the book and set it beside him on the mattress. "I thought your boss refused to work weekends."

"We're having breakfast with the Danish team on Saturday. Thursday and Friday are the meeting days." The lie slid out so easily and left a bitter taste in my mouth.

"Ah, well, you should make some time to see them, if you can. I know how much you miss them." He watched me steadily. "You okay?"

I nodded. "Just tired. It's been a long day and now I have to get up early tomorrow."

"Come to bed."

"In a minute. I'm nearly done packing."

Niklas peeled off his shirt and tossed it at me. It landed in my suitcase. I shook my head and moved it aside.

"Come to bed and I'll make it worth your while."

He grinned at me and began easing his boxers off. I zipped my suitcase and then set it on the floor. I tried not to feel guilty. I was living with a man who was undeniably sexy. His firm body was still tan from our summer in the US. The golden brown trail of hair that started at his chest drew my eyes downward to the thick thatch of pubic hair along his gorgeous cock. I was so in the mood for him... even if a part of me was still angry with him.

I grinned as I walked over to his side of the bed. "How worth my while will you make it?"

He reached for me and pulled me into bed with him. He unbuttoned my blouse and pushed it away. I arched up to meet his touch as he dragged his palm across my naked breasts. "I love it when you don't wear a bra," he said and then took my right nipple between his teeth and gave it a gentle tug. I pulled at him, not wanting foreplay but still loving the way it felt when he teased me with his fingers and his mouth. As we kissed, his cock stirred and nudged my thigh. I opened my legs wider; I was so ready for him. I whispered for him to fuck me, to take me, begged him to do whatever he wanted to me. My body buzzed for him, I was so turned on that when he finally slid inside me, I was trembling and anxious to feel even more of him.

We made love, and then curled around each other, drifted off to sleep, woke up, made love again. Later, when both of us were too tired to move or even mind the damp sheets, Niklas kissed my neck and kept his arm coiled around my waist.

"When you come home, we can look into adoption," he said softly. His voice already had that slow, sleepy quality. "It might not be easy...but we should try."

I squeezed his hand and said "okay" softly. I was glad for the dark. I thought for sure the guilt would show on my face.

CHAPTER FOUR

Danish Surprise

Going to Copenhagen released something inside of me. All of the tension dissipated and I felt like could breathe again. It was a feeling I always had whenever I arrived. Was it the city's irreverent grittiness? It was just as beautiful as Stockholm, but less studied. Copenhagen didn't mind if you saw it on an off day, whereas Stockholm always strived for perfection. While my colleagues were more impatient, making bee-lines for the taxi stands as soon as we'd disembarked, I liked discovering the city slowly and opted for the train. I wasn't in the mood for small talk, so I told them I would meet them at the hotel.

Our first meeting didn't start until after lunch, which gave me time to check in at the hotel, and call Copenhagen Cryo to make sure my appointment was still on. I almost felt like a secret agent with all this subterfuge.

And imagining myself as a modern day Emma Peel made me laugh at myself. Here I was, trying to hide from the man who was effectively my husband that I was trying to figure out how to have a baby without him. And my guilt ate away at me. What the hell was I doing? I pulled out my iPhone and sent Niklas a guilty text that said, "I love you so much." I did. So why did I feel like I was cheating on him by even considering using someone else's DNA to help me have a baby?

And why was I so obsessed with a baby being mine? By the time I arrived at the hotel, I'd almost convinced myself to call Copenhagen Cryo and cancel my appointment. But then I thought about it—I wasn't committing to anything. I was just getting information. Information could possibly help me—help us—especially since Niklas was warming up to the idea of us starting our own family. By the time I was on my way to the offices of Jensen, Fogh & Ogilvy, I'd talked myself into believing Niklas would thank me for taking the initiative, and not waiting or simply relying on information found online.

*   *   *

Copenhagen Cryo turned out to be easier to find than I'd expected. It was just around the corner from the Hotel Kong Arthur, in an office block that looked more like a five-star hotel than a medical clinic. I'd expected something very plain, or the cookie-cutter medical offices I was used to from back home; nice enough that you were glad your doctor had one but bland enough to have zero distinction. But this office was very Danish design—all wengé wood and muted colors. It was obvious that the architects and interior designers worshipped at the altar of Arne Jacobssen—there were teal-hued Egg and Swan chairs and sleek edges. A floor-to-ceiling wall of glass let in pale shafts of watery light as it overlooked Nørre Søgade and the bridge to Nørrebrø.

The young woman sitting behind the receptionist desk, who looked more suited to the cover of Elle rather than behind a desk in a clinic, watched me with an expressionless face as I approached her from the elevator bank. As soon as I was close enough, the expression on her face warmed, and she allowed a smile to form. "Welcome to Copenhagen Cryo," she said. "Are you here for an appointment, or an information session?"

"I'm here for an information session with..." I glanced down at the name I'd saved on my phone's reminder app. "Ida Friis?"

"And you are?"

"Laney Halliwell."

The Ice Blonde nodded and tapped away at her computer. "Ah, yes. There you are." Then she called my Client Services Assistant on what looked like the very latest iPhone. "Have a seat, and she'll be right with you."

I chose one of the Egg chairs and tried to look as calm and collected as I imagined Eddy would be in this situation. Nothing ever seemed to faze my cousin. Something completely out of the ordinary happened, and she was more likely to raise an eyebrow than to have a mental breakdown or burst into uncontrollable tears. I was the one who usually lost control, or who froze and couldn't think straight. And she was usually the person who would snap me out of it and make me react. I wished she was with me. I should have asked her to come along for moral support. No doubt she would have criticized the outfit I was wearing—black capri pants, black ballet flats, and a silk pullover sweater—and said it was too boring, too Euro Corporate. That I'd pulled my hair into a bun would have made her grimace, but I had to dress for work, and I'd come to the clinic straight after my last meeting, so at least I had an excuse.

When Ida came out to greet me, I was struck by how young she looked. She didn't seem like she was much older than Siri. She was probably only a few years her senior. But she carried herself with a self-assurance that was enviable. I pegged her at twenty-five. When I was that age, I could only fake confidence. I was good at working it and making people think I was cool as a cucumber, but inside I was shaking. And now, as we greeted one another and shook hands, I tried to channel a little of Eddy's confident persona. Ida led me to her office, which was just as stylish and Danish cool as the reception area. Instead of sitting at her desk, Ida and I sat on the black leather Exposition sofa. On the rosewood coffee table in front of the sofa were several binders and a sleek MacBook Air. From unseen speakers, ambient lounge music streamed in, giving her office the feel of a trendy hotel bar rather than an office at a clinic.

"Now, tell me," Ida said in an encouraging voice. "What sort of man speaks to you?"

"Speaks to me?" I asked. "You mean on a daily basis?"

"No, sorry, I should have been clearer. I meant what sort of man interests you."

"Oh! Well..." I tried to picture Niklas in my head. He was the man I loved so, surely, he would be the man who spoke to me. Instead, I saw a completely different man. Someone a little taller, a little less serious. Someone who didn't slick their hair back every morning with hair gel and who didn't clear his throat whenever he wanted me to hand him the Culture section on a Sunday morning. "I like men who are creative." It was the only thing that came out that wouldn't sound like a withering putdown of Niklas. And he didn't deserve that. Where had all of this criticism come from?

"That's a good start." Ida started taking notes on her computer. "Tell me more."

I closed my eyes and let my mind wander. I thought of the walk I'd taken from the Jensen, Fogh & Ogilvy office in Væsterbrø and envisioned the men I passed. There was a café I passed just as I came up Øster Søgade. It was situated on the corner, and I remembered seeing a man sitting by the window, reading the newspaper. I'd paused long enough to catch his eye. I hadn't meant to. I got a bit distracted by how relaxed he looked, how his reddish-blond hair waved around his face. He wasn't classically beautiful, but he had an interesting face and such kissable looking lips that I could almost feel them on mine just thinking about them. Then I had to stop myself... damn, I already felt guilty, and all I'd done was daydream about another man.

"I'm sorry," I said. "This just feels weird."

So Ida took over and began telling me about why Copenhagen Cryo insisted on potential parents meeting the men who could help them in their quest to become parents. "We wouldn't just let anyone in our homes, so why shouldn't we be selective about whose sperm fertilizes our eggs?"

She made it sounds so normal, so logical. She talked about Dr. Mikkelsen, the woman who'd founded the clinic and who'd come up with the idea of making a sperm bank as transparent as dating. How she thought you ought to know as much as possible about the men involved—even have access to their medical records or police records so that you could be assured you were getting superior genes. It all started to sound a bit like eugenics, and maybe Ida sensed my reticence, because she assured me that this wasn't about creating a master race or a super baby, just making sure that the man whose sample you used didn't have any illnesses or disorders that could prove fatal for your future child.

"This way, you never have to worry about being impregnated by a man with HIV, for example, or with hemophilia or congenital heart problems."

"How many women have used your... services?"

"Well, since we opened ten years ago, we've helped 30,000 women here in Denmark alone. And when we initiated the open sperm donations two years ago, we helped 5,000 more women."

The figure was significant. I nodded slowly and let her words sink in. It was a figure Niklas would respect.

"If you're worried about the race of your child, we have African and African-American donors as well. I'm sure a few of them will come to the mingle."

"Do you get a lot of Danish women who want black children?"

"Quite a few," Ida said, without seeming surprised by my question.

"My partner is Swedish, so I think it's probably best if I have a donor who resembles him."

"It's your decision," Ida replied. "We don't try in any way to steer your choice of donor."

I thought she would leave it at that, but then she began to describe the hormone therapy that every woman had to go through to prepare for artificial insemination. The rounds of shots, the possible mood swings... the insemination itself and then the waiting. The more she told me, the less sure I felt. I wished Eddy were there. I wished I could ask her for advice, hear her reassure me about how pleased Uma was with the choices she'd made. Eddy would know all the right questions to ask. I tried to imagine sitting here with Niklas. He'd listen, he'd nod, he'd say all the right things, but later he'd shake his head and say it was all a bit trite. If I couldn't even imagine my partner here with me, why was I doing this?

"Would you go through all of this to have a child?"

Ida nodded and flashed a beatific smile. "Yes, I would."

"Honestly?"

"I would. Especially if I still hadn't met the man I want to be the father of my children, and I heard my biological clock ticking."

"I don't want to feel desperate."

"This isn't desperation, Laney. You already know you want to be a mother. You've just unfortunately found yourself in a situation where your partner's past decision has put you in this position." Ida slid the binders toward me. "Have a look. You don't have to make a decision now. You can walk out of here whenever you like, without making any commitment whatsoever. This is all up to you."

I flipped open one of the binders and browsed through page after page of men. Some were exceptionally handsome, others average. Some so well-educated—at least on paper—that it was almost intimidating. But none of them in the first binder spoke directly to me, or elicited enough of a reaction that it warranted watching the videos Ida assured me she had of every single one of them. I asked her if there was a particularly popular one. She smiled a little enigmatically and then said, "I could show you his video. He's got magnetism."

I was curious, so I went along with it. I had to see the man who seemed to inspire women to melt.

And the video was very compelling. He was rugged-looking, with the sort of wind-blown, reddish blond hair and pale green eyes that made you think of a young Robert Redford. And when he spoke, he had a deep timbre that resonated inside you and made you think of long sessions of weekend sex and wine, sore muscles. I glanced away, thinking how this man probably helped populate many a Danish town. He was the man I'd seen in the café, the man I'd imagined when I should have been thinking about Niklas.

"He's got a definite appeal." I blushed. I was glad my skin was dark enough to cover the rising heat flaring inside me.

"He does," Ida agreed, still smiling. "You know, you should really stay for the mingle."

"Is it here in the office?"

"No, downstairs at the bar. I think we'll have a good crowd tonight."

Ida changed the subject again; she wanted to know more about me, and how I'd ended up at Copenhagen Cryo. For some reason, I hadn't expected this. I'd thought she would go into hard sell mode and try to convince me to sign up already, pick my sperm donor, and then start the hormone treatments immediately. I found myself telling her about Niklas, about how sometimes he made me feel like the most wonderful, most essential part of his life, and other times I felt like a shadow. I told her about my relationship with Siri and Jesper, and how daunting it was to be the de facto stepmother to teenagers who seemed hell bent on hating me, no matter what I did. And how I'd woken up that morning in New York, with a void growing inside of me, and a sudden desperation to have a child of my own.

I wasn't getting any younger. I was thirty-three. The number scared me. When I was twenty-five, I'd thought that by now I would be back in the US, or maybe in London, with a different man, perhaps. I'd never pictured myself staying in Stockholm for so long. How had that happened? How had I become one of those women who latched on to a man and didn't let go? But that was love, wasn't it? Or at least part of it? When you knew with a certainty that you could not live without the person you were with, or that you didn't want to live without him? I didn't want to live without Niklas. I just wished that parts of him—the part that psychoanalyzed me whenever I was annoyed, or the part that always took Siri and Jesper's side, even when they were wrong—would magically disappear.

"Are you sure you want to have a family with him?" Ida's hand was on my shoulder, and it was a gentle, comforting touch. How could she have such empathy? I didn't think I had it when I was her age, but perhaps that was inherently part of who I was. I had such difficulties being empathetic. I could fake it, but I didn't always feel it.

"I don't know," I finally admitted. "Maybe I want to have a baby on my own."

I had never even considered this. I'd always said I would not be one of those women who would get pregnant and become a Baby Mama. My parents had been pretty adamant in their lectures about not being the Single Black Mom, especially not the single black woman who had no intention of having a father figure for her child. I didn't want to be one of those women constantly moaning about how my man didn't help me with my kids, how I had to be the mom and the dad. But that's what I would be if I had a baby on my own. Maybe not so angry and resentful as the women I saw on TV, or as the women I often saw on the subway, but I would join their ranks. And in a way, instead of being frightened or disillusioned, it felt okay.

How long did I sit there with Ida, rambling on about my life while she nodded and took notes? I knew she wasn't my therapist, but it was easier to tell her what was wrong with my life than the woman I saw in Stockholm twice a month.

"I'm sorry I am going on like this," I said. "It's being here, away from Stockholm and from my step-kids and Niklas... do you get a lot of women like this?"

"Occasionally. Some women come here looking for something completely different. They come to the mingles to meet the men, and they want relationships. It happens sometimes."

"I don't want a relationship. I already have one."

"Good, good. Well, let's focus on finding you a good donor."

I shouldn't have stayed.

Ida let me use one of the more comfortable rooms, where there was a touchscreen monitor set up for virtual viewing of donors and the staff impression reports of them. I probably spent an hour browsing and seeing no one who clicked for me, and then I stopped. The man in the cafe was donor DK-101 52 7315, Mads Rasmussen. Mads. His video revealed that he lived in Copenhagen, and worked as a carpenter and furniture maker. He was single. And his voice was delicious.

I couldn't understand everything he said—my Danish wasn't very good—but he was sexy in that hipster way I'd always thought I hated. He had the most interesting face; not quite symmetrical, with gorgeous, sensual lips and a slow sexy smile. If this were a dating site, I would have sent him an email immediately and requested a date. But I wasn't single. I had Niklas. And I wasn't here for a new partner. I was here looking for someone to be the father of my children. And, if I was honest, I wanted Mads to be that man.

I watched his video three more times, then made myself stop. I was behaving like a love-struck teenager. No, no, no. I stood up a little too quickly, and nearly knocked over my chair. I needed to walk out of here. Staying didn't really feel like an option anymore. I'd screened his video four times. I'd let myself imagine him being the father of my children without even having Niklas anywhere in the picture.

No...

I looked out the window, expecting to see outside but it overlooked the mezzanine and, below, the area set up for the mingle. A few people had already arrived and

were being handed drinks by the wait staff. The icy receptionist was there, too. Was she also a Client Services
Specialist? I stepped away from the window and tried to
figure out what to do. Stay or go?

Staying meant opening myself to something more
than I'd bargained for. Or was I jumping the gun? I'd
only seen the man's picture and watched his video. There
was no guarantee he would even show up tonight, and
maybe I would feel the opposite of attraction once I
spoke to him. I didn't need to feel attracted to him to
think he could be a good donor for me. All that mattered
was that he was healthy and his sperm quality was good.
According to the reports in his file, he was stellar material. That was all I needed to think about. I was not
going into this like I was approaching a long-term relationship. I mean, even the website said the only time
donors met the recipients was at the mingle, and possibly
one or two more occasions in between to sign paperwork.

I was safe. Niklas and I were safe. I just had to make
sure it stayed that way.

*   *   *

Downstairs, the atmosphere was more like a party than a
meet-and-greet. They'd hired a DJ and the music he was
playing had the right of amount of swing and groove to
make you want to dance. Instead of the twenty-odd people I'd assumed would show up, the bar was jam-packed.
I eased my way through the crowd and put on the name-
tag Ida insisted I wear. I could see her at the bar,
ordering a drink. She and the Ice Blonde were keeping

an eye on the crowd, which included a few of the donors I recognized from the files I'd seen earlier. Some looked uncomfortable—this was a strange set-up, wasn't it? I supposed it never occurred to them that Copenhagen Cryo would seriously expect them to follow through and meet the people who'd purchase their donations.

I was still thinking about it—and wondering why they called it donations when the men were getting paid—when I saw him. He'd just walked in, and was scanning the room like he was searching for someone. I wondered if the donors hung out sometimes. Maybe they were like a fraternity, or like brothers in arms. One of the wait staff offered him a glass of wine, but he shook his head. Hmm. Either he was a teetotaler, or he preferred beer, or he was driving.

Ida waved at him and he nodded. I stayed where I was, leaning against the sliding glass door that led to a terrace. My glass of white wine was empty now. Either I braved the crush to the bar again, or I waited for someone to come over and offer me a drink. Neither prospect seemed appealing. But I didn't want to leave, not just yet. I probably should have returned to my hotel and had a drink with my colleagues—who were probably wondering where I'd gone. I should have been in my room, calling Niklas and checking in with him. I should have been ordering dinner from room service and staying away from temptation. I didn't even want to be tempted.

I stood still, trying to figure out what I ought to do, and getting annoyed with myself for not being able to make up my mind when normally I had no problem doing so. But just then, I felt like an indecisive teenager at a party she wasn't quite cool enough to be at. So I put on my game face—the one that got me through boring dinners with Niklas's parents. The one that saved me whenever we bumped into Karolina at parties or on the street. The one that was going to get me through the rest of the evening without making any sort of commitment to this sperm donor idea until I'd had a chance to really discuss it with Niklas.

And that's when Ida found me again and said, "Laney, I thought you should meet one of our donors." She gently nudged me forward. "This is Mads. Mads, meet Laney. She's thinking about starting the process."

We nodded and smiled at each other. Shaking hands felt too formal, and doing the continental cheek kissing felt inappropriate.

"Have you been a donor for a long time, then?" As soon as I asked the question, I regretted it. I sounded so facetious, so ridiculous. Inside, I cursed and groaned, but I kept a smile that surely made me look idiotic.

He returned my smile and it felt genuine. "Around two years, give or take."

We had a stilted conversation, with Ida watching over us like a mother hen. She'd probably already decided Mads was the donor for me.

"Laney came from Stockholm to look into insemination," Ida said. "Didn't you live in Stockholm at one time, Mads?"

"Yeah, that's right." He waved over one of the wait staff and took two glasses of wine from her, one for me and one for Ida. "I studied cabinetmaking and furniture design at the University College of Arts, Crafts and Design."

I nodded though I'd never heard of it. "Is that part of KTH?"

"No, no. It's called Konstfack in Swedish."

"Ah, okay. I know where you mean. I never heard it called by its English name."

Ida sidled away, leaving us to our own devices. He grinned at me. "You know, these mingles are always a little weird for me."

"Why's that?"

"There's always women who show up who... they don't really want a baby, you know? They're just lonely. And you kind of feel like a gigolo here. You're supposed to look good. Charm the women, make them feel comfortable. You just don't have sex with them."

"Oh... yeah, that does sound weird." We moved out onto the empty terrace. We could look out over the water from here. It was one of those unseasonably warm nights that you always hear Scandinavians talking about, but you rarely ever experience. In Copenhagen the air was more humid than in Stockholm. It felt warm and damp, like what I remembered from growing up on the east coast in the US. Tiny beads of perspiration were already glistening on my skin and sliding down my back.

He pulled a crushed packet of cigarettes from the pocket of his jeans and offered me one. I accepted it and leaned in so he could light it for me. As I took that first illicit drag, he said, "I think I saw you earlier. I was in a café and I looked out the window and saw someone who looked a lot like you."

"I saw you, too," I admitted. We both exhaled smoke and watched the milky tendrils merge and swirl. We kept our backs to the bar and looked out over the water again. "And when I saw you in their... books, I was a little stunned."

"I wasn't expecting to see you here, either."

His voice trailed down my spine. I stole a glance at him. I was wrong earlier when I said he wasn't handsome. There was something so masculine about him. I couldn't really find the words to describe him. He was tall and lean, but there was a strength to him. Underneath his clothing was sure to be the body of someone who did not go to the gym, but who had the natural muscles and leanness of physical labor. He didn't have the perfectly slicked-back hair that most Scandinavian men seemed to favor; they wore it like a badge of their social class and their success. Mads's hair was a messy mop of waves and stray curls that looked coppery in the glow of the spotlights. He swept back the curls that hung in front of his eyes and revealed the most beautiful pair of hazel eyes. I bit my lower lip. He was too good-looking for me, and he was smiling at me with such fierceness that I knew he felt something, too. He was watching me.

I could feel the path his eyes took. My body tingled in anticipation.

"I saw you standing there and I thought, shit, this must be some kind of dream. Or maybe Ida was playing a joke on me."

We both laughed. What were the chances?

"So... why do you need me?"

"Sorry?" His question caught me off guard. I was expecting him to say something else—like ask me if I was single, or if I wanted another drink or some small talk that would be the ideal segue to this moment we were having.

"Why do you need me, or any sperm donor? You don't look like you'd have a problem finding a partner."

"I do have a partner." I took another drag of my cigarette. "But he had a vasectomy just before he got divorced. And he doesn't want to reverse it."

"Ah, well, that would explain it." Mads gestured at a group of rattan loungers on the far side of the terrace. We moved there, away from the glass door and the loud music spilling out of it. The sun had already set. The white summer nights of June and July seemed a long way off as the velvety blackness of the sky hovered above us. We sat close together, finishing our cigarettes and letting the tips burn down to the very end. "I didn't think someone like you would be single."

"Someone like me?" I smiled at him. "What's that supposed to mean?"

"You're beautiful. I doubt I'm the first guy to tell you that."

His directness made me blush. He was still watching me, and the steadiness of his stare made my breath quicken. I could almost picture him in my bed, could almost imagine how it would good it would feel to fall asleep in his arms. I blinked and looked away, pretending to focus on the glittering lights of the opera house on the other bank of the canal.

"We're not married, if that's what you mean," I said.

"No, but you've probably been together for a while."

"Five years."

"A long time, then. So where is he?" He glanced over his shoulder. "Does he want to meet the potential donors, too? Or maybe he's inside with the others?"

I shook my head. "He's at home, in Stockholm."

"Does he know you're here?"

"He knows I'm in Copenhagen. I had a business meeting."

"But he doesn't know you're here checking this place out."

"No. I didn't tell him. I wanted to find out what this was about, and then tell him."

He leaned back in the lounger. We were so close. I could feel the heat rolling off his body. Could smell the sexy mix of sweat and tobacco and cologne on his skin.

"Are you married?" I asked him.

"No, not now. I was married. A long time ago. Well, it only lasted a couple of years. A girl I knew from

Konstfack. But I wanted to come back to Copenhagen, and she wanted to stay in Stockholm."

Silly girl, I thought, as he slid his arm along the back of the lounger. I let my head dip back so it was resting in the crook of his arm. He smelled so good... like crushed lime leaves and black pepper and sunshine. He leaned in and let his lips brush my cheek. Tiny shivers prickled my skin. I'd known he would do it, and maybe I'd even willed it. I just remember folding my body towards his and giving in to his kisses as he found my mouth.

I didn't care if anyone saw us there. I just remember how it felt—to feel his arms snaking around me, to lay back on the lounger and suddenly be cocooned in its shield-like sun visor and feel the weight of Mads on me as we lay there together, kissing with the sort of desperation I thought only came with being a teenager. How long were we like that, sliding our hands under one another shirts, exploring each other's bodies as much as we could? I remember snapping out of the fog of lust and realizing I needed to go. I needed to be away from him. I was getting myself in deep trouble.

Then he murmured, "We should get out of here."

And I couldn't think of a reason why I was saying no.

We went back to my hotel. I waited for something like guilt to creep through me, but this burn I felt for Mads kept it at bay. He pulled me into darkened doorways and pressed me against walls, sliding his greedy hands inside my blouse and pushing aside the flimsy cups of my bra while I rubbed against him. Anything to get closer. I was hungry for him. I wanted to taste every part of him. By the time we made it to my hotel room, we'd come close to stripping in too many public places. I wanted to strip away all the layers of clothing separating us and go down on him. I wanted him to grab my hair and force me to take as much of him in my mouth as I could handle, I wanted to claw his back and feel him swelling inside me. I wanted so much of him.

I remembered tumbling into the room and already pulling at the buttons on my blouse before he'd even closed the door behind him. He was on me before I could think about what was happening. His strong hands already unzipping my pants and pushing them away. We fell together on my bed. We didn't speak. We just fucked. I remember how he took me from behind, tasting me first before he finally entered me and how his hips ground against my ass, how his fingers touched me everywhere and sent wave after wave of lust through me. My moans filled my ears. I didn't care if anyone heard us. I wanted more. And when he came I didn't ask myself if we'd remembered a condom. I didn't care. And that's what scared me. I didn't care. I just wanted more and more of him. I would have taken anything he gave me. And then he went down on me again, sliding his tongue and fingers inside of me, nibbling and tasting me, teasing me, and when I came, it was so hard and strong that I gasped and laughed and cried a little.

Afterwards, we lay there on sweat-damp sheets, letting the breeze from the open window cool our skin.

Outside, someone was laughing and singing along off-key with Rihanna's "Umbrella." Would he fall asleep? Would he leave? I barely moved, I was so afraid of slipping out of this spell.

I didn't have to wait long to find out. He rolled me over on my back and kissed me long and hard. "I want you again... could you... again?"

I nodded and gave myself to him completely.

God, what was happening to me?

CHAPTER FIVE

Home Is Where The Heart Is?

Returning to Stockholm felt wrong. I didn't want to go back, not just yet, but I had to. I had the brochures from Copenhagen Cryo; I had Ida's business card. She'd even given me files of possible donors and their backgrounds, just so it would be easier for me to convince Niklas. But now I wasn't so sure. I didn't want to go home to him. There was still this remnant of longing for Mads coursing through me, and it was strong enough that I was afraid it would bleed into my life with Niklas. But now I was in the taxi taking me from Arlanda Airport back to Vasastan, and Niklas, and our apartment on Dalagatan.

It was late enough in the evening that he might have gone to bed already. I hoped he had. I needed to hold onto the memory of meeting Mads, of feeling him kissing and stroking me just a little longer. I needed to convince myself—before I saw Niklas again—that this would never happen again. We didn't have to go to Copenhagen to have the insemination done. We could purchase the amount of sperm we needed and just have a doctor here in Stockholm take care of everything. And then I would never have to see Mads again or leave myself open to falling again. But that was the problem. I wanted to fall. I wanted to run straight back to him, even though I barely knew him.

What was wrong with me?

When the taxi pulled in front of my building, I was relieved to see the lights in our living room weren't on. That was a good sign. It meant Niklas was either in his office or already in bed. If he was still awake, he'd want to talk and then make love. I didn't think I could handle it. Not yet. Not when I was sure Mads's scent was still on my skin and I still felt his presence inside me.

I paid the driver and thanked him for helping me with my bag. I'd probably tipped too much. I almost always did. It didn't matter. There were some American habits that died hard, and that was one of them. I made my way into the building and took the elevator up to our apartment and wished I could make the elevator's ascent even slower than it already was. My phone buzzed in my handbag. I fumbled for it and then saw Mads's number. My breath caught in my throat.

"When can you come to Copenhagen again?" was all the message said.

Shit, this was no good. My body was already responding, twinging and reminding me of what Mads had done and could do again. I typed in a quick "not sure" and pressed send. I should have deleted his message. I just couldn't bring myself to do it.

Niklas was not at home. The entire apartment had a neglected air to it. I wheeled my suitcase down the hall to our bedroom, expecting to find him there, but it was empty as well. Maybe this was better. I could have some time to get used to being back in my normal life. I needed it. I wouldn't have been able to handle Niklas or how trusting he was. I checked my phone again and saw a missed call. I listened to the message. It was Niklas. He'd taken Jesper and Siri out to dinner and a movie, and he'd be late. Well, that gave me some time to adjust, to reconnect. I unpacked and tossed my rumpled clothes into the washing machine in our en suite bathroom. I slid the brochures from Copenhagen Cryo into the drawer of the nightstand on my side of the bed. I showered, too, thinking this would rid me once and for all of any traces of Mads. But when I lay in bed later, I could still smell him on my skin and I knew then that I was in too deep. Already.

*   *   *

Niklas cupped my breasts, kneading them and pinching my already hard nipples and murmuring how much he wanted me. I reached down between us and felt the heaviness of his swollen cock. I could make him come now, so easily. I could just stroke one finger along his scrotum and press, ever so gently, and he'd come. But I didn't want that. I wanted him to grab my hips and thrust inside me. I wanted him to fuck me so hard I would forget everything else. But every time he touched me, every time he kissed me and whispered "I missed you" or "I love you" I didn't hear his voice, I heard Mads's. I kept opening my eyes and trying to see Niklas's face to remind me that I was home again. I was not in Copenhagen. I was in my bedroom with its white walls and whitewashed oak floorboards, with its memory foam mattress, and windows overlooking the park.

I let him make love to me. I needed him to do this. This was the only way to come back to him completely but everything he did just ignited reminders of Mads. I didn't stop him. I couldn't. I needed him to keep doing this, thrusting into me, grappling at me and urging a response from me. And I couldn't deny it; I responded, because he felt so good, so familiar, even when there was this alien presence between us. I closed my eyes and focused on how he raised his hips just enough to plunge deeper in me, and the rush of want it released in me. I pushed remnants of sleep from my head and then slid one finger in his anus. He groaned in my ear as I eased it in and out and whispered in his ear. He came too soon. I needed more. But this would have to do.

When he kissed me afterwards, he muttered a reminder about dinner with his kids the next day. The mood was broken. Whatever euphoria was coursing through me evaporated. And a phantom version of Mads, whose memory had waited patiently in the corners of my mind, climbed into bed between us. As Niklas fell asleep, I slid my hand between my legs and finished what he started. And this time, Mads filled my mind and I came and pressed my lips together to keep from gasping his name.

* * *

We went on like this for several days, seeing each other in passing. Niklas went to London for a conference, returned two days later distracted and moody, and then spent his evenings teaching or at his office. I worked late, telling myself if I worked I wouldn't think about Mads or when I could go to Copenhagen or if I even should. August bled into September and I still hadn't told Eddy about what had happened despite all her attempts to get me to talk about whether I'd broached the subject with Niklas. I held her off for a while with excuses about work and needing to meet a deadline, which was close enough to the truth that I didn't feel so guilty.

But she wouldn't let me get off so easily. She showed up at my office and hijacked me for lunch. I should have known there was only so long she would let me keep this to myself.

"We're going to that sushi bar you like so much," Eddy said. She hated sushi, so this was her way of making sure I came. "We need to catch up. Now."

So we walked to the sushi bar, and I gave her a vague rundown of what happened. I didn't want to share Mads or what had happened between us with anyone. This was my secret. And I wanted to keep it that way, even as I was pretending it meant nothing. Even as I deleted Mads's text messages or sent hasty replies that said nothing but still promised something. But Eddy was shrewd. Of course she was. This was the woman who'd once dated four men at the same time, and managed to keep each of them from finding out about one another. This was the woman who thought infidelity was not as big a deal as everyone made it out to be. But she was also the only person I knew who seemed to come away unscathed from every relationship, even when it broke down spectacularly. The men she left never seemed angry with her. She somehow managed to remain friends with them. I had the feeling that this wouldn't be the case for Niklas and me. If we ever fell apart, there would be no going back, no meeting for the occasional drink and a quick tumble. The end would be the end.

"So you went to Copenhagen, met this services specialist and looked at a few profiles?" Eddy wasn't buying it. I could hear it in her voice but she wasn't about to accuse me of holding back. She waited instead. "Did any of them seem like good prospects?"

"One or two," I said, as I pushed my salmon roll around my plate. I wasn't really hungry, and Eddy was making me a little nervous. If I picked up the roll with my chopsticks, I'd just drop it, so I took a quick sip of my sake and then added, "They had videos of all the donors. It was all very impressive, actually."

"And Niklas is on board now?"

"Not yet."

"I thought you were going to talk to him about it when you came home."

"I was, but he's been away—first in London and now he's teaching that night class again, so he's never around." I cast aside my chopsticks. To hell with it. I picked up the salmon roll and plopped it in my mouth. "We're going to the beach house in Skåne this weekend. I'll talk to him about it then."

"Good. You need to tell him about this so you can make a decision, both of you."

"I know."

"Are the Evil Steps coming with you?"

"I hope not. I told Niklas we needed some time alone." I kept my eyes down and focused on peeling a prawn from my rice ball. "The only thing we've had together is some late-night sex and then falling asleep."

"Better than no sex at all."

"Is that your situation, then? I thought you and Andreas were always at it like rabbits."

"Andreas is too busy right now." Eddy shrugged breezily. "I think his eyes are wandering. It's fine. He'll come back."

"Shit, Eddy. I'm sorry."

"Why? It's not your fault, sweetie. He wants a taste of something new, and then he'll get it out of his system. In the meantime, I can do what I want."

"Which is?"

"Fuck if I know. Maybe I'll go to Paris. I might go to Rome. Colin is there, so I could always visit him." Colin was the man Eddy had once called the love of her life. He was also her fall back guy whenever anything was going pear-shaped. If she was thinking of visiting him, then Andreas and his wandering eye must have really been bothering her.

"Why don't you and Colin just try to make a go of it?" I asked. "How many years has it been of you two bouncing between relationships and still hooking up anyway?"

Eddy pursed her lips together and watched me steadily. "You know that's a forbidden topic, Laney."

"Why?"

"Because Colin and I can never make it work." She let out a sigh that was both wistful and resigned. I knew she still had feelings for Colin. She'd been in love with him for so long and they'd tried—on and off—to make their relationship stick, but it never did. Sometimes I wondered if it was cold feet on both parts or if it was everything that happened when they were together in New York. There'd been so many factors: racial tension, misunderstandings that flared with the merest kindling into something too large to control, so-called friends who disapproved, and then Colin's sudden decision to move back to Europe. And then he was gone, and Eddy—who was so in love that she would have done any-thing for him—followed him to Europe, but couldn't convince him that they were worth fighting for. And then she gave up and looked for someone else to love. They still spoke often; they never let go properly.

"Maybe you could now. You're not kids anymore."

Eddy gave me a cool look. I was treading on thin ice. "There is nothing left there. We're just friends."

"So why are you thinking about going to Rome?"

"To visit a friend," she stressed and then drained her glass of sake. "I don't want to talk about me. I want to talk about you."

"There's nothing to tell, Eddy." I ate my last piece of sushi. Mads flashed through my mind. I pushed him back into a corner. "I went to the clinic and I met one of the specialists. She took me through the entire process. I still need to think about it."

"You know you have to shoot yourself up with hor-mones before they can inseminate you, right?"

I nodded. "She told me about it."

"Are you nervous?" Before I could answer, she shook her head and said, "I would be. I would be, if I were you. You're stepping into something completely new. You don't even know what to expect."

"I expect a child at the end."

"Well, you'd get a child, but you know what I mean. The magnitude of it."

"As long as I don't get a child like Siri, I will be hap-py."

Eddy laughed and slapped my arm. "Girl, you are in-sane! You know what I mean. This isn't just about having a baby. This is about bringing someone into this world and being connected to them in a way that can even supersede whatever you feel for Niklas. You will love your child more than you love him."

"I know. Ingrid told me about how it was for her. She said she had to learn to love Anton again, because she only had eyes for her babies."

I tried to imagine it, though. What would my life with Niklas be like with the addition of a baby? One of the home offices would have to become a nursery. When Niklas was still married to Karolina, the babies slept in their bedroom—often in between them in bed—and he'd hated it. Not because the babies invaded his space, but because he was terrified he would accidentally crush them in his sleep. He was a wild sleeper. I knew it from how many times his arms and hands crashed into me at night. I'd already decided our nursery would also have a daybed, so that I could sleep there if need be.

"That could be you, Laney," Eddy said softly. "You need to think about it. You and Niklas are already going through a rough patch. A baby could make it even rougher."

"I thought you were gung-ho for me to do this."

"I want you to do it, if you think you're ready for it. Not because I said you should do it. Did you meet any of the donors?"

"A few, but none of them really lit any fires for me."

"You don't have to fall in love with them. You just have to like the look of them."

"That's what I meant." I said quickly. "I didn't really see anyone who looked like he should be the man whose... DNA should mix with mine."

"Do you still have the files?"

"Yes, I keep going through them to see if anyone really jumps out at me." I didn't want to reveal that there was only one file I kept reviewing. Only one file was worth reading for me. I sometimes imagined what our children would look like. Because if I went through it once, I would do it again. I wanted two kids. And I knew if I went through with artificial insemination, I would want Mads to be the father.

My phone beeped. I glanced at it; a reminder that I had a meeting in twenty minutes. "I need to get back to work. Meeting."

Eddy kissed my cheek. "I know there's more than you're letting on, sweetie. You're just too distracted."

"I... I'm just nervous about telling Niklas, that's all."

I rushed back to work, telling myself this was for the best. If I told Eddy, it would make whatever was happening between Mads and me too real. As it was, when only I knew, I could pretend it was insignificant. I could compartmentalize everything that had happened, erase his number from my phone, and try to convince myself that Mads was just one of those men who knew how to charm a woman into anything. It would have been so easy to dismiss the feelings I had for him. It wasn't something that was burning inside of me, threatening to tear apart my life with Niklas.

* * *

—I'm not going to keep texting you. I have the feeling you've got regrets.

—No regrets, just confused. I don't know what to do.

—I want to see you again.

—I want to see you too.

—Well, at least we know that.

—I could come next weekend.

—Another meeting?

—No, but I'll tell Niklas I've got meetings.

—Don't lie like that, Laney. Say you're seeing a friend. That's the truth... technically.

—I can't just say that. He knows all of my friends in Copenhagen.

—Okay, Okay. Sorry. I just... I miss you. I feel like we need to explore this.

—Me too.

—I could come to Stockholm.

—No, it's easier if I come to you.

—So you'll come.

—I'll text you when I've booked my tickets.

—Don't book a hotel, stay with me.

—Easier if I book a hotel...

—No, stay with me this time.

* * *

We went to the countryside, Niklas and I. But being there with just the two of us no longer felt like such a brilliant idea. We drove to Skåne early in the morning to beat the traffic, but Niklas was irritable. By the time we arrived at our house in Yngsjö, his mood was so foul I wished I'd stayed home. But I told myself to ignore it. Once we opened up the house and let some fresh air in, he would be fine. Besides, the weather was perfect for a long weekend—the sky was a perfect shade of turquoise. The waves rolled and splashed against the shoreline. I kicked off my shoes and pulled open the sliding glass door. A salty breeze swirled past me. I could see a bumblebee buzzing around the asters I'd planted. I folded my arms across my chest and stood on the wooden slats of the terrace, letting the air fill me. Behind me, Niklas muttered complaints. His sister hadn't kept the house as he liked it. He'd have to spend all weekend rearranging things so they were how liked them.

"It doesn't matter, Niklas," I called out over my shoulder. "We're only going to be here a few days. We can put it right at Christmas."

He swore, ignored me, and started moving things around in the kitchen cupboards. I shook my head. I knew I ought to help him, but I just didn't see the point. He would go behind me, changing whatever I fixed. The tension between us would pull tighter and we'd end up fighting in that way that never seemed like a fight to other people--with me simply avoiding Niklas and putting as much distance between us as possible and him pointedly glaring at me and not saying a word. Fights like that could last for days, or weeks, even. And now didn't seem like a good time to even cross into that territory.

"Should I drive to Martins Rökeri and pick up some fish for tonight?"

He grunted a yes at me. I fished out the car keys and slid my feet into the flip-flops I always left by the front door. I didn't ask him what he wanted. I knew by heart. But the house felt suffocating. I rushed to the car and put some distance between us, following the narrow roads that took me from Yngsjö to Åhus. It was only six kilometers away, but the distance was enough to allow me to disconnect from the tension between Niklas and me. I knew it was my fault. At least, I thought it was my fault. I'd come home from Copenhagen full of a broiling longing for Mads. There was no room in my thoughts for Niklas, and he was clued in enough to sense that some strange impasse had come.

This is temporary, I told myself, as I turned onto the narrow curving road that led to Martin's.

It was late enough in the season that most of the summer people had returned to their normal lives in Malmö and Stockholm. The parking lot was nearly empty. Just a few cars with German license plates, one or two with Swedish plates. I parked close to the door and took a moment to enjoy the silence. Though there was the faint hum of traffic and the occasional burst of Swedish or German being spoken, there was nothing to distract from how beautiful it was in this part of Skåne. Across the creek, graceful houses lined the waterway as trees bowed beneath the weight of the late summer heat. I looked inside the small shop. A group of Germans was trying to make it clear what they wanted with the two girls behind the counter. Two older Swedes, most likely pensioners who lived in Åhus all year, waited with impatient faces that burned red.

I retraced my steps and retreated to the picnic tables by the water. I sat down, facing the water, and listening to the call of the gulls swooping overhead. Going back to the house wasn't an option. Not now, while Niklas was in a funk over things being out of place. This side of him always came out when we left Stockholm and came to either his family's summerhouse in Skåne, or the small house we rented in the archipelago. He liked things just so. Even at home, he was this way. I tried to remember if he'd been like that when we first met. We'd spent most of our time in my small apartment in Kungsholmen. He used to call it cozy, but then one day when we reminisced about those days, he derided my old place, calling it shabby and ridiculous.

I remember being stunned. He used to say how much he preferred my apartment to the place he'd shared with Karolina. How there was nothing unnecessary cluttering it. How lived-in it felt, like a proper home. Maybe he'd only been positive because he knew he needed to sound good to keep getting me in bed. Maybe it was all part of the "courtship." Of course it was, it always was. You said and did all the right things to keep getting closer to the person. I'd been the same. I'd gone into this relationship pretending to be more together than I really was. All I could think was "we clicked, this should be easy." I didn't know the click was just the beginning. I didn't know how awful his kids were. I didn't know about his mood swings. He didn't know how messy I could be, or how I liked to stay in bed late at the weekends and not get up early for morning jogs. All these things we discovered like a lot of other couples. But somehow it felt like our journey as a couple was full of wrong turns and dead end streets. I used to ask myself if everyone else had to deal with a partner's ex like Karolina—who could be charming in parts but was usually rude—or if the other women I knew who were second or third wives spent as much time compromising with teenagers who didn't give a flying fuck about them. Aside from Eddy and Ingrid, I didn't have anyone I trusted enough to compare notes with. And now that Mads was a part of the mix, I didn't think I could discuss it with them, either.

My phone rang, jarring me from the course my thoughts were taking. It was Niklas. "Why did you just leave?"

"I told you I was going to the smokehouse to get some fish."

"I thought you meant later."

"I'm at Martin's now," I said, not wanting to get into a discussion about the semantics of what I'd meant when I said I was going to the smokehouse for fish. "I'm just waiting for the Germans to leave."

"Okay."

"Is everything alright, Niklas?"

"I don't know... yeah. I suppose it depends."

"On what? Is it the kids?"

"No, it's you."

"What are you talking about?"

"I was unpacking our bags and I found some files."

"Sweetie, I told you I would take care of that."

"Why do you have files about men in your bag?"

Shit. Shit. Shit. My hands were shaking. How the fuck was I going to explain that? "It's... it was part of something I wanted to talk to you about while we're here."

"Don't be so cryptic, Laney. What's going on?"

"I don't want to talk about it over the phone," I said firmly, willing a resolve I usually never felt when Niklas and I were arguing. "But it's got to do with us and having a baby."

"My God, don't we have enough going on, Laney? Do we really have to talk about this scheme of yours this weekend?"

"I think we do. It's why we came here, isn't it?"

"I thought we came here because you wanted to have some time alone with me."

"I did. I do. And I thought we could discuss this, too. And we will. Just as soon as I pick up the fish. And I'm guessing we need some wine as well, so I'll swing by Systembolaget." Systembolaget was the state-run alcohol store. At least Åhus had one of a decent size.

"Laney, just get the fish and come home." His anger came through loud and clear. Niklas didn't shout, but his voice always sounded darker, more intense when he was losing his temper. I could imagine the tense atmosphere I'd come home to.

"Do we have wine at home?"

"I don't know. Probably not."

"Do you want wine at dinner tonight?"

"Well, yeah."

"Then I will go to Systemmet when I am done here, and then I'll come home. And then we can talk." I hung up before he could say anything else, then I turned off my phone. It was better this way. And it would give me time to figure out how to tell him about the sperm bank and using someone else's sperm to have our baby, if there was going to ever be a baby.

I came home laden with bags. One stop became several as I tried to use the time as a buffer, a way to give Niklas a chance to calm down and me a chance to come up with good excuses. In a way, I didn't need excuses—he'd said we could think about adoption, so he wasn't against the idea of us starting our own family. Sometimes, I thought the reason he was the way he was acting—especially with the vasectomy—was because, as much as he loved Siri and Jesper, their arrivals in his life marked the end of what intimacy had existed between Niklas and Karolina.

When we moved in together, our sex life was explosive, and then we went from having his kids once a month to every other week, and now they came and went as they pleased. We never knew which nights we'd be alone, or when Siri would show up with a new boy hanging on to her, or when Jesper would show up, wanting a gaming night with his friends because our TV was bigger than his mother's and because she refused to allow noisy, disturbing video games in her Zen-like apartment. So we were forced to accept this. I was forced to, knowing Niklas could never say no to his kids, and he still felt guilt about leaving their mother. Which I didn't understand, since she'd already left him emotionally when he finally decided to leave her.

But I did have a reason to be guilty. I'd slept with another man. I couldn't stop thinking about that other man, even though I loved Niklas. And I was afraid I didn't love him enough. If I loved him enough, would I have been able to give in so easily to Mads? It wasn't as though Mads had needed to do very much to get me into bed. I was already attracted to him before I'd even spoken a word to him. I was still attracted to him. I could still taste him in my mouth and feel his phantom touch on my skin.

I steeled myself and bustled into the house, blathering about the goat's cheese I'd found at one of the local farms, and the amazing flounder and hot-smoked salmon they'd had at Martins Rökeri. Niklas was sitting on the sofa, his head in his hands. I stopped, feeling all my excuses drain through me, and the only thing that spread through me was the slow burn of guilt. I'd done this to him. I was sure of it. I put the food and wine in the fridge, and then I went over to him and sat beside him on the sectional sofa.

"I should have told you about going to the sperm bank."

"Why do you always do this?" he demanded, keeping his body stiff. "Why can't you ever talk to me about things?"

"I needed to find out for myself what sort of options I had."

"I thought we agreed we could look into adoption."

"We didn't actually agree on anything," I reminded him. "You made it sound like it was a long shot. I figured this was something I could do, that would at least get us information."

"Did you sign any paperwork?"

"No! I went there to meet with a client services specialist, and she told me about how they do things there. And she gave me some sample files so I could see what information they have on the donors." I reached out to touch his arm, but he was so tense. I wanted to assure him that we were okay, but I was afraid he'd sense my betrayal. "I just wanted to know what options I had. I found out about this sperm bank and since I was already in Copenhagen, I thought I ought to take a chance and go there, find out how they might be able to help me... us... if we decided to try that way."

Niklas didn't say anything for a long time. He shook his head and then let out a long sigh. "Sometimes I don't understand you at all, Laney."

"What's that supposed to mean?"

"If you didn't sign any paperwork or any contract, then why do you have those files?"

"Ida—the client services specialist—gave them to me. She said she wanted me to go through the sort of information prospective recipients receive so I could feel comfortable with any decision I made. She said it was standard."

"Why couldn't you tell me this before you went to Copenhagen?"

"I thought you would get angry. And I was right. You are angry."

"I'm angry because you tried to hide this from me."

"If I'd told you about it, would you have been okay with me going to the sperm bank?"

"I don't know, Laney. You never even gave me a chance to figure out how I'd feel."

"Would you be okay with me doing this? Using a sperm donor?"

"I don't know. I need to think about this."

But I had the feeling he would say no. Because we hadn't discussed this "properly," because he really didn't want to go through this. And I knew that instinctively, before I even went to Copenhagen, and it made me want to walk out the door. But I stayed. I didn't move from my spot on the sofa. I just sat there, letting the silence grow between us and wondering where we went from here. Niklas left the sofa and went in the kitchen area. Sometimes he needed distance from me to think. He was a therapist by trade, but he didn't often use the tools he gave his patients. Sometimes, he used them on me or the kids, but—and this was something the three of us had in common—we all hated it. If he tried it now, I would go along with it. I was the one at fault, the one keeping secrets. Not him. He pulled out a box wine his sister had left in the fridge from her last visit, and filled a glass for himself.

"I'm going to cook. It'll clear my head."

"Do you want me to help?" I asked. I felt like I needed to do something. I couldn't just sit there. I didn't trust myself to be alone.

"Just... no. Go for a walk, leave me alone for a while. I need to think."

"We should still talk about this, Niklas."

"I said I need to think, Laney." He slammed his hand on the countertop. He shook his head slowly. "Just give me a little space. I'll take care of the fish and everything."

"All right." On the coffee table, the files stared up at me accusatively. I swallowed hard.

The file on top was Mads's.

The mood lightened somewhat after dinner. We sat outside on the terrace and let the sea breeze carry away some of the tension. Niklas became more like his old self, relaxed and easygoing. I didn't like the neurotic part of him that came out whenever we came here. It made me hate his sister, and Ylva was actually a pleasant person to be around. She was just one of those women who couldn't sit still and who needed to have something to do constantly. Finding order seemed to be her cup of tea. She wanted everything nice and neat, but she never considered that her system of organization only worked for her. Yes, I could blame Niklas's mood on Ylva. It was easier than admitting I'd played the biggest role in it. Niklas was more relaxed now that he was in the loop. He'd even taken the step to discuss our options in a way that at least felt proactive. But now I was reticent. As I listened to him, a small part of me became cynical and almost snarky. That part of me—the part that Niklas didn't appreciate very much—questioned why he was so willing to discuss our future family. Why couldn't he have been so open about it a few weeks ago? Why now?

You wouldn't have slept with Mads if Niklas had been open with you from the start, the cynical me whispered in my ear. You wouldn't have even bothered to look up that clinic if he'd been willing to discuss this with you from the start.

I watched him from across the table and slowly sipped my glass of chardonnay. The sun was already beginning to set, and the sky over the Bay of Hanö was soft shade of rose. Soon, the sky would go velvety dark and fill with stars. But for now, striations of clouds mixed and stretched across the evening sky. Something snapped between us. Niklas seemed so self-satisfied. He behaved as though going to a sperm donor was his idea all along, and that I'd simply hastened things along. He patted my arm in a manner that felt almost brotherly. I sensed no sexual attraction or desire. Not from him. Not from me. I didn't want to sleep with him. I imagined lying in bed beside him, the bed rocking as he tossed and turned. And the only thought in my head was to book a ticket to Copenhagen as soon as possible. Explore the possibilities with Mads, and then figure it out later.

It was so wrong. I shouldn't have been thinking about another man. But I couldn't stop myself, and Niklas wasn't doing anything to make me feel like I should want to be loyal to him.

*   *   *

That night, I tried to make love to Niklas, without thinking about Mads. Whenever my mind wandered, I focused only on Niklas and tightening my arms around him or breathing in the warm scent of him. I kept my eyes open so I saw only him, his dark hair now mussed up as he braced his arms on either side of my head... as his cock rubbed inside me, hitting just the right spots to elicit a surprised moan. I didn't think of Mads when Niklas flipped me over and took me from behind. I didn't think about him when I came. I didn't think about Mads until after my body slowly returned to normal, no longer attuned to Niklas's every move, every breath... when the catch of his breath was no longer in my ear, and his hands no longer taking possession of me, my thoughts became restless and my body, though satisfied, longed for the touch of another pair of hands.

I lay beside Niklas, listening to his breathing even out as he fell into dreams. Our bodies were still entwined, but our minds no longer connected. The air in the room was heavy and damp. I tried to inch away, but I was caught.

He murmured in a sleep-heavy voice, "I love you, baby."

"Love you, too," I whispered back.

But the emotions behind the words rang hollow. Oh, babe... what happened to us? When did the love we shared dissipate?

I wanted to go back in time. Back to that night when Niklas and I first met, in the bar at the Hilton Hotel in Södermalm. That night, when he first hooked me and I lost my desire to be footloose, to be free to fuck whomever I wanted when I wanted.

I wished I could return to that moment and figure out just what spell he'd cast over me and recast it, so I could love him more. Because I was scared.

Were we just idling until our relationship died a slow, uneventful death, or would it implode with a ferocity that would leave us both scarred? What would happen to us?

I couldn't sleep that night. Even with Niklas's body curled around mine, I found no solace. I'd set this in motion and now it was spiraling out of my control.

CHAPTER SIX

Lost Weekend

"**D**o you want to go to Kivik?" Niklas asked as we cleaned up after breakfast. It was another impossibly sunny day, still warm though it was mid-September. I'd already walked along the beach while Niklas slept in, but I was restless. I wanted to get away from the house. I wanted to get away from him.

"No, but you go ahead." I stretched and sidestepped him as he absently reached out for me. "I was thinking of riding my bike for a while."

"I could wait for you."

"I don't want to go to Kivik. You go. It's okay."

When he left, I breathed a sigh of relief. What the hell was I doing? I'd wanted this weekend away with him. Now I couldn't wait to be away from him. Instead of leaving the house, I lay down on our bed and closed my eyes, letting myself think of Mads without having to consider Niklas and his proximity. I tried to imagine what sort of future there was for us. Did I really want more with him than an affair? Was that what I was having? In Copenhagen, it had all been so crystal clear. At least in the confines of my hotel room.

I reached under my pillow for my phone and checked for messages. There were none, other than two text messages from Eddy. I scrolled through my contacts until I found Mads's number. I knew I was taking a stupid risk, calling him when I was so uncertain of everything. But I wanted to hear his voice, even if it would do no more than give me a false sense of security. I pressed call and waited as his phone rang. It took five rings before he answered, sounding out of breath and a little irritated.

"It's me."

There was a long pause, long enough that I was afraid he'd hang up on me. But then he said, "I was hoping you would call. I wasn't sure it was a good idea for me to call you."

"It's better if I call you." I tried to imagine where he was. Music was playing, just loud enough that I could hear it was the Rolling Stones' "Gimme Shelter," loud enough to blanket any other sounds.

"Are you still at the summer house?"

"Until Monday, then we drive back to Stockholm."

"Is everything okay?"

"I don't know. No. I think... I think I might leave Niklas. I don't know. I don't know what I want."

"Laney, slow down. What do you mean?"

"I still love him, but I don't love him enough." I took a deep breath to calm myself. My pulse was racing so hard I felt a little lightheaded. "Or... I don't know if I love him enough. And I can't stop thinking about you. I just... I need to see you."

"So come here. Come when you can." His voice set off a thousand sparks along my spine, hitting me in just the right places to weaken me.

"I think I can come on Friday. I can only come for the weekend."

"It's better than nothing."

"I'll have to visit some friends while I'm there."

"Okay... just give me whatever time you can."

"Does this, what we're doing, feel wrong?"

"No. Because it feels like it was always supposed to be me and you."

His words set free a wave of relief inside me. I felt the same, even if it scared me. "I don't know what to do, Mads."

"You don't have to feel guilty, Laney," he said softly. "It was like we were meant to meet each other. Otherwise, why would we have seen each other before you even went to the clinic?"

"Maybe it was just a happy coincidence."

"Maybe it was. But I know I felt so connected to you. And I know you felt the same."

"I keep asking myself what's going to happen with us."

"We don't know if we don't try."

"I don't know if I can just leave Niklas."

"I'm not asking you to. Just come see me."

His request seemed so simple. Just come see him. It was easy enough to go to Copenhagen. Just an hour's flight. I could slip away the same day, come back in the evening. Come back the next morning and claim a meeting ran over. "Okay... I'll come. I'll come on Friday."

"Good. Tell me when you've booked everything, and when you're going to land. I'll meet you at the airport."

"I know I'm going to feel even guiltier, but I can't pretend there's nothing between us."

"No one's asking you to do that, Laney."

"Niklas—"

"He's had five years with you, and you aren't happy. How many more years are you supposed to give him?"

His question hung in the air, unanswered, unanswerable. I had no way of denying Mads's words. The truth was, I wasn't happy. Maybe I hadn't been happy longer than I'd realized, and just blinded myself to it because it was easier than admitting I was drowning. I thought about those early days, when Niklas's children weren't so involved in our relationship—when Karolina didn't want them anywhere near me. That was when they were still young enough that their dislike of me never seemed to touch me. And Niklas didn't feel the need to push me to like his children. He didn't even behave like I had anything to do with them in the beginning. Maybe he thought I was transitory. Maybe I was never intended to be around this long.

Maybe it was time for me to do something different.

Niklas returned from Kivik with bags of heritage apples, bottles of apple wine and apple cider, and jars of apple cinnamon jelly. I was perched on a bar stool by the kitchen island, watching as he unpacked each bag. Apparently, we were going to overdose on all things apple.

"How was your bike ride?" He came over and kissed the top of my head. I wanted the gesture to feel more romantic, but there were no sparks. "How far did you make it?"

"I ended up taking a nap." I smiled up at him, but I couldn't summon any passion or desire.

How long had we been like this? He kissed my cheek and I caught the familiar warmth of his natural scent. Normally, I wanted to bury my nose in the crook of his neck and kiss him there. But now, I held him without craving him, without my fingers automatically raking through his hair or unbuttoning his shirt. He pulled me out of the chair and folded me into his arms. We kissed again, our lips tentative and without their usual certainty. I wasn't sure which of us began moving to the sofa, but somehow we ended up there, falling backwards so I was on top of him. My T-shirt was pushed up, Niklas was claiming me again, with his hands on my skin, with his mouth...

Later, when we were both naked, I was straddling him, riding him and trying to disconnect for a little while from Mads, from the longing for him. Niklas tried to pull me in for a kiss, but I planted my hands on his chest, pressing him down so I could maintain control. I needed to do this, to remain the one on top. He was close to coming, but I was struggling, trying to bring myself to the edge of an orgasm with no success. Then Niklas managed to flip me on my back. He slid down between my legs and kissed my inner thighs. His kisses tickled, and then tempted me. Finally, I began to respond. My muscles loosened as his lips brushed my clit. He sucked and nibbled there, grazed his tongue along its tender nub until I moaned and gripped his hair.

He stroked and fucked me until, finally, my orgasm erupted in waves. First gentle, then undulating into something wilder and untamed. I was panting by the end, and my body was spent. My forearm covered my eyes, shielding me from Niklas and his perceptive gaze. He nuzzled my breasts, kissed a line from my nipples to my shoulders and whispered my name. I couldn't look at him. My God, what was wrong with me? Why couldn't I love him? Or did I love him, and have only a fleeting attraction for Mads?

"What's wrong?" He touched my cheek. "Baby, why are you crying?"

I shook my head, tried to turn my face away but he wouldn't let me. He gently turned my face back to his. "Laney, babe. I know we're going through a tricky patch, but we'll get through this. I love you, babe. We'll get through this."

I let him kiss me again and, after a while, I kissed him back, feeling drained, wanting to be held and consoled, knowing I didn't deserve it. But his reassurances, his calming voice and gentle touch, relaxed me. Maybe he was right. Maybe this was just a rough patch, a premature seven-year itch. Maybe all of this with Mads was a silly aberration.

*   *   *

The rest of our long weekend passed without any unexpected phone calls or interruptions. The kids didn't ring, Karolina didn't text with ridiculous demands. Even Eddy left me alone. There were no messages from Mads either and, in a way, I was glad. I needed to feel connected with Niklas again, and I couldn't do that if I was constantly wondering if every beep or buzz was another text message from Mads.

By the time we drove back to Stockholm, the air between us was almost normal again. He was more affectionate, and so was I. My desire to touch him, to rake my fingers through his hair, to be near him had returned, though not with the same force. By nightfall, we were back in Stockholm, back in our apartment, and greeted by the stench of spilled alcohol and sweat and stale cigarette smoke. I opened windows and tried to air out the apartment.

It didn't take a rocket scientist to figure out that Siri and Jesper had invited their friends over while we were away. We didn't mind when they had friends over—but we did have two rules that Niklas and I insisted on, no matter what: no parties without our prior consent and any detritus or damage from said party is the full responsibility of the hosts. Siri and Jesper were well aware of these rules. Yet they'd chosen to ignore them, again.

"I'll have to talk to them about this again," Niklas said resignedly. He opened the balcony doors and a cool breeze slithered in. The sour cloud of spilled alcohol and vomit still hung ominously, and a part of me wished I could escape it.

"It won't matter," I told him as I picked up a saucer that had been used as an ashtray. "They'll just apologize, and then do it again next time we're away."

Niklas flinched, as if my words stung him. I didn't press the issue. His children were always a touchy subject for us. He didn't like to believe there was any malice in them. He wrote it all down to teenage thoughtlessness. This was probably the case with Jesper, but with Siri I was more inclined to believe it was a misguided sense of entitlement. I'd said so before, and been met with stony silence or a therapist-style questioning about my own teenage years, as if that would magically explain my anger at her behavior. No, there was no point pressing here. Niklas would side with them. He always did.

We worked together, cleaning up the apartment and ridding it of lipstick-stained glasses and cigarette-butt-filled beer cans. Smelly beer stains marred the upholstery on two of our couches. We found a used condom under our guest bed, so we stripped the bed linens after we'd disposed of it. The guest bathroom reeked of vomit and urine. I grimaced. This was my limit. I closed the door and left it as it was. Niklas could clean it up. I'd done enough. When I was a teenager, I never dared have a party in my parents' house while they were away. My father was too strict, and their neighbors were too present, too willing to rat me out. Any illicit partying was done at the homes of my friends, who lived in other neighborhoods, but we never dared to do so as often as Siri and Jesper did. We knew there were always consequences. Punishment or, if your parents were old school enough, an ass whipping that hurt enough to instill a fear of not toeing the line. For Siri and Jesper, the only consequence would be a lukewarm lecture from Niklas and radio silence from Karolina.

"I'm sorry, Laney." Niklas came up behind me and rubbed my shoulders.

"Sorry for what?"

"Sorry I've never really supported you when it comes to them."

"I think it comes with the territory," I said as I turned to face him. "People always defend their kids in situations like ours."

"But they're not always right, and I know this. I should have been better at sticking up for you when you needed me to do so."

"It's okay." I kissed his cheek. At least he was finally saying it. "Roseanne Barr used to say that all kids are thieves and liars. At least your kids aren't thieves." I winked at him and we both laughed.

The apartment was clean now, but the sour funk of old cigarette butts and spilled beer still hung in the air. Niklas wrinkled his nose. "Maybe I'll call the cleaning service tomorrow."

We changed the sheets on our bed, just to be safe.

It took a long time to fall asleep when we finally went to bed. All of my confusion came to the surface again. I lay beside Niklas, holding his hand and trying to absorb his calm. He'd fallen asleep easily. But I lay there, listening to someone in a neighboring courtyard singing out of tune, the faint whirr of night buses, and soft voices as neighbors returned from nearby bars and restaurants. I moved closer to Niklas. He pulled my arm around him as he turned onto his side. Maybe we were okay. Niklas was a good man, and I knew this. It was one of the reasons I fell deeper in love with him after that first encounter. It was one of the reasons I decided to stay here in Sweden, instead of moving on when I'd had the chance. Niklas used to tell me that we were like those half circles in Aristophanes' theory of soul mates, constantly searching for our other halves, and then we found one another in that bar on a Third Thursday. Just then, I wanted him to be right. I didn't want to think that I could fall out of love with him and not even notice it. I wanted to feel that brightly burning certainty again. I didn't want to be without him.

I just didn't know how much longer I could be with him.

In the morning, my body was stiff from having slept in the same position too long. Niklas was already awake. I could hear him in the kitchen, starting the coffee maker. I stretched, trying to revive my stubborn muscles and bring some life back to this old body of mine. My ankles cracked, my shoulders creaked. I hadn't expected my body to be so noisy when I was only thirty-three. These were the sounds of my mother's body, my grandmother's body—not my body. I shuddered to think what it would sound like when I was forty or fifty.

Niklas appeared in the doorway. "I've started coffee. Shall I pop down to Brunkeberg's Bakery and get some bread for us?"

A cozy feeling of warmth swept over me. "Thanks, Nicke. Maybe I'll work from home today."

"You should. We had a long drive, and then all that damned cleaning yesterday. By the way, I called the cleaning service. They're sending someone over this afternoon to take care of the rest of the mess."

"That sounds perfect. I don't think I could stomach scouring the apartment for more half-full beer cans and used condoms."

"I still can't believe they left the apartment in such a state. Siri knows better. Jeppe too."

I nodded in agreement, but the truth of the matter was that neither of them gave a flying fuck about any rules Niklas tried to enforce. They pretended to listen and respect his wishes, and then continued doing whatever it was he'd asked them not to do. It had been this way for the last five years. I didn't see how one more angry lecture would change anything.

But I tried to show my support by suggesting, "It might help if you make them understand the weight of their actions. You could always take a page from my father's book and make them pay for whatever it is they've done. Make them pay for the cleaning service this time. You know how much they hate spending their own money on other people."

"That might just work. Thanks, babe." He flashed a brilliant smile at me, and then he headed down the hallway. A few moments later, the front door opened and then slammed shut. I was sitting up now, my feet dangling over the edge of the bed as I contemplated what to do with my day. I could work from home. It would be nice not to be in the office, to have the serenity of my home office and work relatively undisturbed.

I slipped into my bathrobe and padded down the hallway. My handbag was where I'd left it, on the floor in the hall by my sandals. But when I looked inside it, my phone wasn't there. I went back to the bedroom, still no sign of my phone. Shit... where had I put it last night? I went through the entire apartment, even Siri's room but I couldn't find it. That's when the panic building in me came to an ugly head. Fuck—what if Niklas found my phone? What if he was scrolling through all of my messages now? I dumped out my bag on the couch and

checked every pocket. Nothing. I checked all the bedrooms again--still nothing. Shit, shit, shit... I was still
searching the apartment when Niklas returned.

"What's wrong?" he asked as he unpacked the bread
and fruit he'd picked up.

"I can't find my phone."

"Did you leave it in the car last night?"

"I don't know."

"I'll head back down and check."

"No, I'll do it—" but he was already out of the door.

Please let my phone not be in the car. All I could
think was what if Mads had left a message and Niklas
saw it. This was getting too dangerously close. But I
needed to calm down. I went in the kitchen and poured
myself a cup of coffee. Niklas made his coffee Swedish-
style: robust and flavorful. He was pretty picky about his
coffee and bought it from a special coffee and tea specialist on Odengatan that roasted its own beans. I wasn't
certain it tasted any better than the Gevalia or Löfbergs
Lila we bought at the supermarket, but he was convinced
there was a difference. I added milk to mine, but Niklas
always drank his black. I ended up setting out everything we needed for our breakfast: the crusty sourdough
bread he'd bought, cheese and cold cuts, tomatoes and
marmalade. But I couldn't eat. Not until I knew where
my phone was. I listened out for Niklas. It was at least
another fifteen minutes before he finally returned, my
phone in his hand. He set it down on the kitchen island.
The expression on his face was grim.

"Looks like you've got some missed calls," he said without looking at me. "And your battery's nearly dead. You should charge it."

"Okay. Thanks for finding it for me." I went over to him and kissed his cheek. "Where was it?"

"On the floor, under the passenger seat." His jaw had gone tight. He rested his hands on the marble island top. "Babe, who's Mads?"

"One of my new colleagues." The lie came too easily. I tried to remember if I'd deleted the first set of messages he'd sent me. I thought I had but I wasn't sure. "He's from the Copenhagen office."

Niklas nodded slowly. "So it's not the donor?"

"What? What are you talking about?"

"One of the donors. I saw it in his file. His name was Mads."

"This is a completely different Mads. I think it's a pretty common name in Denmark."

He nodded again. "When did you say you were going to Copenhagen again?"

"Probably later this week. We've got to present some ideas to our client." This was at least partly true. Marius, the art director I worked with, was supposed to present our latest ideas. I didn't really need to be there, but I'd already decided I was going.

"Maybe I should meet you there," Niklas said as he picked up the bread knife. He grabbed the loaf of bread and began slicing off thick slices for his sandwich. "We could go to that clinic and I could meet your... what was she called?"

"Client services specialist," I offered. I scrounged through the catchall drawer, looking for the extra iPhone charger we kept there. "I could book a time for us with Ida."

Niklas checked the calendar on his own iPhone. "No, this weekend is no good. I'm going to a CBT seminar in Uppsala. Damn."

"We could always go together next weekend." I didn't want this, but I was trapped and I just went along with it. "We could visit Anton and Ingrid."

"We should do that." But he'd become distracted by something on his phone.

"Nicke? Should I book tickets?"

"I don't know. I need to check my other calendar."

I plugged in my phone and deleted any remaining messages from Mads. I couldn't take any further chances. After today, I knew I would have to be more on the ball. No more leaving my phone around. If I was going to continue seeing Mads, if I was going to cheat, I had to think like a cheater and know I could be caught out at any moment.

*   *   *

We ate breakfast together without speaking. We'd reverted to our usual habit of reading the newspaper—I read the culture section, he read the main section. Every now and then I felt his eyes on me. What was he thinking? Sometimes I smiled at him, and he'd smile back. But once I glanced up and the expression on his face was tense and tight. He blinked quickly, then glanced away, but the tension remained. He wasn't sure he could trust me anymore. And I didn't blame him.

I went through the rest of the day answering email, revising copy for the indecisive cosmetics company, whose global launch for a new lipstick we were handling. They were one of our biggest clients, and they were also one of our most annoying clients. They never seemed to be able to make up their mind about anything. We'd get them on board with a campaign and two days later they'd get cold feet. It was par for the course but it still annoyed the hell out of all of us. But it was my job. So I revised the tagline for the twentieth time. I wrote another version of the press release, announcing their choice of Noomi Rapace as their new spokesmodel for their Bold Impact Color Range. I did everything I could think of that would keep me busy enough to not call Mads or send him an email. I was glad I hadn't befriended him on Facebook. Niklas always claimed he didn't care about social media, but he had an account there so he could keep an eye on Jesper and Siri. In my office, with the door firmly closed, I could stay focused and write what needed to be written, have the telephone meetings that needed to be conducted.

The only thing I couldn't do was stop thinking about Mads.

The file folders were on my desk again. Niklas had put them there last night. Mads's folder was on top. I opened it and read his profile again. The photographs of him didn't do him justice. In the photos, his square jaw looked heavy and out of proportion, his nose almost too off-center. His eyes were almost colorless. But in person, he was so beautiful, so sexy. And his voice hit me at the base of my spine. It was rough, deep. If I closed my eyes and concentrated long enough, I could just hear him saying my name. And it was a little frightening that I could want him and still be afraid of leaving Niklas. Because I knew I was one of those lucky women. I had a de facto husband who was good to me, who tried to make me happy, whose faults weren't so awful that I couldn't live with them. But I couldn't help thinking that, in some way, we were even. He'd cheated on me with Karolina and I'd forgiven him. Sometimes the truce wobbled, but we'd recovered.

And I was willing to jeopardize it to taste something, someone, new.

I used the arrival of the cleaning service as an excuse to go out. I made sure I took my phone, sliding it into the inner pocket of my handbag as I walked towards the door. Niklas was in the living room, tapping away on his iPad. He barely looked up as he asked, "Are you going to be out long?"

I paused just at the door. "I don't think so. I'm meeting Eddy for a drink."

"Ah. Well, give my regards to your lovely cousin."

"Are we going out for dinner tonight?"

"No, Jeppe's coming over, so I thought we could go out some other time."

"Maybe I'll have dinner with Eddy, then. Give you two some time alone."

"Laney, I'd like it if you were here with us." Niklas finally lowered his tablet. He leveled a stern look at me. "You haven't seen Jesper in two weeks."

"I thought you'd want some father-son time, alone," I said, blanketing my irritation with a falsely bright smile. A part of me said I ought to be there. At least his son and I got along when Siri wasn't around. "I'll be back by around six-thirty or seven," I told him. "Are we eating here or going out?"

Monday was usually our Date Night, the one night a week when we let someone else cook for us, or we walked to the Grand on Sveavägen to catch a film and then have a drink afterwards. We'd agreed on it after the hiccup with Karolina. It was supposed to be our way of reconnecting, and it worked for a while.

"I'm cooking," Niklas said. "Maybe you and I can go out tomorrow."

"All right. I'll be back in a bit."

Then I made my escape down the birdcage-style elevator. I told myself I needed fresh air. I needed to move since I'd been stuck behind my desk all day. Really, I needed a break from the tension in the apartment. Ever since Niklas found my phone, he'd been keeping his distance in a far too obvious manner. I wasn't used to this from him. He wasn't usually the sort of person who withheld affection. And, generally, when I worked from home, he found excuses to distract me. He'd suddenly feel the need to take a nap on the IKEA sofa in my office, or he'd realize now was the time to read a book I'd recommended to him—a book that just happened to be in the bookcase behind my desk. Today, he'd stayed away, sequestered in the room he'd made into his office. I wanted the calm again. The only way I could have it back would be to forget about Mads and focus on making things better with Niklas. God, I needed advice....

So I headed to Eddy. She was my oracle for anything to do with relationships. I didn't have a sister I could call. And moving to Sweden hadn't done much to preserve the friendships I'd had. I'd lost touch with so many people simply because of distance. But I'd also learned not to put much faith in holding on to acquaintances. I only had Ingrid, Anton, and Eddy as the people who were the touchstones in my life. And Eddy was pretty much the only family I had.

I needed Eddy to guide me through this love disaster I'd created.

* * *

Sometimes, when I walked out of our apartment building, I imagined being spirited away—by my restlessness, my inability to connect with Niklas on a deeper level, by anything—and finding myself in another life. The life I had in Stockholm was nothing like my life in the United States. I'd grown up on the periphery of a rough neighborhood in West Philadelphia. My neighbors weren't bankers and artists. They were the descendants of the Great Migration, men and women who'd come north looking for work and for dreams, and were met with the realization that the whites of the north hated them just as much as their southern counterparts. And whatever dreams they'd had of a better life, of picket fences and making something of themselves, were swallowed and worn down by working two jobs to make ends meet.

I only took Niklas there once. We were in Philadelphia for a former classmate's wedding. We rented a car and I drove west on Lancaster Avenue, my knuckles tightening as we left behind the green oasis of Drexel University's campus. All too quickly the run-down houses and abandoned storefronts were upon us. Niklas tensed beside me. He didn't say a word when I turned left and drove along Baring Street. I stopped in front of the two-story row house where I'd grown up. A new family lived there—yuppies from the looks of it. The bricks had been repointed, the stamp-sized garden full of hydrangea in full bloom. They'd hung a seasonal flag outside the front door, which they'd painted a shiny red. I nodded at the house. "I grew up here," I told Niklas. "But it didn't look so nice when we lived there."

"It's... small." He nearly grimaced then seemed to remember why were there and that I was watching him. He winked at me like it was an inside joke we shared, but his initial reaction stayed with me and haunted the rest of our stay.

My hometown lost its luster, and all I could see were its faults. We never went back to Philadelphia together again. I didn't want to be reminded that Niklas was ashamed of where I came from. He liked the nice, shiny version of me. The version of me with no gritty past, just a pristine present that revolved around him and the gilded trappings of his life.

*   *   *

Drottninggatan was crowded with tourists, so my progress was slow. I'd had to slalom my way through clots of Swedish and foreign tourists alike. Getting past them proved difficult and frustrating. It reminded me why I hated coming to Drottninggatan. But there was nothing to be done about it. It was the street all of the tour guides instructed tourists to visit first, despite the fact that it was not very interesting and was clotted with the same stores you could find in just about every shopping mall in Sweden.

I dodged my way to PUB and took the elevator up to floor three, where Andreas and Eddy had their boutique. Eddy was busy with a customer when I arrived. I could tell this was a big-money transaction; one of those trust fund babies who would buy all the most expensive vintage dresses she could find, without caring where anything came from or how beautiful it was. While Eddy schmoozed, I browsed. On one of the racks was the most gorgeous slip dress I'd ever seen. It was so light, so fragile, made of blush-pink silk and, when I held it in front of me and imagined wearing it, a little shiver went through me. I would wear my hair down, the lace edging would frame my cleavage to perfection. The price tag fluttered. Four thousand kronor. More than I wanted to spend, but I had to have it.

But the Trust Fund Baby saw it in my hands, and announced that she wanted it. I flashed Eddy a warning look—it wasn't so often that I became so attached to clothing, so she knew better than to try to separate me from this wispy piece of magic. She made an excuse, found a similar dress, and convinced the Trust Fund Baby to buy that one instead. Once she'd gone, Eddy called Bring Express to pick up the rich girl's purchases.

Eddy eyed me with interest. "Buying a sexy dress. An expensive, sexy dress. Things must be getting better with Niklas."

I shrugged. "Not really. He found my phone."

"And?"

"Eddy, it was full of messages from Mads."

Saying his name, even when it was getting me in trouble, felt so good. I could almost melt just thinking of the sound of his voice and the slow, easy way he stroked me when we lay in bed together.

"Who's Mads, sweetie?"

"The man I met in Copenhagen."

"Whoa—hold up now, I thought you said nothing happened there. You've been holding out on me."

"I wanted to tell you."

"Oh, Jesus. Did you sleep with him?"

I nodded, trying to feel contrite but instead an over-whelming sense of joy bubbled inside me. "Eddy, I was so attracted to him. I haven't felt like that with Niklas in so long."

Eddy shushed me. "Sweetie, you were just supposed to go there for information on Super Sperm, you weren't supposed to go hog wild."

"Well, now I think Niklas knows."

"You told him you fucked someone else? Sweetie, you're never supposed to admit to that. You always say 'There was this guy who was really laying it on thick, but I said no'—even when you actually did do it."

"I didn't tell him I slept with anyone," I said quickly. "I only told him about the sperm bank, but then I could-n't find my phone and it was full of messages from Mads."

Eddy gripped my hand. "What were you thinking?"

"I was thinking... I don't know what I was thinking. I just knew I wanted him."

"He must have been something if you strayed."

"He was. He is. I can't even describe it, Eddy, he made me feel like I was alive again. But Niklas hasn't actually said anything. He's just being weird. Distant."

"Maybe he's using one of his therapist tricks on you."

"God, maybe."

"So you need to figure out a plan." Eddy shook her head.

"I know, and that's why I came to you."

"And the guy?"

"Mads?"

"Yes. Is he worth the mess you're making?"

"I don't know. Maybe he is."

"Honey, you can't just toss away five years with Niklas for someone who might only be a maybe."

And then she launched into a Colin analogy. I knew one was coming. It was more a rant than conversation, but I needed to hear what she had to say. And this was a marathon rant by Eddy standards. It continued until we'd closed the shop together. Its tempo increased as we walked homewards. She only paused when we ducked into Melanders Fisk for a glass of wine. At least there, she spoke in more hushed tones, since it was possible we'd bump into someone who knew both Niklas and me.

By the time she finished her analogy, peppered with nostalgic reminiscences of what she'd lost, what she knew she might never have again, my guilt bubbled over. I blinked away the first tears burning my eyes. I excused myself quickly and retreated to the restroom. I splashed cold water on my face and tried to stop the well of tears from coming. My sobs came in heaving gasps. I hated crying, especially in public places. I was someone who cried in private, usually curled up on the sofa in my office, where I could hide. But now I was in a restaurant, too close to my apartment for comfort, trying to cry away all the confusion and guilt. Yes, that awful word again, that was chafing at me.

I tried to get my emotions under control again, but I was too far-gone. My face was burning up, my chest hurt, and my eyes prickled. Eddy came in the bathroom and took charge. She pulled me closer to the sink and turned on the cold water.

"Put your wrists in the water stream."

I did as she asked. Though my hands were still shaking, the cool water cut through the heat burning inside me. She took some paper towels, wet them and then squeezed out the excess water. She then laid the towels across the back of my neck and spoke softly to me. "Relax, Laney. Just listen to me."

I nodded, letting the cool towels absorb all my anxiety. I felt so lost, and I didn't know what to do about it. I knew I couldn't keep doing this, bouncing between Mads and Niklas, and pretending this was tenable. It wasn't fair to either of them. It wasn't even fair to me.

"You need to end whatever it is you started with this guy. You had your taste of something new. But you know, in the end, you should be with Niklas. You need to commit to your relationship because you know—and I know this is true—you love him."

I nodded again. "I do love him."

"You're just confused. That's all this is."

We stood there murmuring to one another, ignoring the other patrons who came in and disappeared into the stalls. I finally calmed down enough that I could go home. I promised Eddy I would call her the next day.

At home, the apartment smelled and looked better. The beer smell had been replaced with the fresh scent of lavender and pine needles. I ventured further into the apartment and called out to Niklas and Jesper. There was no answer. I went into the kitchen. A Post-It note was waiting for me: "We went to Köttbaren to pick up food. Back in a bit."

I took my loot into the bedroom, and then stripped. I was curious to see how the dress would look on me. I slipped it over my head and let the silk slither down my body. The version of me I saw in the mirror looked sensuous and beautiful. I let my hair down. It fell in unruly waves around my shoulders. Was this how Niklas saw me? An attractive brown girl with bee-stung lips, full breasts, and curvy hips. I looked both innocent and sexual. There was something so titillating about this dress. It was so thin, I would not be able to wear a bra with it. And whatever underwear I chose would have to be skimpy at best. This was not a dress for Spanx or granny panties. This was the dress of a seductive woman, and wearing it made me feel like I could be her. I could be one of those women who wore barely-there dresses that skimmed my curves. I could be one of those women who didn't give a damn about anything other than pleasure. Had the woman who'd owned this dress before me been wanton? Had she been the sort of woman who had a lover? I turned slowly, trying to see how the dress looked from every angle. I loved it.

Now, I just had to figure out who I would wear it for.

CHAPTER SEVEN

Voices Carry

"Why don't you wear your new dress tonight?" Niklas raked his fingers
through his hair and then brushed an
invisible piece of fluff from his shoulder. He was standing in front of the full-length mirror in our bedroom,
examining his reflection.

I wrinkled my nose at the idea. "It's too chilly tonight." I'd already decided that it was not a dress to be
worn for Niklas. And definitely not a dress to be squan-
dered on dinner with Karolina.

"You'd look amazing in it."

"No, not tonight." I was already slipping into a knee-
length sheath in black cotton jersey. It was my go-to
dress for dinners at the expensive French restaurants
Niklas favored, or—on nights like tonight—dreaded
dinners at Karolina's place. I was in the walk-in closet,

one of my favorite hiding places in the apartment. Sometimes, when Niklas and the kids went into their exclusive cocoon of familial love, I retreated to my closet. It was bigger than any closet in my parents' house. It was closer to the size of my childhood bedroom. And I could sit for a while in this closet, that had once been the maid's room in the apartment's previous, pre World War I life. Sometimes I even called Eddy from this closet, when dealing with lonely nights while Niklas was away at yet another conference. I called her from the sanctuary of the closet when I discovered Niklas had cheated on me with his ex. Eddy told me to leave him then. I stayed.

I tried not to think about his transgression. Most days, I could squeeze it to the back of my mind. I told myself it was the alcohol's fault. He'd had too much to drink that night. I'd left him there when he was vulnerable. I should have made him come home with me. But I also blamed him. He still loved Karolina, even if he pretended he didn't. I had the feeling he'd go right back to her if I weren't in the picture, no matter how many times he swore he could never be involved with her again.

It was one of the reasons I hated when she called. It was also why I hated when he discussed our private life with her. I didn't want his ex-wife picking over the scraps of gossip she thought she could get from our life. It was also the reason I didn't want to go tonight.

And I wouldn't wear a sexy dress to show her that Niklas still wanted me.

"Why did you spend so much money on a dress you aren't going to wear?" He was standing in the doorway between the closet and our bedroom. "I want you to wear it tonight."

"I didn't buy that dress to impress Karolina." I practically spat her name out. It had come out too harshly. Niklas flashed me a strange, cautious look. The ghost of his infidelity stood between us, casting a tense pall over us.

"I just thought you'd look good in it."

"I don't want to wear it tonight. It's enough that I'm even going."

"You don't have to go, then."

"Karolina would like that, wouldn't she?"

"Don't get like this. It's Jesper birthday, and she wants a family dinner."

"And what did Jesper want?"

"Laney."

"Never mind. I'm dressed. I'm sorry I haven't tarted myself up so your ex-wife can be satisfied that tonight you won't get so drunk you fall into her bed again."

"My God, why are you even bringing that up now?"

I nearly apologized. The words "I'm sorry" were perched on the tip of my tongue, but my memories of the evening that had led to his relapse with Karolina still ate at me. I couldn't completely forgive him.

We were at an impasse. We could pretend it had never happened whenever we went to New York or

Thailand. Distance could numb it, but it always bubbled to the surface sooner or later.

I turned away from him and concentrated on finding a pair of shoes. As a concession, I slipped into a pair of platform stilettos I knew he liked. He sometimes called them my "come fuck me" shoes. Once, he'd asked me to strip and only wear those heels. I couldn't do that for him anymore. Not since that night when he confessed he'd slept with Karolina. I hated even being in the same room as Karolina, knowing that Niklas somehow could not resist her no matter how much he said he loved me or craved me. She was the real woman in his life, and I was a stand-in. A stand-in he loved fucking, a stand-in who made his life a little more palatable by organizing everything and smoothing out details. But I was not the one he married. And I wasn't the one he turned to when he wanted advice.

I took a deep breath as I adjusted my feet in the zebra print shoes. As I looked at myself in the mirror, I pulled a face at my own reflection. This wasn't how I'd imagined my life would be, not when I first decided to move to Europe, and certainly not when I'd moved in with Niklas. I thought there would be so much more to this, to us. Not this ridiculous game of pretending his infidelity meant nothing.

"Tonight, let's not bring up the sperm bank visit," Niklas said.

I straighten my shoulders and pull my hair into a messy chignon. "I wasn't planning on it."

"Karolina will just blow everything out of proportion."

"I don't care what she does. It's none of her business. It never was."

"No, of course, you're right. I shouldn't have mentioned it to her."

"No, you shouldn't have."

"Laney."

I dropped my hands to my sides and turned to face him. He was giving me an unreadable look. I waited, my nerves building as the seconds passed.

"You know I love you."

"That's what you tell me."

"Why do you have to sound so doubtful?"

"Sometimes, it feels like we don't fit anymore," I said.

"Of course we fit."

"I don't want to go, then."

"I already said we're going."

"Why did you tell her?"

"I told you already. It came up in passing." Irritation colored his voice. He folded his arms across his chest. The tips of his ears burned red.

"When?" I insisted.

"We had lunch."

"You had lunch?" I started but there was no point in continuing. This was an argument waiting to happen. One we'd had on so many occasions. I shook my head. Forget it, Laney. You'll never win this. In the end, you'll be the one with nothing.

We took a cab to Karolina's apartment in Östermalm. I thought it was a waste of money, but Niklas didn't want to lose his parking spot, and he reasoned it would take too long to find a place to park once we arrived. Jesper's birthday presents were in a shopping bag balanced on my feet. I'd bought them. It was one of the things I did, buying birthday presents and Christmas presents for his kids, his secretary. I put more thought into it, he said. I knew exactly what people wanted since I worked in marketing and understood people's likes and dislikes. But really he just didn't want to be bothered. And though I didn't mind being the purveyor of presents, it bugged me that he didn't even try, not even when it came to his own children.

"Did we pick up flowers for Karolina?" he asked as he tapped away on his phone.

"That's your job, not mine," I quipped as we passed the dark green expanse of Humlegården Park and the Royal Library. Back when we were newly in love, we spent a long summer afternoon in that park, lounging over a picnic basket and bottles of rosé. Later we stumbled back to my apartment and made love in a feverish rush. Thinking about it took the edge off heading into enemy territory. I wasn't going there for Karolina's sake. I was going there because of Jesper, who was a sweet kid, even if his sister too easily swayed him.

Tonight, I wouldn't let Siri or Karolina get under my skin.

Karolina lived in an extravagant apartment on Strandvägen. The apartment took up an entire floor of the building, and had a view of Lake Mälaren, the bridge to Djurgården and the majestic burnished brick facade of Riksmuseet. It was the sort of grandiose apartment regularly featured in Elle: Interior or Living, Etc and Karolina liked to brag about how many times she'd entertained her famous friends there. She had a lot of famous friends, thanks to her family's cultural connections. Her parents were theatre legends with aristocratic backgrounds. And, just by the way she looked at me, I knew she thought I wasn't good enough for her ex-husband. And sometimes it ate away at me, and made me wish I could be with someone else, someone without so much baggage.

"Nicky, darling!" Karolina flashed him a brilliant smile as she ushered us in.

"Hej, Karro." Niklas was smiling back at her a little too hard. I noted how his eyes lingered on the plunging V-neck of her caftan, at the exposed skin and shadow of her cleavage. Only Karolina could get away with wearing a silk kaftan and looking drop-dead gorgeous. In my black jersey dress, I felt like a dowdy aunt who was trying too hard.

Niklas and Karolina held each other a smidgen too long. She kissed the side of his chin and left a perfectly formed crimson lip print. Jesper groaned at the sight of his parents hugging. "Move, Dad. I want to say hi to Laney."

He sprang away from Karolina as if suddenly released from her spell. A flush of red crept up his neck. I flashed him a look, and then hugged Jesper and wished him a happy birthday. Jesper grinned at me. With his mop of dark hair and strong jaw, he looked so much like a younger version of Niklas. I told him he was getting handsomer every day and handed him his bag of presents. "From your dad and me."

"I know they're both from you," Jesper said. "He never remembers anything."

"I always remember your birthday," Niklas protested.

"Oh, now...come, come," Karolina interrupted. "Let's move through to the dining room. Everyone's waiting."

Karolina had seated me at the far end of the table, next to Niklas's brother-in-law Oscar. Already, he'd tried to slide his hand along my thigh as he bored me with long-winded descriptions of his kitchen renovation. I slapped his hand away and hissed "stop!" at him. Niklas was with Jesper and Karolina at the center of the table. Karolina was holding court, gesturing with her wine glass as she reminded everyone of how many hours she'd spent in labor with Jesper. She was laughing, her graceful neck exposed as she swept her hair back with her other hand.

I kept my eyes trained on Niklas, hoping he would be attuned enough to turn to me and reassure me with a smile. If he turned to me and there was a return of the smoldering intimacy he once felt for me, I could hold on. I could call off everything with Mads, I thought. But he was watching his ex-wife with such an intensity that I knew he'd forgotten I was even there. And the way he was drinking her in was how he used to look at me. I blinked and looked away. I didn't say no when Oscar refilled my wine glass.

New York seemed like such a long time ago.

I told myself I imagined how he drank her in. I even convinced myself he couldn't make love to me at night if he'd started sneaking around with Karro again. But I sensed it in the strange vibe between them. The smiles they directed at one another. The looks that lingered a little too long. I knew Niklas too well. He'd been this way with me. And whether it was alcohol that fueled his inability to keep Karro at a distance or something else, I could tell he'd slept with her again.

Karro caught me watching them. Instead of glancing away, she held my stare and then smirked. She angled her body closer to Niklas's and whispered in his ear. The neckline of her caftan gaped and displayed the tops of her breasts. And Niklas, oblivious to anyone around them, kissed her on the side of her mouth. His hand slid beneath the table.

What the fuck was going on? I gulped down my wine and looked away. I was sure of it now.

He was fucking her.

We were even now.

Even if it didn't make me feel any better.

CHAPTER EIGHT

Sharing Someone Else's Pillow

Going to Copenhagen again, even with the return of this weird mood between Niklas and me, filled me with a secret thrill. I shouldn't have been so gleeful at the prospect of having to keep track of more lies to cover the lies I'd already told Niklas, but I was. It got me through the rest of the week. It got me through the dinner with Jesper, who'd been sullen and not exactly friendly now that Niklas had actually taken my advice and was making his son and daughter pay the cost of the cleaning service. After a few half-hearted protests, Jeppe gave in to Niklas's calm delivery of the punishment. And Niklas's firm stance impressed me. I was so accustomed to his giving in to his children's protests whenever they did anything wrong, that I'd stopped believing he could ever be strong in the role of the disciplinarian. But I stayed out of the discussion and just listened and observed as Niklas laid down the law.

At the end of the evening, Jesper was contrite, and apologized, but his reddened face and thin frown revealed his anger at being caught out, at being forced to take responsibility for breaking the rules. Before he went to bed, Jesper asked me why his dad was being so hard on him. His anger had subsided enough that he looked more like a lost little boy than an arrogant teenager. I touched his shoulder and said, "Honey, he didn't like what he found when he came home."

But Jesper still seemed confused.

I tried to put all of this out of my head as I boarded the flight to Denmark. In my suitcase was the wanton dress, just waiting to be worn for Mads. I would check into the hotel, then I would call him at the workshop he shared with three other furniture makers. I wondered how long it would take before we would end up in bed again. My body was already responding to the idea of being naked with him again. A slow heat crept up my neck and along my arms. Would he kiss me? Would he still meet me at the airport?

I settled into my window seat and told myself this could be a new beginning. I could fall in love with someone else. I didn't need to settle for being an afterthought for Niklas. And that thought alone was enough to calm me.

When the plane finally landed in Copenhagen an hour later, and Mads was waiting for me in the arrivals hall, holding a sign that said "*Elskede* Laney"—Beloved Laney—any doubts eating away at me receded.

I felt like I'd come home.

"I need to make a quick stop. It won't take too long. After that, I'm all yours for the weekend."

We were driving away from Copenhagen, taking a curving northbound road that wove its way through pretty suburbs with clapboard and brick houses and fields of green. I was too enchanted to ask him where we were going. Sitting in the passenger seat, letting him take me where he wanted...

A huge paper-wrapped package took up most of the backseat. "Is that for me?" I joked. I let my hand stray to Mads's right thigh, savoring its firmness.

"No, not this time," he said, grinning. "They're for my grandmother. It's her birthday."

"Are you going to see her later?" I was anxious to touch him, to feel his hands on me again.

"We're going there now. Is that okay?"

I nodded, even though I'd envisioned us in bed together, picking up where we'd left off. But maybe this was a good thing. He was forcing us to go a little slower, even if it was unintentional. I was still reeling from our first meeting. Sometimes when I thought about him, my body reacted as though he were already near me. Twice I'd almost called Niklas by Mads's name, and caught myself just as it was slipping off my tongue.

"Why do you do it?"

"Do what?"

"Donate sperm."

"I was wondering when you'd finally ask me." He sounded grim, almost defensive. But he kept his eyes on the road and gripped the steering wheel tightly. I reached out my hand and stroked his denim-covered leg. His thigh muscle was taut under my palm.

"I'm not judging you, Mads. I'm just curious."

He nodded slowly. I saw how his jaw tightened. I didn't want to make him feel nervous or uncomfortable, so I turned on the radio and fidgeted and gave him some time to think. After a while he said, "I needed the money so I could have my workshop. And Ida convinced me it was an easy way to get enough money to set up my business."

"Does your family know?"

He didn't answer, not at first.

"Mads? I promise you, I'm not judging you. I'm just curious. That's all."

"My grandmother knows." He glanced at me, a nervous smile on his lips. "I haven't mentioned it to my cousins or my aunts and uncles. Didn't really see the point."

"Do your friends know?"

"Some of them. It's not really something I talk about with them. It's too... private."

I tried to imagine how it felt for him, going to the mingles, knowing that one of these women would carry his child. I wanted to ask him If he ever thought about the kids... but all of this felt too new to dig very deep. His knuckles whitened as he gripped the steering wheel. I loved his profile, the ridges in his nose that betrayed it had once been broken, the sharpness of his cheekbones.

"I can never judge you for what you did," I said softly. "I went to that clinic hoping I would find someone who could help me... and I found you."

He grinned. "We found each other before that. When I saw you through the window of that café and you looked straight at me."

"And the rest was history."

"It'll be a good story we can tell someday." And then he kissed me quickly, and inside I soared.

"Who is this?" Though her eyes were milky with cataracts, Alma Rasmussen peered at me and reached out a hand and touched my cheek. "Mads, have you finally fallen in love?"

Mads—my strong, beautiful, Mads—blushed. He grinned at his grandmother and said in Danish, "If I could, I would keep her with me all the time." He didn't look up at me, but the shy, boyish smile spreading across his lips told me everything I needed to know.

His grandmother chuckled. "Well, this pleases me. I have worried about you, alone since you returned from Sweden."

She had a musical voice. Even with the unfamiliar cadences of Danish, Alma Rasmussen projected an openness that pulled me in. I wanted to hold her hand, sit close to her, and listen to any advice she'd give me.

Her love for her grandson shined bright, filling the room with a warmth I'd rarely experienced with my own family. As I sat there, sipping the glass of strawberry-rhubarb cordial she'd served, I listened as she quizzed Mads about the goings-on in Copenhagen, and his family. And I was envious. This was what I'd missed when I'd been shuffled from one relative to another, until Eddy took me under her wing when we were in college.

"Hvordan er det at du mødte min søde barnebarn?"

My mind went blank. On the drive up, Mads had filled me in on how he'd spent so much of his childhood in this house with his grandparents when his parents divorced, but we'd never touched on how either of us would answer that question if it came up.

She noted my confusion and said in English, "How did you meet my sweet grandson?"

"*Farmor*, I told you, we met at a party." Mads leaned forward and refilled his grandmother's glass of cordial. "It was a few weeks ago."

"Mads, you let the girl speak for herself." His grandmother let out another tinkling laugh. I glanced at Mads. She knew he was a sperm donor, but I was pretty certain telling her we'd met at the mingle wasn't a good idea. His knee brushed mine as he leaned forward. I wanted to nestle closer to him. There was something about his calmness that told me we could be good together.

But I needed to answer his grandmother. So before he could answer for me, I said in careful Swedish, "It's like

Mads said... we met at a party. I thought he was the handsomest man there."

Apparently, this was the right answer. Alma's smile widened and her face lit with joy. "He is a handsome boy, isn't he? Even with his broken nose."

"It's been like this for twenty years." Mads grinned at her and tapped the uneven ridge of his nose. "Sooner or later, you're going to have to accept my pugilist badge of honor."

"Oh, I have, my dear." She laughed softly. "And it just makes you handsomer."

I nodded and added. "We spent the whole evening talking and... we just clicked."

"That pleases me. He's been single too long." She spoke English now, her words carefully enunciated. She patted Mads's cheek again.

"*Farmor*, it hasn't been so long." His cheeks bloomed red and it made me smile. I'd never seen him blush before, but it softened the rugged angles of his face, melting away a little of his roughness so I could see the shy boy he'd once been.

"If anyone knows how long you've been alone, it's me. I don't understand how that silly Swedish girl ever divorced you in the first place. I worry about him. I want to see him married and happy."

It was the perfect milieu. The three of us sitting in her cozy living room with the French doors open to her garden. All of my impatience to get to the hotel, to be alone with Mads, dissipated as we chatted with his grandmother and she regaled me with stories from his childhood. How different it was from mine. How different this was from when I'd first met Niklas's family. We'd had a tense dinner at Restaurang Gondolen with his taciturn father, who barely spoke other than to ask pointed questions that were either unanswerable or hid an agenda to belittle or embarrass. I thought back to when Niklas first met my aunt Cecily, during our first summer in New York, and how she'd disapproved of him instantly.

"He's too old and too smooth for you," she'd said, despite there only being a seven-year age difference between us. "Too smooth, too rich. This won't last."

But sitting here with Mads, I could almost imagine my deceased mother's reaction. She would have liked him. She would have appreciated his love for his grandmother. God, this is what I'd missed for so long in my life. I wanted a family. I wanted grandparents I could spend Thanksgiving and Christmas with. I didn't have anyone left. My grandparents had died before I was born, and both of my parents were gone by the time I was fifteen—my dad was with his new wife, my mom dead after losing her battle with breast cancer. The only points of certainty in my life were Eddy and Niklas and his kids. Then something vibrated against my leg. Mads had settled back now and was telling his grandmother about a new commission he'd received. He paused and glanced at me. "Is that your phone, Laney?"

"Sorry?" Then the vibrating and humming got louder. "Oh! Sorry... I'll just... take this."

I stood, a little too abruptly, and excused myself. I opened the French doors and stepped out into the overgrown garden, glad for the breeze and this moment alone. I could smell the salty sea air even without needing to see the narrow Øresund Strait separating southern Sweden from the northern tip of Denmark.

Niklas's avatar filled my display screen. I walked further out into the garden and then clicked on the answer button.

"I can't really talk right now," I said in a hurried whisper. "We're in the middle of a meeting."

"This won't take long. I just wanted to be certain you'd remembered Siri's birthday."

"You left me a note."

"Well, I thought since you're already in Copenhagen, you could pick up a present while you're there."

"I'm working, Niklas. I'm not here shopping."

"I doubt you're working every single second you're there."

"I'm actually quite busy." I tried to keep my voice low, but I could hear my anger crackling through. "I've got to get back to my meeting so just spit out what you want."

"I'm going to ignore your tone. You don't need to be so sharp with me."

"Niklas, I don't really have time for this. What do you want me to pick up for her?"

"Laney?" I swung around quickly. Mads was in the doorway, worry blurring his face.

"Sorry, I'm coming." Then I hissed at Niklas. "I have to go. They need me again."

"Fine. Just pick up a Lulu satchel from Piet Breinhom's shop on Nansensgadde."

I wanted to protest, but he added, "It shouldn't be out of your way since your hotel is near there."

Then he rang off before I could even think of a way to say no. I shoved my phone back in my pocket and stalked towards the house. Mads was still waiting for me in the doorway. As soon as I was close enough, he pulled me into his arms and kissed me, setting off a stampede of butterflies through me.

"Thank you," I said softly. "I really needed that."

"Don't think about him." He kissed me again. "It's just you and me this weekend, okay?"

I nodded and let his words soothe me. But when we stepped back into the living room, I felt his grandmother watching me. I couldn't meet her eye. I was pretty certain she'd heard every word I'd said.

Alma Rasmussen adored her grandson. There were pictures of Mads everywhere. Old school portraits with Mads at various ages hung on the wall leading to the kitchen. One picture in particular caught my eye. A teenaged Mads glared at the camera, the bump on the bridge of his nose red, swollen and angry-looking, and violent bluish-black smudge under his right eye. His straw-colored hair hung lank around his face. I wanted to reach into the picture and tuck it behind his ear. This teenage version of Mads was full of anger, and his pale eyes seemed to challenge the photographer. But there was a story there; what had happened that led to the bruises on his face.

"He was sixteen then."

I nearly jumped out of my skin. I hadn't heard his grandmother leave her chair or even walk across the creaking oak plank floors. She patted my shoulder, and then sighed as she looked up at the photograph. His face was thinner but he was already beginning to look like a man and not a boy. "What happened to him?"

"A fight," she said and shook her head. "The poor thing, trying to defend a girl. He was so angry then." The older woman sighed again.

"Why? What happened?"

"His mother died. She had a terrible accident," she said softly in English. "He hasn't told you this?"

"We haven't known each other that long," I admitted. The truth of it jarred me. We'd shared such a deep intimacy but we didn't really know much about one another. "It's still quite new."

"Mads must have strong feelings for you, then," Alma surmised. "You are the first woman he's brought here since his divorce."

A scintilla of surprise sparked inside me. I tried to keep my face from revealing anything, but Alma was perceptive. She linked her arm with mine and led me back to the living room. At her bookcase, she showed me a framed photo of Mads on his wedding day. The sylph-like woman at his side was laughing at someone just beyond the camera. Her golden hair was decorated with flowers, and looked perfect with the thin, gauzy dress she wore. Her delicate features gave her a childlike fragility but something told me she wasn't as whimsical as she appeared.

"That is Karin," his grandmother said, switching now from Danish to English. She tapped the dusty glass. "She was a sweet girl, but she and Mads weren't a good fit."

She showed me another picture of Mads, a candid shot taken in what looked like her garden. He was laughing and his eyes twinkled with energy and joy. Beside him was an older man whose face was also alight with laughter. Mads was the spitting image of the man. They had the same nose, though the older man's was straighter than Mads's.

"His grandfather, Henrik," Alma said. "Handsomest man there ever was, and the kindest too. Just like his grandson."

"Mads resembles him," I said carefully, trying to use the Danish I'd learned. She nodded in encouragement at me. "They have the same eyes... the same nose."

"They were very close." Alma eased herself back into her chair. "Henrik was more a father than a grandfather to Mads. Mads's father... he didn't know how to be a father."

Nor mine, I thought. So we had that in common. Fathers who didn't know how to be fathers. "My father didn't know, either," I said. "He left my mother around the same time she found out she had breast cancer. When my mother died, he said I wasn't his responsibility."

She fixed her milky eyes on me and said in a low, clear voice, "I know you have something unfinished at home, my dear. And I know you feel very strongly for Mads."

"I do," I assured her. "I'm ... trying to sort things out at home. I want to be with Mads. I do."

"Then promise me one thing. Don't you break his heart. Whatever you do, don't you hurt my grandson."

"I won't. I promise." There was a stammer in my voice, even though I'd wanted to sound confident. Alma Rasmussen didn't look away. Her smile was gone now, and it didn't return until Mads came back.

"*Farmor*, are you telling tales?" Mads returned bearing a tray with more cake, and flowers he'd arranged in jam jars. "I hope you're at least telling Laney nice stories about me."

"I only have nice stories," she said as she beamed at him. When she turned back to me, I couldn't meet her eyes. All I could think was what would happen if I never left Niklas, if somehow he managed to convince me to go through with the sperm donation and the insemination. Everything drained out of me. I didn't want to lose Mads. But that's what would happen if I didn't do something soon. And we'd both end up hurt.

Later, as we drove back to the city, I watched Mads's reflection in the window and imagined him in a house by the sea, like his grandmother's. He had her eyes, startlingly pale green one moment, warm and flecked with coppery tones the next. I angled my body closer to his and brushed a strand of hair behind his ear. He grinned at me.

"You're going to cause an accident if you don't stop," he teased. And as he said those words, something in his tone touched me and spiraled around inside me. I saw us bathed in golden light, our lives spread out before us like little books waiting to be discovered and read. The children we could have together, the life we could have if I would just take a leap of faith and let go of the gilded trappings of life with Niklas. I blinked quickly and turned my head away so I could stare out the passenger window. I didn't want him to see the confusion tumbling around inside me.

But that unsettling feeling was still there. Mads was inside me, even when he was not. Unfurling like a flower and taking root. I couldn't dispel him. I didn't want to. He reached across the space between us and stroked my cheek with the pad of his thumb. His touch branded me and left me breathless. I was his.

"Do you want to go to the hotel, or to my place?" he said so casually that I nearly missed the twinge of uncertainty in his voice. We were on Øster Søgade now. The sign for my hotel was a few meters ahead. The sky had already darkening and streetlights were flickering on, casting a sulphur glow on the black asphalt streets.

"Let's go to your place." I let my hand slide down to his thigh. His muscles tensed under my fingertips. "I want to see where you live."

"Good, I was hoping you'd say that."

"Why? Have you got a surprise planned for me?"

Mads shook his head. "I was just hoping we wouldn't have to spend all our time together in hotel rooms. There's more to life than hotel beds."

"Though we have had fun in them."

"We have," he agreed. "We'll have fun in other places, too."

His apartment was on the other side of Dronning Louise Bridge, in the Nørrebrø district. I'd only ever passed through this part of Copenhagen en route to Ingrid and Anton's house. It had a different flavor from the rest of the city. It was gritty and lively, with kebab shops and hair salons specializing in African hair vying for space with trendy fusion bistros and designer bike shops. Nestled between all this chaos was a down at its heels, umber-hued turn of the century brick warehouse. And on the second floor of the warehouse was Mads's apartment. We climbed the uneven marble steps to his floor, and then he opened the door and let me into his life.

I wasn't sure what I'd expected. A pokey studio apartment, maybe? A utilitarian Funkis style apartment with perfectly square rooms and no wasted space? It was nothing like the sprawling apartment Niklas and I called home. Mads had taken what looked like raw, industrial space and converted it into a loft, dividing it into what was absolutely necessary for him. A living room, with walls lined with bookshelves he'd made himself, a galley kitchen that proved he never really ate at home, and sliding paneled doors that separated the bedroom and the bathroom from the rest of the apartment. The gracefully arched windows jarred with the modern loft style, but somehow it fit.

There was a warmth here that felt very familiar and welcoming. I wanted to sink into his sofa and curl up with a book from his shelves. I wanted to stay here with him and never leave.

"So this is home?" I trailed my fingers over the planes of his cheeks.

He set my bags down by the bedroom door. "This is home. Not as nice as a hotel, but you're always welcome here." He grinned at me, a nervous, boyish grin that made me want to melt into him and forget everything else. And for a little while I did.

Mads pulled me up from the sofa and said, "Come on, or we'll be late."

"Late? I thought we were staying in," I teased as I wrapped my arms around his neck. I didn't want to go anywhere. Being along with him was all I'd thought about the entire week and now we were finally away from everyone. "Can't we just stay here and order some takeout?"

He planted a quick kiss on the tip of my nose. "No, we're going out on a date. It's what proper couples do."

I smiled up at him. "So we're a proper couple?"

"We could be." He unwound my arms and led me towards the hall. "It all depends on you and what you
want."

His words hung in the air between us as we put on
our jackets and shoes. It was up to me.

He made me wait.

All through dinner, I wanted to feel his hands on me.
Each smile promised more. A raised eyebrow set my
heart racing. I crossed my legs, trying desperately to
quell my desire for him.

"Why do you stay with him?"

The question slid so easily from his well-formed lips.
Our shared dessert was now nothing more than chocolate smears on a white porcelain plate. A tiny chocolate
crumb dotted the left corner of his mouth. I wanted to
lick it away, but I needed to concentrate. His lips were so
beautifully curved. It was hard not to stare.

"That's not a simple question to answer."

"Sure it is." He was stroking the back of my neck,
drawing lazy circles with the tip of his index finger.
"You must have your reasons for why you've stayed so
long."

"I don't want to talk about Niklas."

"Laney, I just need to know what we're going into. I
need to know how you feel." His touch branded me,
claimed me as his own. My muscles unknotted for him.
My blood pulsated for him.

"Maybe I don't know the answer anymore."

"I think you do."

"Sometimes it's... easy to stay with him. When you've been together for so long, you know each other inside and out. You know what to expect," I said, carefully choosing my words. We were in a minefield. It would be too easy for either of us to get hurt. "And Niklas, the way he lives, it's what I always thought I wanted. The expensive vacations, the apartment in the right neighborhood, the never having to worry about money because there's always more than enough. I never had that security before."

"So... why are you here with me?"

"Because I like you, and you make me feel good."

"That's good. You do the same for me."

"I thought I wanted to marry Niklas. I thought I wanted to spend the rest of my life with him. But I'm not so certain anymore."

Our waiter refilled our coffee cups and then asked if we wanted anything more. Mads shook his head and asked for the check. He'd abandoned my neck and was now playing with the springy curls escaping from my bun. I nestled into him, my head resting on his shoulder. He curved his arm around me and the scent of him cocooned me. Niklas never held me like this in restaurants. Not in Stockholm, anyway. In Stockholm, he frowned upon public displays of affection. I closed my eyes and let myself enjoy being so near him and feeling his warmth and desire.

Mads's lips grazed my forehead. I closed my eyes and wished I'd met him in Stockholm, before I'd ever walked into that Third Thursday, before Niklas ever left his imprint on me.

"If you aren't certain... if you want another option, choose me."

We slowly retraced the path back to his apartment building and marveled at the fog rolling across the lake. You could barely see the island of Christianshavn and each step felt like delving deep into a dream. But, oh... how wonderful it was to walk beside him, to feel his palm slide against mine and our fingers lace. The heat of his skin kissing my skin. The gentle pressure of his thumb. We walked along the harbor without speaking. Fog lights blinked in the distance and the damp air chilled my skin. I wanted to tell him this was something new for me. Niklas never held my hand anymore when we were out walking together. He said it made him feel uncomfortable. I tried to remember the last time anyone had held my hand like this. I was not the girl boys walked home. I wasn't the woman they walked home either. I'd let myself become a booty call so I could have sex like a man and not let messy emotional attachments get in the way, and I'd convinced myself it was so I could be independent. Now, Mads was holding my hand, and all I wanted was for him to smile at me again and make me feel like the most beautiful woman alive. And it wasn't long before he did.

By the time we arrived at his doorstep again, I was more than ready for him, but he wouldn't let me rush. In the dark portico that separated the main entrance of his building from the inner courtyard, he stopped and pulled me to him. He pressed me against the wall and kissed me so long and hard, I thought my knees would buckle. I held onto him, reciprocating his fervor with equal measure. I loved the taste of his mouth, the faint razor stubble grazing my cheek as he kissed the curve of my neck, his strong hands gripping my hips and sliding down my thighs. When we finally pulled away, my lips felt swollen and hot and ached to be joined with his again. We laughed and rushed across the courtyard, knowing that soon we'd be able to savor one another again. Upstairs, in his living room, we stripped and fucked standing up. Afterwards, my back was sore from rubbing against the textured wallpaper. We retreated to his bedroom and made love again, though this time we took things more slowly. Mads whispered in my ear as his hands explored my body. I claimed him with my lips, my tongue, my fingers. There was something delicious about this rediscovery. It erased the traces of my week with Niklas, rendering it so faint and diaphanous that I could almost pretend it had never happened.

"I've missed you." His breath was hot against my skin. I arched up to meet his lips as they grazed my shoulder. "I don't know how long we can keep being separated like this."

"I don't know, either," I gasped as his fingers slid inside me. The heel of his hand moved in slow, deliriously wonderful circles. My hips moved of their own volition. He grinned down at me. "Don't stop."

"You should spend a week here with me." He slid another finger inside me, then stroked me gently. "Do you like that?"

I nodded. "You're driving me crazy." My nipples were so swollen and hard. "My God..."

"Stay with me, Laney. Don't check into your hotel tomorrow. Stay here... with me."

I was so turned on, I would have given in so easily. I did give in. He took one nipple in his mouth and sucked deeply on it. "Stay a week. We could figure something out."

"Niklas..."

"I don't care about him. I don't think you do, either."

His words stung, but just then I didn't care about Niklas or what was going on in his mind now that I was away. He knew there was something wrong between us. We couldn't be fixed, and I didn't care anymore. Niklas knew our relationship was falling apart and he wasn't doing anything to make me want to be faithful, to make me want to stay.

A faint draft of chilly air passed over our naked skin. I lay in Mads's arms, letting the scent of his skin fill me. Every part of me was attuned to him, sensing his every movement, his every breath. I belonged to him... and he belonged to me. And this moment, lying in his bed and knowing that tomorrow I could wake up with him—that, if I wanted, I could do this again and again, thrilled me. But how could I walk away from Niklas when I'd invested so much in our relationship? Sometimes, I thought he was on the verge of asking me to marry him, and then the moment would pass and I couldn't figure out what had even made me think it was possible.

"It's hard to just walk away from him."

"Laney."

I looked up at him. He kissed the tip of my nose.

"How can we ever know if we've got something special, if we never give it a chance?"

"I just need some time."

He answered by shifting his body. He nudged my thighs open a little more, and now his cock replaced his fingers, coaxing me closer to another orgasm. I kept my eyes open as I hung on to him. Our eyes locked and the intensity between us excited me even more. Mads lunged for me, kissing me deeply, using his forearms to hold me in place as his body claimed me. And I wanted him to claim me. I wanted him to obliterate my life with Niklas since I was too much of a coward to do it myself. This was not going to end well, not if I continued to ricochet between two men. Sooner or later, I would have to decide who I wanted to continue my life with. And I was afraid to let go of Niklas. He was a safe haven for me. Even with his ridiculous kids and his even more ridiculous ex-wife. He'd given me the physical and financial security I'd never had and didn't even know I'd needed.

Mads murmured something in Danish. I couldn't understand him but the deep timber of his voice hit every
synapse in me and made me want him more. I tried to
remind myself of Eddy's words, that Mads was just a nice
new flavor to try, but that I would eventually want the
familiarity of my favorite flavor, Niklas.

I didn't really like thinking of either of them as ice
cream.

We must have fallen asleep afterwards. I was one of
those annoying people who could drift off, smiling with
satisfaction, within seconds of having an orgasm if there
wasn't some stimulation to keep me alert. The air had
cooled, but the room wasn't chilly. The last vestiges of
summer were still holding on, unable to disappear completely. I stretched, and then moved closer to Mads.
Lying here with him felt so natural. I could imagine
waking up with him every morning, and going to bed
with him every night.

Could you imagine raising a family with him? The
niggling question filled the room. Obviously, I could
imagine him giving me children. He was the only one of
the donors who'd piqued my interest. Even before we'd
met properly, when we made eye contact through the
café window, I'd felt a charge of recognition and want.
But could we be one of those couples who could have
children and still have this sort of love life? Would we be
able to stick it out with one another, or would we fall

apart, just as Niklas and Karolina had? Just as it felt like Niklas and I were?

Before I could even think of leaving Niklas, I needed to know. But it was early days, wasn't it? Could I just ask Mads if he wanted to have a baby with me? I stroked his cheek, let my fingers drift along the curve of his neck and along his shoulder. His eyelids fluttered. *"Hvad er klokken?"* he murmured in Danish.

I knew enough Danish to understand him, but sometimes I tripped over the words when I tried to answer, so I spoke English instead. "It's almost midnight. Maybe we should go out for a drink?"

"We could do that." He spoke slowly, enunciating the words so I would understand him. Even though Danish and Swedish were similar, they sometimes sounded like they had no common origin. "Maybe..."

"When did you do this?" I trailed my fingers over the tattoo on his upper arm. The skin around the inked words was still red and painful-looking.

"A few days ago." He took hold of my fingers tips and kissed them. "It's your initials and the date we met."

I smiled at him and bit my lower lip. No one had ever done anything like this for me before. "You must like me a lot," I said in a breezy tone, but I felt the weight of this. This meant there was more to us, that neither of us had imagined our connection.

"I like you very much." His lips grazed my fingertips again and sent little shivers through me. "And I think you like me, too."

"I do. Very much so."

"Do you speak Swedish with Niklas?"

"Sometimes."

"Are you thinking about him now?"

"I was thinking about us... if we could be one of those couples with a baby."

"We could. You already wanted to have one with me." He grinned.

"But would you want to have one with me?"

He kissed me for an answer.

I wanted to hear it from his lips but I would accept this for now, how luscious it felt to be kissed by him, to be so close to him. We could have stayed like this all night, slowly kissing, this cocoon of tenderness enveloping us. I don't think we would have left the bed at all. But then my mobile rang and startled us apart.

I answered it with an uncertain, "Hello?"

"It's me."

"Niklas? Is everything okay?"

"Everything is fine, they cancelled the seminar in Uppsala. I thought I'd come down tomorrow."

I froze. Mads lay still, waiting to see what would happen.

"What time?" My voice caught in my throat.

"I'm landing at noon. Is your hotel near the train station, or do I need a taxi?"

"It's a bit of a walk." The truth was, he could take the train to Nørreport, but Niklas never took subways or commuter trains.

"Okay, then I'll take a taxi. I think this will be good for us, Laney. We need to get back on track, you and I."

"I know."

But when I hung up I felt sick. I didn't know what to do. I lay there shivering. Mads pulled me closer to him. "He's coming, isn't he?"

I nodded. "Tomorrow afternoon."

"So that was it for this weekend?" His disappointment came through loud and clear.

I nodded again. "I'm sorry, Mads."

"It's okay. At least we've got the rest of the night." He kissed my neck. "Let's just enjoy what we've got."

We woke early the next morning and, after showering together, after fucking in his shower, after fucking one more time in his bed, we got dressed in tense silence and then Mads walked me to my hotel. At first, there was a chasm separating us, but then his hand sought mine and our fingers entwined. We were just a few meters from the turning to the hotel when he pulled me aside and said, "I'm not used to this. I don't like putting you in this situation, or even being in this situation, but I can't stay away from you."

"I'm sorry."

"Don't be," he said, his expression still grim. "I just need to know it won't be like this forever." Then he cupped my face in his hands and pressed his lips to mine. His fingers trembled against my skin. I squeezed my eyes shut. I couldn't bear seeing the uncertainty growing between us.

"I don't want to go."

"You have to."

"We could go back to your place."

"You can't avoid him forever, Laney." Mads kissed me lightly. "Sooner or later, you have to decide what you want. *Who* you want."

Checking in at the hotel after spending the night with Mads cast a pall on the spell we'd created. I wished I'd never answered my phone. I could see the disappointment etched across his face, in the tight line of his grimace, the flatness of his eyes. I thought Mads would say goodbye to me in the lobby, but he took my suitcase and escorted me to my room. Before he left, he gave me a slow, furious kiss that almost felt like a break-up kiss. I watched him as he lumbered down the hall to the elevators. I couldn't just let him leave like this. I called out to him. He stopped. It took a few seconds before he turned to face me.

"Next weekend, come to Stockholm?"

"Are you sure?"

"I'll figure out something." I wasn't sure what solution I could come up with other than booking a hotel room in Stockholm and telling even more lies to Niklas. There was also an element of danger in that we might be found out.

"All right. You tell me how you want to do it, and I'll come." Then he disappeared around the corner. I wanted to follow him, to drag him back to my room and tell him I'd go along with whatever he wanted. But how could I? And even now as I stepped back into my hotel room and closed the door, I felt like someone who'd been glamoured and was awaking from the spell.

All I knew was I wanted Mads.

*   *   *

By the time Niklas arrived, I'd unpacked and hung up all my clothes. My computer was set up on the desk, and my work files were scattered around the room. There was no trace left of the night Mads and I had spent together. Not externally. Inside me, a kernel was growing. I hid it under layers of the old me. The me who would never do something like this, and who still wanted to work things out with Niklas. The front desk clerk called me when he arrived, and alerted me that Niklas was on his way up. When I hung up, I wondered if she was the same clerk who'd handed me my key when Mads and I arrived. A tiny bubble of panic formed inside me, but vanished just as quickly. I'd worked as a chambermaid at a five-star hotel while I was in college. It had paid my tuition and my living expenses, since I didn't qualify for very much financial aid. I figured out pretty quickly how things worked. You saw things and you didn't see them. We learned this from the very beginning. Never divulge in-formation, never judge, never see. The society ladies who came in with their thug lovers, the business men who'd picked up underage hookers and treated them to a little shopping, swank lunches, and drugs before disappearing upstairs for an hour or two of fucking, and then back to their respective lives. Hotels were safe havens for the unfaithful.

Now, though, Niklas was in the room with me, smiling confidently and letting his presence take possession of my room. He gave me a perfunctory kiss and then declared he needed to shower and get rid of the airplane grime. He hated how dirty he felt after a flight, no matter how short it was in duration. I sat on the edge of the bed and watched him undress. This was his precursor to making love. He would let me drink in the sight of him naked, and it was a sight to behold. He had an enviable body, thanks to the hours he spent in the gym, never letting his weight fluctuate, always in control. Watching him strip used to be enough to rev me up so that I could think of nothing more than joining our bodies and giving each other pleasure. But I was sated. And he was invading what should have been my hideaway. He knew, he had to know—otherwise why would he come? Things between us had been strained for months, so why pick this weekend to surprise me?

But I pretended I was in the mood, because anything else would have roused his suspicions. I kept a smile on my face and tried to think saucy thoughts that didn't involve Mads. I was wearing a loose sweater and shorts, but was naked underneath. It was too hot for layers, even now in September.

152 · KIM GOLDEN

"You're quiet today," Niklas noted as he draped his pants over a chair. He pushed his boxer shorts down and then kicked them aside. "Anything on your mind?"

"Work," I said automatically. "I was up late last night working on some ideas for the launch."

"Well, now I'm here, I'm hoping you won't have to work all the time."

"No, nothing like that," I said. "I finished my meetings yesterday. Just need to nail the tag lines."

"Should we call Anton and Ingrid?" he called out from the bathroom. He was already in the shower. I could hear water splattering against the tile walls.

"I've already done that."

I stood up and went to the window. Instead of the previous day's pristine weather, the watery-gray sky was thick with clouds. Soon, it would rain. Was Mads out walking? Was he meeting friends now? I knew so little about him. That was what scared me. I'd memorized the cartography of his body: the pale lines of scars on his hands, the small black-inked tattoo on the inside of his left arm, the thin scar on his stomach from an appendectomy, the puckered burn mark on his right shoulder that was a remnant from when he tried to steam away wallpaper and the steamer leaked on him. I knew these things. I had no clue where his workshop was, or who his friends were. I knew he had a cousin called Ragnar who lived in Malmö, but his life away from the time we spent exploring and enjoying one another's bodies was a mystery.

Niklas's singing in the shower shook me out of my thoughts. I knew so much about him. He was, essentially, an open book for me to skim at my leisure. Niklas Lundqvist had no real secrets from me. I knew which schools he'd attended, I knew who his friends were, knew even where he ordered his custom-made shirts. I'd sat through dinners in Uppsala with his father's side of the family and gone to France with him to meet his mother's relatives. I knew he was afraid of spiders, even though he thought therapists shouldn't be afraid of something so trivial. I knew he cried sometimes in his sleep. I knew he was secretly worried Jesper was too much of a slacker, and too easily led astray by Siri. And he worried Siri traveled in too fast of a crowd, but he didn't know how to put a stop to it, or if he even could. And there were times when he could elicit from me a tenderness that caught me off guard. I didn't think of myself as someone capable of being so affectionate. Yet, there were moments when I simply had to catch sight of Niklas bent over a conference paper, his dark eyebrows knitted together in concentration as he chewed on the top of a pencil, and I couldn't stop myself from going to him, draping my arm across his shoulders and leaning in to him or sliding into his lap and distracting him.

He emerged from the bathroom wrapped in one of the thick, fluffy hotel bathrobes. "Now, I feel like a new man."

"Good."

"Should we make an appointment at the clinic?"

"Why?"

"I want to find out more about this sperm donor idea of yours." He lay down on the bed and then patted the spot beside him. "Come here. Let's talk about it."

I went over to him. "I thought you didn't want to do it."

"If I say no, what are you going to do?" He slid his hand up and down my back in slow, easy strokes.

I shrugged. "I hadn't thought that far."

"I know you, Laney. After five years, I think I know you well enough to say you would go ahead and do this without me." Niklas kissed the top of my head. "You're pretty stubborn sometimes."

"I'd rather do this with you than without you," I said softly, even though I wasn't sure if it was still what I wanted. I'd always imagined that any child I had would be the perfect mix of us, but that was never going to happen.

"So let's go to this clinic on Monday before we head back. We can rebook our tickets so we fly back on Monday evening."

"I can't do that," I said quickly. "I have an important meeting on Monday morning, that's why I'm flying back tomorrow afternoon."

"So now work is more important than our future family?" His hand dropped away from my back.

"This isn't fair, Niklas."

"I could go myself. I'll talk to this... what was her name again?"

"Ida," I said, trying not to sound too cautious.

"Of course. Ida. And then she can let me know what's what, and how we'd proceed. And the cost, of course. Did she say how much it would cost?"

"It's fairly steep," I said, trying to figure out in my mind what number would be too high even for Niklas's blood. "If I remember correctly, it's going to cost us at least 40,000 Danish krone."

"Well, that's a number we can live with," Niklas said with a shrug. "We've spent more on a weekend in Paris."

"Couldn't we come back some other weekend and arrange a meeting with her?" My voice betrayed the panic building in me. "It's not as though we have to rush. I've got the files. I'll need to send them back soon and make a decision, but I don't think we need to really do anything until we've decided."

"Have you changed your mind?" Niklas asked.

"No, no. I just don't think it makes sense to rush it this weekend, when we could come back next week, or the week after next." I said quickly. "We could even have a Skype call from Stockholm with Ida and she could explain everything."

Neither of us said anything for a while. Niklas let out a long sigh and watched me evenly. His fingers toyed absently with my hair. I inched closer to him. I didn't want us to argue. Even if his intrusion had put a damper on my weekend, I didn't want us to argue.

"I know something's not right between us, Laney." He finally said. "I know there's something else going on with you."

I couldn't deny it. Of course, I couldn't. "Niklas."

"Just get it out of your system, babe. And come back to me." I heard the quiet desperation in his voice and it scared me. He didn't know what he was asking me to do. If he knew, he wouldn't want me to do this.

"I can't."

"You can. If you still think we can have something together, then you can. I don't want us to fall apart."

I didn't know what to say. How could I want to leave him when he knew me this well?

"Just... do whatever it is you need to do. But come back to me."

I squeezed my eyes shut tight. I was crying already. I didn't deserve him. Not now, maybe not ever. Because even as he was giving me a green card to fuck around on him, I was still thinking about what I could have with Mads. And it didn't involve going back to Niklas in the end.

We took a cab from the hotel to Anton and Ingrid's house in Husum, a cozy residential neighborhood just twenty minutes from downtown Copenhagen. Visiting them there always made me wish I could have their life. They were both teachers. Ingrid taught art at a local elementary school and was a freelance illustrator, and Anton taught English and math at a high school in

Nørrebrø and commuted by bus or bicycle every day. They had three children—all daughters—who were so calm and friendly, especially when compared to Niklas's kids. Whenever we were around them, I wondered what Niklas and Karolina should have done differently so that Jesper and Siri wouldn't have turned out so rude.

Anton greeted us with hugs and said, "Come on in, it's a mess, as usual." He always said this, but the house was never as messy as he intimated. He led us into the kitchen where Ingrid was just taking the salmon out of the oven. I shooed Anton and Niklas out of the kitchen, saying I would help Ingrid.

We brushed cheeks quickly, and then I began pulling plates from the cabinets. "Sorry we just sprang this on you. Coming over, I mean," I said as we began bringing the food out.

"Laney, you know you're always welcome here. Doesn't matter how last minute it is."

Anton and Niklas were out in the garden, drinking beer from the bottle and smoking. The only time Niklas ever smoked was when he was around Anton. Maybe it was because Anton looked like the laid-back, free spirit Niklas always claimed to be. Anton was lanky with wild curly hair and hipster glasses. There was a languidness about Anton that Niklas sometimes tried to emulate. Maybe it came from growing up in California and being a surfer. Anton never took anything too seriously, and whenever Niklas was around Anton, it wore off on Niklas.

"Where are the girls?" I asked Ingrid. I'd only just noticed how quiet it was. I'd set the table for seven, but maybe it was just the four of us.

"They're out. They're at that age now. They'll be back later." Ingrid set the fish at the center of the table. "Oh, we can take away two of the place settings, then."

"Who else is coming?" I collected two of the place settings. It was always a toss-up with Ingrid. She didn't believe in planning ahead when it came to dinner. If Anton invited an extra person, she took it in stride. Niklas could never deal with that sort of spontaneity. If we'd already decided that only Eddy and her boyfriend were joining us for dinner, and I suddenly wanted to add two extra people, he'd dissect my reasons for the new additions and get stroppy about having to pick up more food, when there was more than enough. Afterwards, even if he'd enjoyed the evening, he'd complain and find more reasons to question why the new additions were necessary. It wasn't worth the bother.

"Anton invited a friend of his to join us. He figured you two wouldn't mind."

"No, that's fine with me. Is it Adam?" Adam was also American. He lived across the street from them and was a teacher at the local community college. Niklas didn't like Adam. He thought Adam wanted to sleep with me, but Adam was gay. He always mistook Adam's enthusiasm for hanging out with Ingrid and me as a latent desire to be with us sexually. Sometimes, it made me wonder just how good a therapist he really was.

"Adam's in the States again. His sister's getting married," Ingrid said as she stacked two of the plates. I uncorked a bottle of white wine and set it in the wine chiller. "I don't think you've met this guy. He's a new friend of Anton's, but I think he's a good egg."

The doorbell rang, and Anton came in from the yard and answered. I was just putting the flatware on the table when I heard the voice from behind me. I turned quickly. Standing there, holding a bottle of red wine was Mads. I glanced quickly at Ingrid, but she was oblivious to my attempt at eye contact. Mads hadn't seen me yet. He was laughing with Anton and speaking Danish. Why had I never noticed how tall he was? He was taller than Anton by a good three or four inches. Niklas was just coming in from the garden. He went forward and introduced himself, and then gestured at me. That's when Mads turned and saw me.

I tensed inside. Everything in me wanted to run to him, throw my arms around his neck and greet him with a long, deep kiss. I wanted to feel his lips against mine, and the pleasure of his arms encircling my waist. But I couldn't. Not now. And panic was taking hold inside me. What if I said the wrong thing? What if Niklas figured out that Mads and I knew one another already? Or if he recognized him from the Copenhagen Cryo files? I opened my mouth to speak, but for the briefest of moments no words came to me. What was he doing here? I was happy to see him, even if I couldn't be with him, but

I was scared of making a mistake. I rushed forward and shook his hand, "Nice to meet you."

He gave me a puzzled look but went along with the charade.

God, was Fate playing tricks on me?

We all moved back into the dining room and chose seats. Niklas had a possessive arm around me, and was using a chummy voice I had never heard from him before. I moved away and pulled out my chair. Mads sat directly across from me. He was staring at me, not bothering to hide anything. Under the table his knee brushed against mine. Images of the previous night flashed through my mind. The life I'd imagined with him shimmered tantalizingly between us. I blinked quickly and it vanished without a trace. Mads looked away from me and turned to talk to Anton, but the pressure of his leg kept me tethered and unable to ignore him or even pretend I didn't want to be near him.

"How do you two know each other?" I asked as we passed around the serving plates.

"Mads is helping me make a new table," Anton said. "He's got this wicked workshop... it's amazing what he can do."

"Anton's doing most of the work." Mads was still watching me over his glass of wine. "I'm just supervising."

"What kind of wood are you using?" This came from Niklas. I could tell from the expression on his face he was impressed by Anton's new hobby. He had an innate respect for craftsmen that I'd never quite grasped. At home, he never showed any interest in using his hands to create anything but the moment he was around a stone-mason or a carpenter, his degree in psychology was forgotten and he'd wax nostalgic about the time he helped renovate his grandfather's house in southern Sweden.

"Oak. Finest wood there is."

Mads glanced from me to Niklas. I saw the questioning look in his eyes, but I couldn't respond, not when Ingrid was leaning toward me and telling me an anecdote about one of the children she taught. I tried to pay attention but I could barely even eat. Both of them in the same room...

"Is Mads a common name?" Niklas

Mads shrugged. "It is here in Denmark."

"I thought so. You've got to be the...third, fourth person who's called Mads that Laney's met." Niklas grinned like it was a joke, but I thought I heard an edge to his voice.

"It's a very common name," Ingrid assured Niklas as she refilled her glass. "I must have at least three cousins called Mads."

"How long have you and Laney been together?" Mads directed the question at Niklas. I flashed him a warning look but he ignored it.

"Five happy years," came Niklas's reply. His cheeks were flushed already from the heat and all the wine we'd had. "We met at this ridiculous American mixer."

Niklas winked at me. He was trying to be jokey, but hearing him recall the mixer as ridiculous—even if I agreed—jarred me. I angled my body away from him and let the distance between us grow. I thought he'd stop there, but he continued. "I'm not sure what Laney was even doing there, but I saw her and I thought, here's a girl who looks like she knows how to have a good time."

"That's me, the good time girl," I said, my tone dangerously close to turning cynical. "You make me sound like a slut, Niklas."

Ingrid saved me. "Now, Niklas, when I asked you that question, you told me you couldn't take your eyes off Laney." She kept her voice light and airy, but there was a steely edge creeping in. "You said she was everything your ex-wife wasn't, and you knew you had to have her in your life."

"I say a lot of things." Niklas grinned. He leaned toward me and rested his hand on the back of my chair. "But it's true. I thought she was someone I had to have in my life."

"And now?" Mads's jaw tightened. I wanted to switch seats and sit beside him. I wanted to be the girl who could kiss away all that tension. And I hated that I was the one causing it. I didn't want it to be like this.

"Now, I'm someone who keeps track of things for him," I said lightly. But the words hurt. I didn't want to be anyone's glorified assistant. And when I looked at Niklas, the man I'd fallen in love with wasn't there. The man sitting beside me was a stranger.

"You know you're more than that, Laney." Niklas laughed. He was so loose now. He'd undone his collar and his hair was slightly mussed. I'd lost track of how many times he'd refilled his wine glass.

"I'm not sure about anything anymore," I said, more to myself than anyone else. But Mads heard me. And the look he gave me—questioning, yet full of something like love—made my breath catch. I bit my lower lip and glanced away.

"Mads, where's your special lady?" Niklas asked. His hand slid along the nape of my neck. His damp fingertips grazed my skin. I brushed them away, but they returned. "You're the odd man out."

"She's occupied tonight." He drained his glass and then set it down. He was still looking at me, his eyes dark and flat. "Maybe next time." Anton refilled it, and wondered if anyone wanted a joint.

"I didn't know you were seeing anyone," I said stupidly.

"Well, you wouldn't. We only just met, didn't we?"

"Have you met before?" Niklas's fingers tensed on my shoulder. "I thought you hadn't met before?"

"We haven't met," I said tightly. "We just met tonight."

"Niklas, it's the wine talking." Ingrid laughed. "Anyway, you still haven't told us about New York."

I raised my glass to take a sip, but the wine sloshed over the rim and splattered on the tabletop. I mopped it up quickly with my napkin. While Ingrid distracted

Niklas with reminiscences about New York, Mads's hand was stroking my knee. I tried to start a conversation with him that would be neutral enough that neither of us would feel uncomfortable. But the situation was too weird. Neither of us knew how we should interact; not when Niklas was there, not when we were in the home of two of my closest friends. I tried to remain calm, laughed whenever I knew I should, told stories Anton and Ingrid prompted from our college days.

"Is that how you know Ingrid and Anton, then?" Mads cocked his head to the side. "From college in America?"

"We all lived together," Anton said. "It was a house share with some other students."

"One of the girls... what was her name, Ingrid? Do you remember? The one whose grandmother actually owned the house?" I prompted. Mads was still stroking my knee. It took everything in me not to look up at him and lose myself.

"Chelsea, I think." Ingrid laughed and shook her head. "I remember she was a pain in the ass."

"Laney and her cousin, Eddy, had rooms on the second floor, and Ingrid and I had the attic bedroom." Anton poured more wine in his glass. "We couldn't afford cable TV, so we spent all our evenings hanging out at the local bars or looking for free nights at clubs."

We all laughed as we reminisced about those pauper days in New York, but something felt off. The air was charged with a strange undercurrent, and I wasn't the only one who noticed it. Ingrid, who was usually as languid as Anton, seemed squirrelly and nervous. A few times, I caught her exchanging odd looks with Anton. What was going on here? And Mads was behaving like all of this was a lark. He was asking Niklas so many questions, almost interrogating him. I knew what he was doing—assessing Niklas and trying to figure out what was there between us—but I wished he would stop.

I shivered, though the room was humid and almost too hot. Our now-empty plates stared up at us. The conversation had turned again, and now Niklas was telling Mads about our vacation in the United States. Mads was nodding, though occasionally his hazel eyes slid my way. Ingrid touched my arm and asked if I wanted to have a cigarette in the garden. I nodded. I needed a break.

Ingrid led the way into the garden. We went through the kitchen instead of the doors leading out to it from the dining room. "This bit is nicer, more private," she said over her shoulder. I pulled the kitchen door shut behind me, and followed her to a stone bench shrouded by an ivy-covered arch. Tiny, white lights were threaded through it, giving it a lovely, ethereal feel. Once we sat down, Ingrid took out a silver cigarette case and offered me a hand-rolled cigarette. I gladly took it. The tobacco smelled fresh, aromatic and it reminded me of summers in Richmond.

"You should come more often." Ingrid sighed and took a first drag from her cigarette. "I miss our late night chats."

"So do I." I took a drag. The smoke eased down my throat and spread through me, relieving the knots of tension in me. "Sometimes I feel like I'm living someone else's life, not mine."

"Mmm. I understand. I never thought I was going to be living in the suburbs with three kids. Can you believe it? I have three teenage daughters."

"You and Anton are lucky, though," I said, letting myself imagine for a moment that this was my life and I was living it with Mads, not Niklas. "You have what I want, this... easiness, this certainty you belong together."

"You make us sound so much more romantic than we really are." Ingrid kissed my cheek. "Sometimes, I still wish we were living like paupers in Vesterbrø." Ingrid shook her head and smiled wistfully.

"Really?" Their old apartment. It was cold, cramped. But there was so much love there. I wanted that. I wanted some of what they had.

"Sometimes. I miss the freedom. I miss not having to worry all the time about whether the girls are okay, or trying to decide if I should treat myself to something I want, or put the money in our renovation fund so we can fix the roof."

"Is everything okay with you and Anton?" I asked cautiously. Were they going through a similar rough patch as Niklas and me? They weren't as affectionate with one another as they usually were. Normally, Anton found any excuse to touch or kiss Ingrid, but there was a definite chill between them.

Ingrid, though, shrugged. "I think it's simply a case of being too used to one another. We've been together so long."

"But... it's nothing serious, is it? You're not getting a divorce or anything like that, are you?"

"God, no. I promise, it's not as catastrophic as all that, Laney. We just need to have some alone time, like we used to. I've already booked a trip to the coast for next weekend." She squeezed my hand. "But I think it is with you and Niklas... unless I am reading the vibes wrong."

I didn't say anything. I took another long drag from my cigarette and exhaled slowly.

"I saw how you and Mads were looking at each other... and I saw how you reacted when he arrived."

Still, I said nothing. I didn't know how to tell her, despite how long we'd known one another. From the other side of the garden, the men's voices drifted to us along with the resinous scent of marijuana smoke. Niklas usually refused to smoke pot. Would he do it now since both Anton and Mads were doing it? His little rebellion?

"Laney, what's going on?" Ingrid said in a lower voice. "You know you can tell me anything."

"Mads and I know each other."

"Why didn't you say so? You didn't have to pretend you were strangers."

"Yes, we did. We do."

"But why? I still don't get the need for subterfuge, darling." Ingrid tossed her red hair over her shoulder and fixed me with a questioning look.

"Because I'm fucking him behind Niklas's back." I said softly, but firmly. I didn't meet Ingrid's imploring eyes.

Ingrid gasped. "Did I misunderstand you? You used to always say you weren't the cheating type."

"I didn't think I was, either." I shook my head. "And then I met Mads when I was here for work a few weeks ago."

"He's working with you?" Ingrid asked. "Anton said he was a carpenter."

"No, he's not working with me." I bit my lower lip. "I told Niklas I wanted to have a baby, and then he suddenly announced he'd had a vasectomy before he met me..."

"I still don't understand how Mads fits into this, honey."

"I went to a sperm bank."

"Wait, wait... did you go to Copenhagen Cryo? Is that where you know Mads from?"

I nodded. "I met him at the mingle."

"I thought it was all done artificially."

"It is, Ingrid. But I haven't signed anything yet. Because I met Mads and it just... it just happened. I want to be with him, I don't want anything else. Just him." It came out almost too quickly, the words tumbling from my mouth so inarticulately. I took another drag from my cigarette and wished for a moment it was marijuana instead of tobacco. At least it would have uncoiled the tension and made me relax more. "I came here this weekend... I lied to Niklas and told him it was for work, but I came here to see Mads, and then Niklas decided he was coming down to meet me. I'm in such a fucking muddle, Ingrid. I don't even know if I still love him. I think he's still fucking Karolina. I barely know Mads, but I want to be with him all the time."

"I knew something was bothering you." Ingrid took my hand and squeezed it. "I wasn't expecting this, but I knew there was something."

"I don't know what to do." My chest tightened. I took a longer drag from my cigarette and exhaled slowly, hoping it would relax me. I watched the smoke curl skywards. "He's always in my thoughts. He's like a drug for me."

"Does Niklas suspect anything?"

I nodded and then I told her about his finding my phone and then what he'd said this morning. "Is he telling me I'm allowed to do this as long as I don't let him see it?"

Ingrid was quiet for a moment. She squashed out her cigarette butt on the flagstone and then she put her arm around my shoulders. "What do you want, Laney?"

"I want to be happy."

"Are you happy? Right now, I mean, with Niklas?"

I shook my head. "Not for a while. It almost felt normal between us when we went to the States, but as soon as we were back in Stockholm it all went wrong again."

"So explore this thing with Mads. He gave you permission as long as you don't flaunt it in his face."

"Eddy says I should just focus on Niklas." But I knew, deep down, I didn't want to follow Eddy's advice this time. I wanted to unfurl my wings.

"You could. You've been doing that for five years, though, and it doesn't seem to give you any satisfaction. It never has." The cold edge of Ingrid's tone caught me off-guard. I blinked at her.

"I thought you liked Niklas," I said cautiously.

"I do like him. He's charming, he's handsome, he's the perfect guest." Ingrid stood and shook her strawberry blonde hair back from her face. "But I just don't like how you stop being you when you're with him. And I don't think he appreciates you, not really. I think you're his pretty American girlfriend he likes to show off. But I don't think you'll ever be more than that for him."

She walked toward the edge of the house, and I followed her. From where we stood, we could see the trio of men, standing by the open French doors to the dining room, passing a joint and talking. For once, Niklas looked perfectly relaxed. His hair was mussed, his clothes less strict. He'd unbuttoned his shirt at the collar and removed his blazer. Why couldn't he always be like that? Mads was the only one who sensed we were watching and looked over his shoulder at us. I raised my hand in a discrete wave. He smiled back at me. Niklas didn't turn. I heard him say something about babies, and how I wanted one. He made it sound like a silly joke, like something insubstantial and whimsical. I asked myself why I was still with him, but then he finally looked my way and the smile he gave me sent me reeling inside. It was that secret smile he used to give me when we were first dating, the one that seemed to encapsulate every passionate moment we'd ever had and concentrate it in the slow slide of his lips.

I blinked and looked away.

No, this was crazy.

Inside again, I retreated to the small powder room in the front hall. I turned on the cold-water tap and let the water cool down my wrists, but it didn't seem to help. I still felt on the verge of tears. There was no point in crying. Not really. Niklas was behaving as though there was nothing out of the ordinary taking place. Even though he'd studied the sperm donor files, he didn't recognize Mads. They were back inside now. Mads and Anton were in the hall, just on the other side of the door, speaking Danish together in hushed tones. I heard my name. I froze. What were they saying? I wished I'd paid more attention all those times Ingrid had tried to teach me Danish. I opened the door and stepped into the hall. Mads stopped in mid-sentence. He was flushed, his neck burning pink, his stance tense. Anton stopped too.

"Hi," I said to Mads. I focused on him, on the grim line of his mouth, of his dipped head and the way he wouldn't look at me. "Small world, isn't it?"

"Don't joke, Laney."

Anton glanced over his shoulder. "I'm not sure I want to know what's going on... but does Niklas know?"

I gestured at the door. "Where is he?"

"He's in the kitchen, helping Ingrid load the dish-washer."

"He suspects... look, I didn't want to bring you and Ingrid into this, but now you know."

"This is too close for comfort," Mads muttered. "I'm going home."

"I'm out of this," Anton announced. "Mads, thanks for swinging by."

"I'll see you at the workshop." He and Anton bumped fists and then Mads cast a look my way. His eyebrows furrowed, his mouth formed a grim, tight line. "Tues-day?"

Anton nodded. "Yeah, on Tuesday. See you then." Then Anton shook his head at me and returned to the kitchen.

I opened the front door and went out into the night. The air was milder now. Tiny goose bumps dotted my skin as I stood by the gate. When Mads came out, he was shaking his head.

"This was a little weird." I said with an embarrassed grin.

Mads edged closer to me. "This was too weird, Laney."

I nodded. "Just... kiss me before you go?" The look on his face scared me. If this was too weird, would he pull away? I needed him. I didn't want to be with Niklas, so why couldn't I just tell him and leave?

He took my face in his hands and brushed his lips across mine. We stood there like that—my hands gripping his jeans-clad hips, the two of us kissing each other lightly, tenderly—until from somewhere down the road we heard the staccato laughter of a couple passing by. I stepped back and whispered goodbye to him. Mads pulled me closer again for one more kiss, this one deeper and more passionate. When we parted, he opened the gate and stepped out onto the uneven pavement. My lips still ached for his. I brushed my fingers over them and watched as he walked away and disappeared around the corner. I turned and went back inside. Someone had turned on music, and Nina Simone was singing how her baby just cared for her.

I sat down on the couch and let my head fall back on the cushion. In the kitchen, Niklas was laughing at something Anton had said. Ingrid's soft voice added another layer to the music as she wondered when the girls would come home. It was closing in on midnight. I ought to go in the kitchen and join them. Ingrid called for me and I answered, "I'll be there in a second," but I didn't move from the couch. I needed a few more moments, to re-imagine Mads's lips on mine, the roughness of his palms and fingers as they touched my face, how for a moment the world froze and there was just us.

*   *   *

That night, I couldn't sleep. I told myself it was because I'd had too many glasses of wine, but that was an empty excuse. Beside me, Niklas slept peacefully. Maybe it was the marijuana. But I couldn't think, I couldn't sleep. I climbed out of bed and went to the window. Niklas had closed it before he went to sleep, and now the air was too still. I opened both windows and was rewarded with a cool breeze. Niklas stirred. I returned to bed and tried to absorb some of his sleep vibes. I moved closer to him, draped my arm over his waist and kissed his shoulder. He slept so deeply, his breathing coming in long, slow draws. Normally, lying close to him was enough to help me drift off, but there were too many thoughts crowding my mind. But one treacherous thought troubled me most—I knew Mads's address. I could have slipped away and gone to him. And no matter how easily I could have been caught, I was convinced it would have been worth it.

CHAPTER NINE

A Slight Wrinkle

By the time we returned to Stockholm, Niklas seemed more confident than ever. He was affectionate again, though he was not as watchful of me. I couldn't relax. Whenever he spoke to me, I expected him to mention meeting Mads and finally making the connection, but I focused on work, trying to meet my deadline without having to work late too often. I kept telling myself that work would keep me from being idle enough to text Mads. Things were silent on his end. I didn't want jealousy to spring to life in me and have me wondering if he'd met someone else. I didn't want to second-guess him. But then our client sprang some last-minute rejections on us, and my team and I had to scramble to re-sketch our concept. In the chaos, I'd nearly forgotten about Mads's proposed visit, but then he sent a text midweek, saying he'd booked a room at Hotel Rival near Mariatorget and wondered if this was okay.

I closed the door to my office. I was working from home again. Niklas had been in and out of the apartment all day. I called Mads and spoke to him in a hushed voice, "When do you arrive?"

"Tomorrow evening. Is that too soon?"

"No, it's perfect. We should be able to have a lot of time together."

"What about Niklas?"

"He's got some kind of seminar in Göteborg. He'll be gone Friday and Saturday."

"Good. I don't want a repeat of last weekend."

"Neither do I." I said softly.

"We're taking a really big risk, aren't we?"

"We are," I admitted. "This is crazy. Why are we doing this?"

"I'm doing it because I want to be near you."

"I want that, too." The words felt so true. It was no longer the thrill of doing something illicit. I don't think it ever was simply about the excitement of being unfaithful. I knew as soon as saw him. I knew with a certainty that he was the one I wanted to be with.

We spoke a few more moments, finalizing our plans, before we ended the call. The rest of the afternoon went by in a blur. He would be here tomorrow. No more longing and pretending I could still hear his voice in my head. No more zoning out Niklas as I tried to hold on to a memory of how Mads had kissed me before he left Ingrid and Anton's house. I couldn't wait to be in his arms again, to feel his warmth enveloping me. The anticipation sparked and crackled inside me. I was taking a ridiculous risk. Stockholm was too small. It liked to think of itself as a metropolis, but it was really a small town dressed up in big city clothing. So many times I bumped into colleagues or Niklas's friends in hole-in-the-wall bars that were too hipster for them. There was always that uncomfortable moment when we all had to stand around and pretend we were enjoying the surprise encounter. I didn't want to chance it this weekend. This time, I wanted to have my full weekend with Mads, that wouldn't be interrupted by unwanted company.

"I'm taking Siri and Jesper to London next weekend," Niklas announced over dinner. "Would you like to come with us?"

I loved London—its frenetic energy, the crush of people, the shopping, and the museums—but I couldn't stomach the idea of going there with Niklas and his kids. Even though they were old enough now to take care of themselves, weekend trips with them always ended up with arguments and hissy fits. Siri would do something wildly inappropriate, and then Niklas's usually even temper would flare into embarrassed fury. Jesper, not wanting to be the odd man out, would then do something equally ridiculous, and Niklas would transform into the version of him that I hated—Mr. Psycho Babble, the super therapist version of him that could spend hours asking you therapist-like questions as he tried to get you to see the root of your actions.

The kids usually never fell for it—he'd done this to them too many times when they were younger—but this was his modus operandi, and he tried it nonetheless. I hated it. I steeled myself and pretended I was not with them. I'd leave them to it and hole up in a café or in the hotel bar with a good book and my phone. I'd sit there for hours, until Niklas finally called and was calm again. The worst part about it was the awful tension that permeated the rest of the weekend. Siri and Jesper formed a united front of teenage indignation, while Niklas pointedly avoided talking to them. It forced me into the role of the mediator or ringmaster. I ended up being the one who had to maintain civil dinner conversation.

"I think it's better if you and the kids go on your own." I was already trying to figure out if I would be able to go to Copenhagen that weekend. "We're still trying to finish the Ogilvy project, so I'll probably be working all next weekend."

"What about this weekend? Do you think you can meet me in Göteborg?" He refilled his wine glass, and then topped up mine.

"I've got to finish the brochure text and the press junket material," I said quickly. "That's probably going to take all weekend."

"We're not going to be able to continue like this if we're going to have a baby, you know." The smugness in his voice grated at me. He often worked longer hours than I did. His patients called at all hours of the night. I doubted that would change even if we had children. It hadn't changed in the years we'd raised his children together.

"I know."

"Did you make an appointment for us to meet with Ida at the clinic?"

"She didn't have any free appointments until the second week of October, so I booked one for Friday the tenth." I set down my glass of wine and started scrolling through my phone's calendar.

"Shit, that doesn't work... I promised Jesper I'd take him to Manchester for a football weekend." He was scrolling through his phone now, checking his calendar. "What about the weekend after that?"

"I'm free," I said. "We'll have to check with Ida."

"Will you book it?"

"Yes, of course I will."

Niklas refilled his wine glass. "You know, I'm really impressed with Anton."

"Why's that?" I watched Niklas carefully, curious to see where he was going with this.

"Well, he's found a new passion with woodworking," Niklas explained. "I never saw him as a hands-on sort of person. I thought for sure he was more of an 'art from a distance' person—the person who writes about something beautiful without creating something beautiful."

"His poetry is beautiful."

"It's not the same thing. Poetry is still from a distance. You simply use words—something abstract, not something concrete—to create something of beauty. But wood... now that is something tangible."

"Maybe the next time we visit, we'll get to see this table of his." I said very casually. I didn't want to dwell too much on it too much. It would bring Niklas too close to Mads, and I didn't want to discuss Mads with him. "Ingrid says it's coming along nicely."

We both finished our glasses of wine. There was a strange silence between us. I waited for Niklas to continue with his train of thought, but he was now reading a text message on his phone screen. The longer the silence continued, the more the tension seemed to grow. I cleared the table for something to do.

Finally, I asked him, "Are you thinking of taking up woodworking?"

Niklas chuckled. "No, no. Nothing like that. I thought it was interesting."

I loaded the dishwasher and then put the bottle of wine back in fridge. Niklas pushed away from the table. "I'm surprised you're taking Jesper to Manchester," I said.

"Well, I did promise him."

"Isn't it a bit like rewarding him for bad behavior?" I asked. "I mean, he and Siri disregarded a rule you've always said you hold dearly, and you said you were going to make them accept the consequences of their actions."

"Jesper's already paid his share of the cleaning bill."

"What about Siri?"

"She's going to pay, too. She just couldn't afford to do it this month." But Niklas didn't sound very convinced. We both knew the likelihood of her paying for anything was rather low. She'd already made it clear she didn't think she'd done anything wrong, and that we were being unreasonable.

I didn't want to push the issue any further. I could see the terse look forming on Niklas's face. But I was still annoyed that, even after Niklas had stood up to them, Siri was still flagrantly disregarding his wishes by bringing strangers home to us. Last night, she'd come in at two in the morning with a young man she'd met at a Stureplan bar. I'd woken Niklas and let him know it was happening again, but he only knocked on Siri's door and asked her to quiet down.

"When are we going to do something about Siri and her nighttime visits?" I asked.

"She's eighteen. I can't stop her from sleeping with her boyfriends."

"Niklas, these aren't boyfriends. They're one-night stands. And why does she have to bring them to our place? Does she do this to Karolina?"

"Laney..."

"It's not right, Niklas. It's disrespectful to us."

"So now you're concerned about 'us'?"

I faltered. "What's that supposed to mean?"

"Forget it, Laney. Forget I said anything."

"No, I want to know what you mean." My hands were balled into fists. I steeled myself for whatever he had to say. I knew it would come back to that strange conversation we'd had in my hotel room. "I've always been concerned about us—even when I knew your kids came before 'us'—I've put them before 'us' so many times, and they still treat me like a visitor in what's supposed to be our home."

"This isn't really about them, though, is it?"

"If I ask you what's going on with Jesper and Siri, and the consequences of disrespecting our house rules, then it is about them."

Niklas shook his head and walked out of the room. I watched, angry that he was just walking away, but not surprised. There was nothing to be gained in following him. This would just swell and fester. I cursed and slammed my hand on the kitchen counter. Sharp pain coursed through my fist and I cursed again. Why was I even starting such a silly argument with Niklas? Even if I was upset by how disrespectful Siri was towards us, it had nothing to do with my reason for bringing it up. I knew it, Niklas knew it. And it didn't make me feel like a very nice person. I was beginning to think I wasn't very nice at all.

* * *

Later, when our tempers had calmed and it was time to go to bed, I wandered through the apartment, looking for Niklas. I found him on the balcony, staring down into the inner courtyard of our building. The small garden seemed to shimmer under the glow of light spilling out of the apartments, and the web of white fairy lights co-cooning some of the hedges.

"I'm sorry," I said to his back and touched his shoulder.

"Me, too." He didn't turn. His shoulders sagged. "We seem to be apologizing a lot these days."

"I know."

"Maybe we should wait a little while longer with having a baby, Laney. It doesn't feel like this is the right time. For you, for me. It feels like we're in flux, and I don't know if we should even try if we're so unstable."

I couldn't argue with him. He was right. We shouldn't have been thinking about bringing a child into a relationship like ours. I wound my arms around his waist and leaned into him. The fragility of what was between us didn't prevent me from seeking some sense of security from him.

"I feel like you're not here one hundred percent, Laney. I know you're not satisfied. And I want to make you happy. But I don't know what you want anymore."

Tell him, was the thought going through my head. Tell him what's wrong. But the words were like dust in my mouth. And maybe there was no point in telling him if I was already mentally with someone else. But that was the thing—I wanted to be with Mads, but there was still a part of me that didn't want to walk away from Niklas. I still loved him. But I was in love with—or maybe I was in love with idea of—Mads. I still barely knew him, but when I thought about the kiss we'd shared by the gate, that moment when the whole world disappeared and there were only us and the taste of his mouth and the touch of his skin on mine, I couldn't just ignore it. I didn't know if it was love. I didn't know anything more than that his body made mine spark to life.

"I still love you, Niklas." I took his hand and led him back into the apartment. "I do."

We made our way to our bedroom. We didn't make love, but we held each other until sleep began to weave its web around us. At some point, I heard Jesper come into the apartment. He called out for Niklas and me, but when neither of us answered, he crept into his room, closing the door quietly. I wished it could always be like that. But I knew there was another storm looming in the distance.

"It's been decided that you, Marius, and Johan are going to have to work more closely with the client."

I shifted in my seat, trying to get comfortable as I waited for Jens to continue. I'd planned on working from home again, but he'd called me and said I needed to show everyone I hadn't disappeared off the face of the earth. From anyone else, it would have sounded like a severe reprimand, but Jens was laid back enough in the way he said it that you didn't feel like you were being coerced into anything.

"We already work very closely with them," I reminded him. "We've been back and forth to Copenhagen so many times, working through the weekend..."

"That's why we think it's more productive if the three of you work more intensively, on location, with the Fogh group." Jens adjusted his glasses on his slightly off-center nose. He flopped down into the chair beside mine and stretched out his legs. "Actually, they requested it. They'd rather work with you guys on a daily basis until the project's complete, so it means you'll have to stay in Copenhagen until just before Christmas."

Until Christmas? I was a little dumbfounded. I wasn't expecting that at all. "I'll need to talk to Niklas about this."

"Why? If it was his career, he'd go in a heartbeat." Jens wasn't one of Niklas's biggest fans. Mainly because Niklas was the reason our Friends-With-Benefits status had ended. "Besides, you can fly home at the weekends, or he can go visit you there. And if the project ends well, the big bosses are saying they see big bonuses and promotions ahead for all three of you. So. Are you game?"

I nodded. He was absolutely right about Niklas. He wouldn't consult me if an opportunity like this was in his grasp. He would say yes, and then tell me about it when the wheels were already in motion. Any of my concerns would be disregarded or downplayed. So I nodded again and told Jens I was most definitely game. Niklas and I needed a break, but neither of us was willing to take the next step. Now it was done.

There was already a packet of information waiting on my desk when I left Jens's office. He'd known I would say yes. The only thing I had to do was book my airline tick-

ets and pick the hotel-apartment I wanted to stay in. So
I booked my flight and chose a two-bedroom apartment
near Rosenborg. And then I sent a text to Niklas with
the news. I waited for an answer, but there was none.

Eddy wasn't and I met for a late lunch at Restaurang
Publik in PUB, hoping we could avoid the crowd. When
I arrived, Eddy had managed to secure a table for us and
was battling off the latte mammas looking for tables of
their own. She'd already ordered for us and, from the
looks of it, she wasn't in the best of moods.

"I fucking hate these women" Eddy muttered as she
attacked her plate of *raggmunk*: Swedish-style potato
pancakes served with back bacon and lingonberry sauce.
I was picking at the "health plate" she'd ordered for me.

"Are you trying to tell me something?" I gestured at
the sad-looking plate of mixed greens, topped with cottage cheese and tasteless chicken. "Have I started
getting a little roly-poly?"

"No. They didn't have any *raggmunk* left." Eddy grimaced. "Jesus Christ, what is that smell?"

We both looked at the woman sitting at the table beside ours. She was changing her infant right at the table.

"Are you fucking insane?" Eddy snapped at the woman. "You don't change babies in the middle of a
restaurant! That's what bathrooms are for!"

A waitress rushed over and escorted the young mother to the ladies' room, preventing another Eddy
meltdown. Now that she was calm again, I jumped right

in and told her, "Jens is sending me and my team to Copenhagen until we finish our project."

Eddy gave me a suspicious look. "And you didn't initiate this?"

"No. That would be a little extreme, don't you think?"

"Not considering how Copenhagen-crazy you've been lately." Eddy smirked. "How many times have you been there?"

"Not as often as you're implying."

"So what does Niklas say?"

"Nothing so far."

"Haven't you told him?"

"I sent him a text, but he didn't answer."

"A text? Come on, Laney, you need to talk to him face to face."

"I will. I'm not just going to pack and move without telling him."

"You talk like it's permanent."

"I'm only there for a few months."

"Mighty convenient, all things considered."

"Okay, you know what? Let's forget it. Tell me how you're doing. Everything okay with you and Andreas?"

"No," she said tersely. "He said he wants to take a break from us."

"Oh, sweetie, I'm so sorry!" I took her hand in mine and gave it a gentle squeeze. "Why didn't you say anything? Why haven't you called me?"

She shook her head. "It's embarrassing. I can't believe he's doing this. And the girl he wants to 'explore things with' is like... twelve, practically!"

"Eddy... really?"

"No, but she looks it. She's a model for Elite Stockholm and she can't be any older than maybe eighteen or nineteen. How am I supposed to compete with that? I can't. And that bastard expects me to just continue running the business, while he gallivants around Europe with her."

I held her hand and listened as she told me about how long she'd suspected he was being unfaithful, how it brought out her old insecurities and made her so crazy that she'd finally moved out of their apartment and was borrowing a friend's apartment in Södermalm while he was in Singapore. "The worst part of all of this is that it makes me miss Colin."

"Have you heard from him lately?"

"No, not since Rome." She brushed her bangs back and let out a long sigh. "Shit, Laney, none of this is really about that stupid girl or Andreas. Not really. It's because I still love Colin. Shit. You told me this a while ago. I should have listened."

"Did you tell Colin how you feel?"

"He's seeing someone now," she said quietly. "He told me he'd always have feelings for me, but he didn't know if he could go through everything with me again."

Eddy blinked quickly. "I hate this. I hate that I've been living with Andreas and getting caught up in his bullshit, when the person I really want is Colin and he can't take my bullshit anymore."

We sat together for a long while without saying a word. I wasn't used to Eddy being the vulnerable one. Of the two of us, she was the one who always had snappy comebacks, who never overanalyzed comments or life in general, she was the one who used to prompt me to just go with the flow. When she and Colin were together their instability never seemed to affect her—she always laughed it off or joked about how their fights always led to great make-up sex—but now I understood it was always an act.

I was on my way back to the office when Niklas finally returned my call. He was brusque with me. I didn't blame him. He probably assumed I'd initiated this temporary move to Copenhagen. And when he finally insinuated it, I corrected him.

"I didn't initiate anything, Niklas. Jens and the client decided this was best. And it's not just me moving. Marius and Johan are going, too."

I was nearly at the office and stood in the centre of Dandelion Park. Around me, tourists milled, maps clutched in their hands. A few were poised to ask me for help but I avoided making eye contact with them, and headed for the crosswalk.

"So when is this move supposed to take place?"

"As soon as possible. I told Jens I needed to speak with you about it, but he was pretty insistent."

"What if I'd said no?"

"Niklas, this is my job. It's not like this is some whimsy of mine."

"You don't need to work. I could take care of everything."

"I like my job. I want to work. I don't want to be one of those ladies who lunch."

"I just don't like this, Laney."

"I know, sweetie, but it's work. And it's only for a little while. You could always come down at the weekends to see me, and I could come back to Stockholm."

"I feel like I'm losing you."

"Baby, you're not losing me." I retorted quickly. "I'm going to Copenhagen to finish a project. And when the project is over, I'm coming back to Stockholm."

"Will you still be here when I come back from Göteborg?"

"I don't go until next Wednesday."

"We'll talk about this on Sunday, when I'm home again." His voice was distant. I could imagine him standing by the window in his office, staring down at the food hall Östermalmshallen and its rich red brick facade.

I said okay, but it didn't matter if he was annoyed about my going. I'd already agreed to go, and so had my team. I knew that Sunday would be a litany of complaints about why I was going. I had the feeling Niklas would turn the discussion into an analysis session, but I wanted to avoid that. I didn't want to justify going. I loved my job. Writing copy and working with my team of art directors satisfied me. And we both knew that if the tables were turned, he'd go without consulting me. And he'd expect me to simply accept it.

My temper was a bit short when I finally walked into the office. I'd already relived in my head the conversation with Niklas and found myself wishing I'd had far more assertive arguments. I should have confronted him about his own ambition but it would have done no good. I dropped my bag on the floor by my desk. The soft leather sagged and my iPhone clattered onto the floor. When my phone beeped, I thought it would be another message from Niklas. Instead, it was a text from Mads. It was short and simple.

—I'm here now.

And that was exactly what I needed to make me smile again.

He was waiting for me in the hotel bar. My heart danced a little when I saw him, but I didn't rush over to him, or scream with delight, or any of the other reactions my body was trying to coerce me into. I listened to my brain as it said, Play it cool. Don't make a scene. Wait until you're upstairs to do anything crazy. So, instead, I sidled in beside him and said a casual "*Hej*" and kissed his razor-stubbled cheek.

He wrapped his arm around my waist and kissed my lips. "Can't believe I'm here with you."

"It feels weird." I was glad it was so crowded in the bar. I was still afraid I'd bump into someone who knew

Niklas and me. "I'm so used to you and me in Copenhagen."

We kissed again. Mads held me closer, his hand slid from the middle of my back to my ass. He gave it a good squeeze. "You've got the most amazing ass," he said, his lips just barely grazing mine. "Maybe we should skip these drinks, and go back to my room."

"Maybe we should," I agreed, and then we went downstairs to the bustling lobby and headed for the elevator banks. Mads kept his hand on the base of my spine and his touch filled me with a longing to be naked and at his mercy. We were nearly at the elevator when I heard someone calling my name. I recognized the voice.

I stopped and turned. There was no point in trying to avoid a confrontation. My de facto stepdaughter, Siri was striding towards me. Her impossibly high heels clicked on the floor. "What are you doing here?" she said. She trained her eyes on me, then Mads. "I thought you were going to Göteborg with Dad."

"I'm meeting some colleagues." The lie rolled quickly from my tongue. A little too quickly and easily. I gestured at Mads. "Siri, this is Mads. Mads is from the Copenhagen office."

Siri, with her perpetual pout, tossed her blonde hair back and flicked her eyes over Mads. She said a quick hi and then regarded me again. "I'm surprised to see you in this part of town. You usually never come to Södermalm."

"Yes, well, like I said, I'm meeting colleagues. We're actually on our way upstairs for a meeting."

"You skipped spending time with my dad for a meeting?"

"I have to work, Siri. I think your father understands that."

Mads interrupted. "We should go. Hillevie and Jonas are waiting upstairs."

"Yes, of course. Look, Siri. I've got to go."

Mads and I boarded the elevator, keeping a safe distance until the elevator doors slid to a close. I was shaking. I had barely laid eyes on Siri in weeks, and now she'd shown up when I was with the man who was the reason I was betraying her father. I flinched when Mads tried to take my hand. "Not yet," I murmured. "Not yet."

"Was that Niklas's daughter?"

I nodded. "And she's probably calling him now."

I tried not to think about Siri. I wanted to forget about her completely but the arrogant expression on her face, the way she'd flicked her eyes at me and then Mads, rankled me. I was convinced she'd sussed us out— otherwise why would she ask me how I could ditch her father for work? She'd never cared before what I did with my time. Mads did what he could to distract me. He had an arsenal of tricks, but none of them were working tonight. My brain was fucking with me, and there wasn't much to be done about it.

I couldn't relax; couldn't just wipe my mind clear and stop worrying.

"Maybe we should just stop," I said suddenly.

"Laney, she's not going to say anything."

"I don't know that."

"It doesn't matter now though, does it? She's not here in the room with us. You told her I was your colleague."

"Maybe she saw us in the bar. We don't know how long she was there or what she saw."

"So what if she saw us kiss! You said you wanted to leave Niklas. This is your out. I am your out."

It was hard to think when I was lying naked in bed with a man whose body made mine sing. I rolled away from him, but he didn't let me get too far.

"I'm your out, Laney," he said again. "When the shit hits the fan with Niklas, I'm here."

"We hardly know one another." But then I laughed. Saying it when I'd just let him go down on me was ridiculous.

"I know I like how you taste," he said and then rolled me over on my back again. He slid down between my legs and teased me with his tongue, with his lips and adept fingers.

By the time I was able to tell him my news, he'd pushed Siri far enough out of my thoughts that I'd finally relaxed and we'd made good use of the bed.

"So you're moving to Copenhagen?"

"Temporarily. I'll be working, but it'll make things easier for us."

"You could stay with me."

"The company's already arranged an apartment for me, and until things are resolved with Niklas, it's better this way."

Mads muttered under his breath. "How much longer do we have to be in limbo?"

I didn't know what to say. I wanted to be able to say "tomorrow" but it wasn't that simple. I'd never imagined I would be in this situation. I'd always assumed that, at some point, Niklas would propose to me, and we'd be married. I'd assumed we would have our own family, even if I'd always behaved as though children weren't part of my future. And I'd behaved that way because Niklas's involvement in his kids' lives and his career was always more important than mine. I'd let my own wants take a back seat. Maybe I'd always done it.

So instead of giving Mads an exact time, I said, "Once I'm in Copenhagen, I'm yours."

* * *

We spent the entire weekend in bed. Leaving the room felt too risky, and Mads wasn't in the mood for sightseeing. Besides, autumn had settled over Stockholm with a vengeance, and sheets of rain battered the city.

Room service was our salvation, and Rival's room service was phenomenal. Mads had booked a deluxe room, and the wall of windows and balcony overlooked Mariatorget's verdant urban escape. I lay there in bed, stretching like a satisfied cat, while Mads showered. This was our last day together and he'd ordered a late check-out since his flight didn't take off until six in the evening.

I checked my phone. Only two messages from Niklas, and both were vague. None mentioned Siri. The first said he was in a meeting until 9:00 p.m. The second message said he was going to stay in Göteborg an extra day, and visit some friends. He was lying. I was certain of it, but at that moment I didn't care. I tossed my phone back on the bedside table, and then focused on Mads. The wall separating the bedroom and bathroom was made of glass and only venetian blinds afforded any modesty or privacy. Mads had left the blinds open. His body was too beautiful. I didn't seem to be able to get enough of it. I only hoped that once we were together in Copenhagen, the novelty wouldn't wear off. There was a connection between us, and it was amazingly strong, but I hoped it wasn't just the sex that held us together. And there was no way of knowing until we finally took the plunge.

I hated for the weekend to end. Hated even more having to return to my life with Niklas when every part of me still ached for Mads. We ate breakfast in bed, paid the extra fee for a late check out so we could make love one more time before he left.

Mads seemed to read my mind as we rode the elevator down to the main floor. He gave my hand a gentle squeeze and said, "It's not much longer."

I smiled up at him, anxious and still happy that we had something we could hold onto. This weekend wasn't the end of something, not for us.

"In Copenhagen, you're mine," he reminded me.

"I'm yours." I leaned into him, feeling relieved that soon we wouldn't have to sneak around. We could be a couple. I could go home to him whenever I wanted.

But when I walked back into my old life, I felt haunted. Doubt trailed me as I tried to reacclimatize to the sterile world Niklas and I had somehow created. I moved through the apartment, turning on lights to chase away the autumn darkness. Niklas wasn't home yet. Jesper was in his room listening to music. He'd left a Post-It Note saying he wanted pizza if I decided to order in. Siri was thankfully not around. I closeted myself in the bedroom and waited for the unease to leave me.

For the first time in a long while I found myself thinking about my father. He would not have approved of any of this—not my living with Niklas, not my involvement with Mads. Sometimes my father or some phantom version of him became my conscience. It didn't matter that he was still very much alive, still not interested in the daughter he left behind. I imagined him watching me with those hyper-critical eyes, his mouth pulled into a grim disapproving line, shaking his head at me the way he used to when a younger version of me managed to disappoint him.

I was glad my mother was not around to see what was happening. After what she'd been through with my father and his infidelity, I doubted she would have been very supportive of what I was doing. Even if she liked Mads, she would have tried to convince me to call it off with him. I could almost hear her gentle voice in my head urging me to work things out with Niklas.

"But he's still in love with his ex-wife," I murmured. "And I'm in love with someone else."

I waited for a reply, but silence was my only answer.

CHAPTER TEN

Mistaken for Strangers

The first few days I was in Copenhagen, I didn't think about Niklas at all. I worked late nearly every night, met Mads at his workshop, and then we walked together to his apartment. I loved it there. The exposed brick walls were a dusky shade of red that reminded me of Philadelphia row houses. I could imagine living there with him. And, during the week, I did.

We'd lie in bed together at night and he'd tell me things I'd wanted to know since I'd first met him. And the more he told me, the greedier I became. Sometimes he teased me and asked if I was memorizing his life for a pub quiz. We were both memorizing one another's lives. He prompted me for stories of my childhood. And sometimes it really was like a pub quiz.

"Who was your first love?" I asked him one night. We were lying on his sofa, listening to one of his playlists on

Spotify. Outside it was chilly and rainy. Neither of us wanted to do anything more than kiss, and touch... then kiss a little more.

"My first love? That's easy—a girl called Adriana." Mads grinned. "She was from Cuba. She moved into the house across the street from my grandparents' place. I used to follow her everywhere."

"How old were you?" I traced the ridges on the bridge of his nose.

"I don't know. I think I was... fourteen? I made a mix tape for her, but she didn't have a tape player."

"Silly girl."

"Yeah, that's what I thought, too. Didn't she know that all declarations of love are made with mix tapes?"

"She missed the memo, apparently."

"So who was your first love?"

"A boy called Billy, but he had zero interest in me. I used to try to get him to notice me. But he just never looked my way."

"Stupid boy." Mads pulled me into his lap and nuzzled my neck. "You should have made him a mix tape."

Mads and I fell into a routine pretty quickly. Every morning we walked to what had become our café, where I'd first glimpsed him. We'd sit by the window, perched on bar stools with our feet resting on a toasty warm radiator, drinking our morning coffee while he read *Jyllands-Posten* and I read Justin Cronin's latest novel, *The Twelve*. Sometimes I'd lift my head from my book and catch Mads watching me. He'd take the opportunity to gently massage the back of my neck or steal a quick kiss that sparked into something more. His touch erased whatever residual doubts I might have about being there instead of going home, chastened, to Stockholm and Niklas. On the other side of the glass, the world kept moving: Copenhageners flew by on their bikes, oblivious to the pouring rain and heavy gray skies; buses rumbled past and lines of tourists in matching rain jackets braved the elements in search of Tivoli or the Little Mermaid.

If there was time, we either met for late lunches at a small café near my office, or I'd ride my borrowed bike to his workshop, and we'd eat *smørrebrød* at his work-bench. Our idle conversations danced around our future. Sometimes we touched on it, never mentioning Niklas or when I'd have to return to Stockholm. Other times we avoided it completely and focused on the here and now. When the other carpenters who shared the workshop joined us, the conversation switched from English to Danish. I couldn't always follow it, but listening to Mads and hearing the confidence in his voice reminded me that I didn't need to over-think what was going on be-tween us. It was only when his workshop mates slid curious looks at me or ignored me completely that doubt crept in, and I felt like an aberration in his life. Other women had probably met him here, showing up unan-nounced, giddy with their ache to be near Mads. I was sure of it. I was one of those women. I hoped I was the only one now.

202 · KIM GOLDEN

After work, Mads met me at a pub halfway between my office and his apartment. We'd have a beer there and then go home, where dinner was sometimes forgotten in our desire to continue exploring one another's bodies. By the time we'd remember to eat, it was late enough that we opted for grilled cheese sandwiches or scrambled eggs. We lived like newlyweds.

In a way, I guess we were.

Of course, our idyll was short-lived. Niklas called one night and said he missed me, that he needed to see me. I couldn't tell him to stay in Stockholm. We were still technically together. I suggested coming to Stockholm, but he countered with "I know you're busy. I'll come to you."

Mads wasn't too happy about it. We were eating breakfast together in a café near his workshop when I told him the news.

"Why does he still get to demand anything of you?"

He didn't raise his voice, but his tense posture and the stony expression on his face revealed the anger inside him.

"I just need to—"

"Do you remember what you said to me in Stockholm?"

I nodded guiltily. I'd promised him that I was his once I was in Copenhagen. And I wanted to keep that promise, but I needed to figure out a way to end things with Niklas without it turning ugly. That was the worst part of it. I didn't want to hurt anyone's feelings, but I was doing it anyway.

"If you can't follow through and give us a chance to get to know each other better, to be a couple, then what are we doing?"

"I'm just trying to do this the right way."

"Is there a right way, Laney?"

"I don't know, but there must be. I don't want to hurt Niklas, I don't want to hurt you. It's not like this is easy for me. I love you both."

"The thing is, though, you can't have us both. I don't want to share you. I doubt Niklas wants to share you."

"I know."

"Maybe you should tell him this weekend."

"I'm supposed to go to Stockholm in a couple of weeks. It would be better if I did it then. I could move my things out at the same time."

"Are you tied up in the apartment?"

"My name's on the lease, but it's never really been mine."

The tension began to fade. Mads kissed the side of my face, his fingers grazing my neck and shoulder. "You don't need to be a good girl, Laney. This is your life."

We drank our coffee in silence. It was something I'd learned after so many years in Stockholm. In the US, I was one of those women who always needed noise around her. I had to have my iPod or a TV on in the background or friends to chat with. I couldn't simply sit and enjoy quiet. That never felt right. I'd grown up in a noisy house, where silence was unnerving. Silence marked the beginning of the end of my parents' relationship. But living in Stockholm—and especially those years of being with Niklas—had taught me to accept how calm, how reassuring it could be to sit quietly with another person, and let the vibes we emitted speak for us. If I was reading Mads properly, he was no longer annoyed, just cautious. He didn't want to get hurt. He didn't like opening himself to me, not knowing if there was any sort of future ahead of us.

*   *   *

Niklas arrived the following day. I'd given him directions to the hotel-apartment complex where I was staying, and told the front desk clerk to let him in just in case I was running late. I spent so little time at the apartment that there was hardly anything to clear away. Mads and I never stayed there. We always slept at his place. I preferred it that way. This apartment was one of those glass modernist cubes, and it reminded me of living in a fishbowl, or someone's wacky idea of a museum exhibit with me as the subject under observation. It made me feel exposed.

I managed to leave the office early enough to make it to the grocery store and wine shop before Niklas pulled up in his cab. I was already upstairs when the front desk clerk rang and said my "husband" was on his way up. Husband. The word bristled inside me. For more than five years, I'd been faithful to him, helped him with all the trials and tribulations of raising teenagers, while his

ex-wife escaped to Antibes or Seychelles or Goa for yoga
retreats and getaways. I'd accepted his frequent absenc-
es for conferences and taken care of making his life
easier, and he'd never proposed to me, never slipped a
diamond solitaire on my ring finger, never seemed to
consider moving our relationship to another level. And
now he was calling himself my husband.

He let himself in, and then made a big show of calling
out for me and reuniting. He'd tucked an overly large
bouquet of hothouse flowers under his arm. This was
new. He hadn't surprised me with flowers since the early
days of our relationship. Or since the night I found out
he was fucking his ex-wife.

"So this is where you live." He strode forwarded and
grabbed me in a bear hug. I scrambled away, but he
caught me again. This wasn't the Niklas I knew.

"This is it," I said as he pressed a kiss to my cheek. I
stepped back and gestured at the living room area. "Do
you want a tour?"

"No. I want to show you how much I missed you."
Niklas was still smiling that charismatic smile of his,
trying to woo me with those chocolaty eyes. A glimmer
of the old Niklas shined through. He was wearing the
cranberry-red cashmere sweater I'd given him for
Christmas, and it brought out the natural tan he seemed
to have all year. He'd also worn the black corduroy jeans
and monk strap shoes I'd talked him into buying when
we were in the US. It was a nice change from the wool
dress pants he usually wore on weekdays. But it didn't

206 · KIM GOLDEN

make me feel a renewal of attraction or desire for him. It was too late for that. "It's strange not having you around all the time."

I took a few more steps away. "It's not the first time we've been apart," I reminded him. I didn't want to delve into our history and revisit the arguments, the times I walked away from him, or he walked away from me. That path only led to an emotional minefield and I was already too unmoored. Instead, I showed him around the apartment. He murmured his approval at the sober colors and luxury hotel feel the apartment afforded. He wasn't a man who liked a lot of color on walls. White and beige were good enough for him.

I opened the door to the guest bedroom, with its uninterrupted view of the harbor and stood aside to let him take it in.

"Nice," he said approvingly. "I like the view."

"It's one of the perks of this apartment." I crossed my arms over my chest. "If you're on the balcony, you can see the opera house."

The room was furnished with the usual Danish, modern style furniture—a platform-style bed in dark wood veneer with a sleek glass bedside table. The walls were painted a creamy beige that reminded me of steamed milk in a caffe latte. Niklas wasn't interested in it, though. He touched my elbow and I felt nothing. No spark. No thrilling tingle of desire or love.

"Show me where we'll sleep."

"I thought you could sleep in here." I tried to keep my face impassive. I didn't what him to misread me. I had to do this for Mads and myself. I didn't want this, him, anymore.

"I don't want to sleep in a different room from you," he said cautiously. "And why, exactly, do you want me to sleep in a different room?"

"It's better this way," I ventured. I tried to edge a way but the firmness of his touch kept me in one place. "We both know it is."

"I'm not sure I follow you, Laney." Niklas's fingers tightened around my elbow.

"Nothing... never mind. Are you hungry? I made dinner."

"Laney, what the hell?"

"We can talk over dinner, Niklas. Let's eat. I'm hungry." I was also a coward. I dodged away from him and headed back to the open-plan living room. My chest felt tight with guilt and I'd already set the table. All I needed to do was open a bottle of wine, so I took a bottle of Verdicchio from the fridge and set about looking for a corkscrew. Niklas was lurking in the living room, keeping his distance.

"Laney."

I started. I nearly dropped the bottle of wine, but I regained my composure. I pretended instead that I hadn't heard him and continued with bringing our meal to the table. He came into the kitchen area and said my name again.

There was no avoiding him now. "Siri told me she saw you at Hotel Rival. That weekend I was in Göteborg."

I swallowed hard. "I was there for a meeting."

"I'm not stupid, Laney. You think I don't notice how distant you are with me? You don't want to touch me. Now you don't want me to sleep with you."

"I'm sorry, Niklas." Why was I such a coward? This was when I should have taken the plunge—told him the truth, he'd even handed me a perfect opening.

"So, what's going on, babe?"

I needed a glass of wine. I tried to pour one, but my hands were shaking. Niklas took the bottle from me and filled my glass.

"We should eat," I said.

"No. You should tell me what it is that has you pulling away from me."

I took a large gulp of my wine. The crisp chill hit the back of my throat a little too quickly and I nearly coughed.

"She saw you kiss him, Laney." The smile, that wonderful smile of his that used to fill my heart with light, had faded. He looked so drawn. "She saw you kiss him... so, please, don't lie to me anymore. Don't tell me she made it up, or that she misinterpreted anything."

I shook my head. I couldn't get my mouth to form the words. My hands were still shaking. Inside, every part of me tightened. "Niklas."

"Just fucking tell me the truth. Who is he?"

I let out a long sigh. I was already crying and I tried to wipe away the tears as quickly as possible. "It's Mads."

"Mads? Anton's friend? But you just met him..." his voice trailed off. "Shit. You knew him already."

"I met him in August." It came out as a whisper.

"Did Anton introduce you? Is that why he invited him to dinner?"

"No, no, no.... he didn't know Mads and I already knew each other."

"So when did all of this start?"

"When I came here to go to the sperm bank... I met him at the mingle."

"He was one of the donors?"

I nodded. "We just... clicked." I hated saying it. It was such a cliché but that was exactly what happened. Every particle, every atom, every part of our being slid into place as soon as we'd met. And I couldn't deny it any-more. "And... I kept telling myself it was just temporary, that this feeling would disappear, but it keeps getting stronger. I want to be with him."

"Laney, no. Don't do this."

"We don't work together anymore, Niklas. I'm not what you want."

"Of course you're what I want. Who I want."

"If I were, you would have told me from the start there was no chance we could have a family together."

"We are a family, Laney. Me, you, Jesper, Siri..."

"We're not a family. They're your kids. I am just an observer. I don't have any place in your family. They don't even want me there."

"I want you there."

"No, you don't," I spat out at him. "You still want your ex-wife. I see it every time you look at her. I know you've been fucking her—so what is the point of keeping me around?"

"Laney, I was drunk then—"

"You weren't very drunk the night of Jesper's party," I said. "And yet you still couldn't keep your hands off her."

"That was a mistake."

"You call her for advice, you never ask me my opinion of anything. You talk to her every day, Niklas. You may as well still be married to her."

"So you're fucking someone else because you're mad at me?" Niklas looked as though he were ready to laugh in my face. "Is that what you're saying?"

"I fucked him because he made me feel alive, and he made me feel like I was the only woman he wanted. I wasn't competing with his ex. He wanted me, he wants me. I'm not enough for you, I never will be."

"Babe, you are enough for me—"

"No, I'm not, Nicke." I shook my head and retreated to the kitchen. I poured a glass of wine for myself and gulped it down quickly. "Stop lying to yourself, stop lying to me—"

"You're one to talk about lying!"

"Yes, I lied! I lied about going to Copenhagen, I lied so I could spend time with a man who loves me. And where were you? Were you really at conferences? Were you really at seminars? Or were you meeting Karolina in hotels?"

"You think I was seeing her?"

"You were. It's obvious. I don't know how I missed the signs before."

"And you think that justifies... this?"

"I am not who you want, Nicke. And you... why do you call yourself my husband when you've never even asked me to marry you? I'm just some fucking perpetual girl-friend. And your daughter despises me, your ex-wife looks down her nose at me or treats me like I don't exist. And... I... don't exist. Not for you. But with Mads..."

"We're only going through a rough patch, Laney. We can get through this."

"No, we can't." I countered. "I love you. I still love you, but there's no passion between us—"

"You can't say that... we've made love so many times since you met him, and I've felt the connection between us, Laney. I'm not blind. I saw how you reacted to every-thing we did together."

"Niklas, stop... this isn't helping." I sat down at the table. Our bowls of food were going cold. "We should eat... we can talk more once we've eaten."

"I don't want to eat." Niklas sat down across from me. He was furious but somehow he remained calm. "I want answers."

*   *   *

The rest of the night was spent in what felt like an extended therapy session. I tried to eat, but the food held no flavor. I felt wrung out from all of his questions. Sometimes he'd go quiet and tell me he couldn't look at me. I went for a walk in the rain, hoping to clear my head, wishing I could stop crying and feeling so miserable. I should have been happy, shouldn't I? I was free now. I should have been calling Mads and telling him the news but a part of me was in mourning. Niklas was more than just my former lover, he was also my friend, and now I was losing that part of our relationship and there was no way we could preserve it and keep it separate from the dissolution of us.

When I returned to the apartment, I changed out of my damp clothing and took a hot shower. I changed into a pair of yoga pants and a French terry shirt. The apartment felt cold and empty. I wandered the rooms, looking for Niklas, but he was gone. No note, no left behind mementos of our relationship. I retreated to the bedroom and sat down on the edge of the bed. The rain beat against the windows. I picked up my phone and called Niklas. He didn't answer. I sent him a text asking where he was, but it went unanswered. I was getting what I wanted so why did I feel so alone? And why hadn't I called Mads?

I lay down and pulled my duvet up to my shoulders. I didn't want to think. So I closed my eyes and waited for sleep to come.

Sometimes sleeping was better than thinking.

*   *   *

I shouldn't have been surprised when the next morning the incessant ringing of my iPhone awakened me. I fumbled for it. Eddy's number flashed on the display. I pressed the button for speakerphone, and muttered a drowsy hello.

"Sweetie, you could have given me a head's up."

"Sorry," I mumbled, wishing futilely I could have a few more hours of no one else knowing. "It was sort of sudden."

"Yeah, well, I wasn't expecting your boyfriend to bang on my door last night. He seems to think I'd encouraged you to fly the coop."

"Eddy, shit... I'm really sorry about that. This isn't your problem. He shouldn't have done that."

"A lot of women would say you were fucking crazy for dumping Niklas."

"Are you one of them?"

"No," she admitted. "I think you could have handled it a little better, but you and I know you were in a holding pattern with Niklas. So, what prompted the big scene? Did Super Sperm make you realize there is life outside of Stockholm?"

"I was thinking that I needed to give Mads and me a chance."

"Niklas says you ripped his heart out."

"That doesn't sound like him."

"It was the alcohol talking."

"He had an idea it was coming." I said. "Siri saw me with Mads and told him about it. I think he knew, even before, but he chose not to see it."

"When did she see you? Was she in Copenhagen?"

"No... in Stockholm."

"Laney! Tell me you didn't sleep with him in your apartment."

"No, we were at Hotel Rival. That's where she saw us."

"Sweetie, you should have known better. Stockholm isn't that big of a town."

"I know... it was stupid of me, but I needed to see Mads. I missed him."

"He asked me to pack up all of your things that are still in the apartment."

"I'm sorry, Eddy."

"Just so you know, you owe me big time."

"I know. I'll make it up to you... I promise."

"Just tell me this, Laney. Is he really worth all of this?"

"Mads? I think so. I won't know until I at least give us a chance."

"I hope you won't regret this. I don't think Niklas will give you a second chance."

Later, on my way to Mads's workshop, something Niklas said popped into my head. When we were last in Copenhagen together, just a few weeks ago, he told me he wanted me to be happy. "Get it out of your system, and come back to me." And now I was following his advice, and he was making sure there was no way I could ever go back to him.

"I told him," were the first words out of my mouth as soon as I walked into Mads's workshop.

He stopped sanding the surface of a table he was working on and asked, "How did he take it?"

"Not very well." I walked into his open arms and breathed in the sweet scent of wood and sawdust. He enfolded me in a tight embrace and kissed my cheek, whispered that everything would be okay. Why was I crying? Shit, why was I crying when I was getting exactly what I wanted?

"It's better this way, *min elskede*." He kissed the tip of my nose. "We don't need to hide anymore."

His strength soothed me. He was right. We no longer needed to hide or lie to anyone. We could finally see what it felt like to go on proper dates and hold hands in public.

*   *   *

Our first outing as a proper couple was a dinner party being thrown by two of Mads's oldest friends, Trine and Adam. Trine was a dancer in the corps de ballet with the Royal Danish Ballet, while her husband Adam was an IT specialist for Den Danske Bank. I was both excited and nervous about going. I was looking forward to meeting Mads's friends and being a proper couple, but my Danish was not very good, and I wondered what they would say once they heard how we'd met. As we were getting dressed, I asked Mads if he'd told them how we met. His answer was a noncommittal shrug.

"They haven't asked."

A typical guy answer, I thought. I stared at my reflection and wondered if they would compare me to his previous girlfriends. Of course, they would. Maybe they'd even compare me to the Swedish woman he'd married when he was studying at Konstfack. I didn't know much about their relationship, only that it hadn't worked.

"Do they know I'm black?" I asked, out of habit. It was a question I always had to ask when I was dating back in the US. I was an equal opportunity dater; I dated men of all skin colors and ethnicities. And more often than not, there was someone whose friends tried to dissuade them from dating me because "It isn't easy dating someone black."

But Mads seemed more perplexed than anything by my question. "No one cares about skin color like that, at least not my friends."

Everyone in Scandinavia said variations of the same thing when it came to skin color. They said racism didn't exist there, or that people weren't as obsessed with skin color as Americans, and then recounted how good immigrants had it in their countries, compared to the United States with its history of slavery and segregation. It didn't matter if you tried to argue your point, that racism existed everywhere, or that people just weren't as open about it here. With the exception of neo-Nazis and members of *Sveriges Demokraterna*, no one would admit that they sometimes muttered "*svart skalle*" at immigrants or ranted about how Sweden never had problems with crime until so many immigrants turned up.

Maybe that was why it was going through my head, even though I figured Mads's friends were as blasé about race as he was. Maybe it was just because I was out of practice with meeting my partner's friends for the first time. The last time I'd done it was when Niklas and I first met. And it had been a trial by fire, since the very first person I met was his ex-wife. And it was a nightmare. She insulted me, insinuated I was the reason her marriage fell apart when she and Niklas had been divorced for a few years before we even met. It made me gun shy of meeting his other friends, but I did because he wanted me to and, it didn't help that they were also Karolina's friends.

We were late leaving, mostly because I was procrastinating. Mads had started losing his patience, so I stopped changing outfits and hairstyles and settled on bullying my hair back into a curly ponytail and slipping into the dress I'd bought to wear for him. I topped it with an angora sweater and hoped I would be warm enough. Summer had moved on, and the air in Copenhagen was beginning to bear the chill promise of the coming winter.

We picked up a bottle of wine on the way, and then walked the rest of the way to their apartment. My shoes pinched my toes. I wished I'd worn ballerina flats instead of these platform pumps. I'd thought the heels would fill me with more confidence, but now my toes were screaming and I was irritable. I didn't think this was going to be a good omen for the evening.

They lived in a turn of the century building not far from the Round Tower and the University of Copenhagen campus. I was glad we didn't have to climb any stairs. My toes and heels were sore but I pretended I was fine. Mads pressed in the security code and then we went inside. The building reminded me of my old apartment building in Stockholm, with its birdcage elevator and stone stairs.

I'd thought it would be a small party, but from the noise level before we even opened the door to the apartment, I could tell it had spiraled into something more. We entered a house party in full swing. There were at least twenty people in their living room, and a song I remembered from the first summer I lived in Stockholm—"Summer Sun" by Texas—was blasting from the speakers as a trio of clearly drunk ballerinas screeched along. Mads laced his fingers with mine. I smiled in relief. I'd thought for a moment that he would wander off in search of his friends. It was what I was used to from Niklas. We'd arrive at parties and, as soon as our coats had been taken care of, he'd vanish, reappearing only when it was time to sit down at the table for dinner, or when I'd finally given up looking for him and was on the verge of leaving.

But Mads took me around and introduced me to Trine's ballerina friends. He called them the Bunheads, and they giggled. They were all tiny and delicate-looking, with doe eyes accentuated with wings of thick false lashes and liquid eyeliner.

"We came directly from an afternoon performance," one of them—Sara, I think—explained.

One of the others, a brunette with honey skin and coppery eyes, added, "We're doing *Romeo & Juliet* this season. It's so demanding."

Standing next to them made me feel old and fat. I was in good shape from running every morning, even though I hated exercising, but these women with their lithe bodies and their deceptive fragility made me feel... bulky. I knew they were appraising me. It's what women do at parties. They suss each other up, comparing notes as they wonder how you managed to bag the gorgeous guy at your side. One or two of them gave me looks that confirmed I was right.

"Did you date any of them?" I asked Mads as we moved further into the crowd.

"Nope, none of them," he said and gave my hand a re-assuring squeeze. "They never eat. I like a woman with curves."

We threaded our way through the apartment, with Mads introducing me to countless people whose names I quickly forgot. Some of them greeted me with cheek kisses, others nodded and simply said hello in Danish. By the time I met Trine and Adam, my nervousness had subsided. Adam was easy to like. He was effusive and a little goofy, like a boy who'd suddenly realized he was supposed to be a grownup. He didn't ask any uncomfortable questions, or make any comments that alluded to knowing the how's and why's of how Mads and I had met. Instead, he babbled about how Mads was probably driving me crazy with wood chips and sawdust. Trine, on the other hand, was aloof. She gave me a tight smile that was neither friendly nor welcoming. She wasn't exactly rude, but she gave off an air of disapproval. And when Mads and Adam went out to the building's courtyard to smoke, Trine seemed ill at ease with me. She made idle conversation with me, but didn't ask anything about me or how things were with Mads.

It was only when she offered me a glass of wine that she finally said, "I don't understand how you could meet Mads at that clinic and then decide to leave your husband."

"Did Mads tell you how we met?"

"He told Adam, and Adam told me." She took a sip of her wine and shrugged. "We tell each other everything."

"I'm not married," I corrected.

"I don't really get it, though." Trine swept a loose strand of hair away from her high forehead. She folded her slender arms across her chest and stared me down. "I know Mads is a great guy, but it's hard to believe you dropped everything and left someone for a man you met at a sperm bank."

"Maybe you should discuss this with Mads, since he's your friend." I didn't want to let Trine's words affect me, but she was already getting to me. It reminded me too much of that first dinner party I'd attended as the new woman in Niklas's life. The only thing missing was Karolina, a little drunk from too much Chablis, and telling everyone how I'd lured her husband away with whatever black magic I was working with my pussy—when they'd been divorced for four or five years by the time Niklas and I met.

"So how does this work now? Are you still going to have a baby with him? Except now you don't have to pay for his load?"

"You've got to be kidding me." I set my glass of wine on the counter. Some of the ballerinas wandered in, searching for wine. One of them winked at me as she grabbed a bottle. She said something in Danish that I couldn't understand. "Sorry? I don't really get Danish yet."

The Bunhead giggled and touched my arm. "I just said how envious we are, you get the delectable Mads."

"And you get all of him," one of the other ballerinas added. "Not just the part he leaves at the sperm bank."

I shook my head and walked out of the kitchen. In the living room, someone was passing around a joint but I waved it away. My ankle wobbled but I kept walking. Mads was still outside, smoking and laughing with Adam. Two of the Bunheads had joined them. I couldn't stay here. I picked up my shawl from the sofa and walked out. I would rather be alone than spend another minute in this apartment. I didn't get very far though before I bumped into someone else I didn't want to see. Ida from Copenhagen Cryo was just emerging from under the stone arch that marked separated the main house from the courtyard. She stopped suddenly. "Ms. Halliwell... what are you doing here?"

I shrugged quickly and tried sound blasé as I answered, "Some acquaintances are having a get-together..."

"You know Adam and Trine?" Ida narrowed her eyes.

"Not very well, no."

She nodded. "You know, I've been wondering if you and your partner have decided..."

"We're no longer together," I said abruptly. "I've got to go. It was so nice seeing you again."

I walked away as quickly as I could, even with my feet killing me, and I didn't stop until I was back in the lobby of the hotel-apartment complex. The doorman said something to me, but I shook my head and boarded the elevator without seeing anything than the idea of retreating to my apartment and erasing the evening from my mind.

In my apartment, the air had the stale stillness of a place left neglected. I had barely spent any time here since Mads and I had stopped sneaking around and could be out in the open. I opened the balcony door and stared out at the harbor. Below me, drunken tourists stumbled towards Nyhavn in search of microbrewery pubs. I was almost tempted to join them, just link arms with them and throw back pints until I was so drunk I wouldn't remember my name. It would have been a nice feeling, to obliterate the night and even my name from memory, but the only thing that would happen was that I'd wake up ill and nauseous with shame.

I sat on the stiff, uncomfortable sofa and listened to the night settling around me.

I didn't care what those ridiculous ballerinas said. I didn't even really care what Trine thought. All that mattered was that Mads knew it wasn't like that.

Who was I kidding? I'd wanted them to like me, to approve of me as the woman in Mads's life. I'd forgotten how maddening this part of being a couple could be. I wanted to go back to the little bubble where there was only the two of us, caught up in the euphoria of simply being together. Most of all, I wanted to feel like his friends could embrace me in his life and look past how we'd met.

I picked up my phone.

No missed calls. No texts.

For the first time since I'd arrived in Denmark, I felt incredibly alone.

*   *   *

"Where are you?" I'd fallen asleep on my sofa, and my vibrating phone startled me awake. It took a few minutes for my eyes to adjust to the grainy darkness.

"At my place." I hated how I sounded, like a spoiled, petulant child.

"*Elskede*, I'm coming over."

"No, Mads. I think I need to be alone tonight." I tried to smooth away my embarrassment and anger. None of this was his fault. He hadn't known his friends would be so judgmental.

"I don't think so," he said. "We said we'd never do this, just walk away from one another when we're upset. So I think we should meet. And if you won't let me come to you, then you can at least meet me somewhere."

"It's late, Mads."

"Laney, I could meet you outside your building. We could go to my workshop together. I've got something I want to show you and I want to make sure you're okay. Is that so wrong?"

"No... it's sweet, actually." I bit my lower lip to suppress the silly smile threatening to spread across my face. "You don't have to come here. I'll come to you."

"I'm only a few minutes away. I could be there in five minutes."

"No, it's fine. I'll ride my bike over."

"So, I'll see you in ten minutes. At my workshop?"

I nodded, and then remembered he couldn't see me. "Yes, I'm on my way now."

I propped my bike against the wall just inside the entrance to his workshop. Further in, I could hear Mads's humming along with the radio. Above my head, the pendant lights buzzed and popped on. I shivered a little. Since no one had been in the workshop all weekend, the heat was off and a chill had permeated the thick stone walls. Mads called out to me from the back of the workshop, "Come on back. I'm just moving some things out of the way."

I followed his voice into the darkened workshop, keeping one hand out to avoid bumping into his shopmates' equipment and leftover bits of wood. I was still wearing the dress, though now it was crumpled from sleeping on the sofa. But even if it was no longer pristine, I didn't want to snag it on anything sharp.

Mads emerged from behind a metal shelving unit piled high with binders and smudged boxes. He flashed an uncertain smile at me. "I made something for you," he said as I came closer. "I wanted something you could use, you could touch... and it would always remind you of me."

"You make it sound like we've come to the end."

"Have we?" I heard the uncertainty in his voice.

"I hope not," I said softly. The words came so easily. I didn't want this to be the end of us. But how could we keep it together if even his closest friends were against us? Every time I thought about Trine and the disgusted expression on her face, the venom she'd trickled in my ear. My chest tightened.

"I don't want this getting between us. It's going to be like this sometimes, Laney." Mads reached for me and pulled me into his arms. His calm acceptance lulled me. He stroked my hair slowly. "There's always going to be someone new who finds out how we met and who's going to judge us. But they don't matter."

"They're your friends."

"Trine can go to hell," Mads murmured. "Adam is my friend. He's the one who's been with me through thick and thin. He doesn't care how we met. All he cares about is that we make each other happy. And you make me happy, Laney. Just you."

He held me a little tighter, and the clean scent of his skin soothed me. I nestled into him, wishing we could always have moments like this when there was no one else around.

"Come," he murmured. "Let's go see what I made for you."

He guided me to the small anteroom where he stored all of his finished work. He turned on the ceiling light and then I saw it, amidst the custom cabinets waiting to be delivered was the desk. My dream desk.

I approached it slowly, not letting go of Mads's hand as I took in the sight of it: so simple and beautiful with its cross base in ebonized oak and the desktop in the same wood, though whitewashed. I ran my fingers over the surface, imagining how many hours he'd spent making this for me. I thought of my old desk, the one languishing in a storage unit in Stockholm. The one Niklas bought without asking me what I liked or what I needed. I bit my lower lip.

Then I saw the words, small, perfectly carved in cursive script: *Uanset hvad framtiden byder os, vil jeg altid være gled for at du åbnede døren til dit liv og lod mig elske dig.*

My breath caught in my throat as I imagined Mads saying these words to me. Tears were already welling in my eyes as I asked him, "What does it say?"

"You know." He kissed my neck softly. "Your Danish is better now."

"Tell me." I wanted to hear him say it to erase any doubt clouding me.

Behind me, he smiled. I could hear it, feel it, the way his body relaxed against mine. The way his lips brushed my skin. His breath was hot on my neck as he said, "No matter what the future has in store for us, I will always be glad that you opened the door to your life and let me love you."

A tiny shiver went through me. He loved me. Neither of us had come out and said these words yet, but they trembled in the air between us, waiting to be acknowledged and held dear. I turned to face him and smiled up at him. "I'm glad, too," I said as I laced my arms around him. "*Jeg elsker også dig.*"

"The next time you get scared, think about me. Think about this desk, and what it says to you every day."

I nodded and whispered, "Okay."

We held onto each other for a long time, swaying together to music playing in the other room. I relaxed in his arms and enjoyed the comfort of being loved, and knowing I loved him too.

CHAPTER ELEVEN

Consequences

I didn't want to face up to reality. Not yet. There was something so comforting in still being stuck between dreams and reality. But then Mads climbed back into bed with me, fully clothed. He smelled fresh and clean like soap.

"I picked up breakfast. Come. I'm hungry," he said in between kisses.

"Couldn't we stay in bed all day?"

"After we eat, yeah. I'm starving."

"What have you told Trine and Adam about me?" I asked, keeping my face buried into his chest. "Why does she think I am just some floozy who's just with you to have a baby?"

"I haven't told her anything like that about you, Laney." He kissed me softly. "The only thing I ever said to her or Adam was that we met at the mingle, and we hit it off. Anything she said was just an inference on her part."

"She was awful, Mads," I murmured. "I know I have to meet her again. Am I the first person you've dated who came to the clinic?"

He paused long enough for it to become awkward. "I haven't really dated anyone from the clinic, no."

"It sounds like there is a 'but' coming."

"A few weeks before we met," he said, finally. "I'd just met one of the women from the clinic for coffee. She'd looked me up in the phonebook. I thought she was nice. She had one of those faces everyone says is honest and open. We had coffee, and then she told me she and her husband couldn't afford the sperm donation fee. She was desperate. They'd used all their savings on three other IVF attempts and she said I was her last chance. She wanted me to just... you know, sleep with her, and not tell anyone we'd done it."

"Did you do it?"

He nodded. "I wanted to help them. The clinic had said they could help by giving them a payment plan, but then they said they weren't eligible for it. Ida said Sabina and her husband made too much money but... if you see how they live, you know they couldn't afford the clinic."

"That was... weird." I waited for his confession to explode inside me. I should have been upset he'd slept with another woman, but all I could think of was how anxious and desperate she must have been to search him out and beg him to do this. "Did... did you do it the same day? Or after me?"

"I went with her to her apartment. I thought it was weird, thought maybe a hotel would have been better. The first two times I was with her, we met at hotels. But she said she wanted to do it at home so it wouldn't feel sordid."

"How many times did you do it?"

He glanced away. His skin flushed red. "I slept with her three times. And then she texted me last week and said it worked, she was pregnant."

Three times? He'd fucked another woman three times. I kept telling myself it didn't matter. He'd probably slept with a lot of other women before we met. She was before me. She didn't matter. But... it was a kink. I didn't want to think about how she'd touched him. Or if he'd liked fucking her.

"Were you still fucking her when we...?"

"No, it was done by then. That time in the café... it was the last time."

"It's okay, Mads." I kissed a tiny trail from his shoulder to his chin. "I'm glad you did it. She needed your help. Just... don't..."

"I won't do it again," he confirmed as he pulled me closer. "I'm all yours now."

"She must have really wanted to have a baby."

"So do you, don't you?"

"Maybe not right now. But I do, before it's too late." I squeezed my eyes shut and tried to picture my family in my head. I didn't have anyone.

"In the beginning, I just did it to pay bills. I didn't really think about how I was helping people. It took a couple of months before reality set in."

We lay there for a while, holding one another. Mads stroked my hair.

"Are you going to go inactive?"

"Do you want me to?"

I nodded. "I'm selfish, aren't I?"

"Then we're both selfish. I already told Ida I don't want to do it anymore."

"Good, I'm glad."

"I'm sorry about Trine." He watched me unbutton his flannel shirt. "Adam liked you, though. He thought you were too good-looking for me. He figured you'd break my heart."

I paused. "Why does everyone think I'm going to break your heart? Maybe you'll break mine."

"I wouldn't do that." Mads cupped my face in his hands and then kissed me gently. I wanted to believe that we could never hurt one another, but I had too much experience in the game of love.

"Sooner or later, everyone's heart gets broken." In that instant, all the men I'd dated flashed through my mind. The London City Boys, the New York hipster who wanted to be the next Scorsese. A few of them didn't have hearts to break. One told me I didn't have a heart. It was one of the London City Boys.

His name was Rufus. We dated for seven months when I was living in London. The longest amount of time I'd spent with anyone at that point in my life. I was twenty-five, and the thought of being one of those girls who was counting the dates until a proposal came my way was not for me. Rufus was one of those beautiful London boys who wore suits for his day job as a risk analyst, and spent his weekends playing rugby.

From the first time we met, he was clear he wanted to find a woman to settle down with. For a while, I let myself think that woman was going to be me. And when he took me away that weekend and we arrived at the most picturesque village in Kent, I was certain he was going to take things too far. I liked fucking with him. I didn't want to play happy families with him. Every time I tried to imagine us moving in together, or taking our relationship beyond simply fucking, I knew we wouldn't be happy. But then he didn't propose. He took me to that beautiful place to tell me he'd met someone else.

"I want to love you, Lanes," he said as he delivered the final part of his it's-not-me-it's-you speech. "I want to be that guy who makes you happy, but I can't. And... let's face it, I don't think you saw this going any other way."

And he was right.

But it didn't stop me from feeling like he'd ripped me apart. And when I returned to London, I let a layer of ice crust my heart. I wasn't going to fall in love. I didn't even realize it had happened, that I'd fallen for him, until he said he didn't want me.

Later, when Mads fell asleep, I crept out of bed and wandered into his living room. There was only one picture of his ex-wife around, and it was a framed picture of the two of them standing on the steps outside Stockholm's Rådhuset. A ten-years-younger Mads squinted against the sun. One of his arms was looped around his then-wife's slender waist. Her face was turned away from the camera, and the wind had caught her long blonde hair. Neither of them looked dressed for a wedding. She was wearing tight white jeans, a lace T-shirt and ankle boots. Mads was wearing faded jeans, a white shirt, and white Converses. His hair was shorter and his face much thinner.

I wondered what he was thinking when his friends snapped this shot. Was he thinking he and Karin had a love that would last forever? Was he stunned that they'd actually gone through it? Niklas always said men didn't think that way. Women were the ones who believed in that sort of fairytale. Men asked women to marry them because they were good company, or because they liked fucking them and didn't want anyone else to have a chance. I hoped there was more to it than that. And I hoped someone would look at me and think, Now there's a woman I want to spend the rest of my life with.

But so far, none of the men I'd ever been involved with had proposed, and I'd begun thinking no one ever would. Maybe I was impossible to love. It's what my father used to say about me. Whenever he was furious with me or on the outs with my mother, he'd turn on me and berate me the same way he went after my mom. He'd tell me I was his biggest disappointment, he'd tell me I wasn't worth the effort anyone put in me. And then, once he'd ripped at every part of my self-esteem, he'd deal the final blow and say, "One day, you're going to look around and realize no one loves you, and no one ever will. You're too cold inside to be loved."

And I was always afraid this was true. Maybe it was. Maybe it was why Niklas never wanted me enough to marry me. Maybe Mads would never see me as someone who was worth holding on to. I shook my head and closed my eyes, hoping the darkness would wash away my doubts. I needed to stay focused on now. My dad was dead to me. When he left my mother, he cut off all contact with me. Whatever he thought about me didn't matter anymore. I didn't have to be the type of woman he said I'd become.

Mads was still living in Stockholm when I moved there to work for Jensen, Ogilvy and Fogh. He left two years later, once his divorce was final. And as I sat there on his sofa, trying to read every detail of his one and only wedding picture, I wondered what would have been if we'd met one another that night in the Hilton Slussen. That night when I met Niklas seemed so long ago. I tried envisioning Mads in that bar, striding toward me, approaching me the same way Niklas had done. Would he have seen something, anything, special in me? Or would he have looked at me and seen a woman desperate to be noticed, even as she pretended she wasn't interested?

"*Elskede.*" Mads stood naked in the doorway. He rubbed his eyes with the heel of his hand. "Don't sit there alone. Come back to bed."

I nodded. It was late. In a few hours, I'd need to be ready for another day at the office. It was too late to put his wedding photograph back in the bookcase. I left it on the trunk he used as a coffee table and went over to him. He folded me in his arms and held me tightly. The strong rhythm of his heartbeat steadied me.

"Are you all right?" he asked in a whisper.

I nodded again. "I think so."

"I'm not going anywhere, Laney," he said softly. "I'm in this with you for the long run."

It was exactly what I needed to hear.

As news of my defection from Niklas's life spread, the number of "concerned" emails and telephone calls increased. I ignored most of them or sent text messages promising to call once things calmed down. Most of the calls were from our mutual friends. They were probably only interested in getting the inside story so they could report back to Karolina. The only call that gave me pause was Jesper's. I hadn't expected him to call. I was in a brainstorming meeting with my art director when the call came. I excused myself and took the call in one of the private conversation rooms.

"Is everything okay?" I asked him. "Is your father okay?"

"He just works. He doesn't talk to me, he just works." Jesper said in a strange voice. "Why did you leave? Was it because we had that stupid party? I didn't want to have it. It was Siri's idea."

"It wasn't that, Jeppe."

"I told her it was a stupid idea, but she said it was your rule that we couldn't have parties when you guys weren't home, not Dad's."

"Actually, it was your father's rule, not mine," I said. "But everything that happened between your dad and me... it wasn't all about you and Siri."

"Siri said you were playing Dad for a fool."

"Siri says a lot of things."

"Laney, are you breaking up for good with Dad? He's really unhappy without you. And I miss you, too. I was going to ask you to come to Manchester. I thought you'd like the football match. I just didn't say anything to Dad, because he said we needed some father-son time."

He sounded so despondent. I wasn't used to my step-son—l had to admit it, he was my stepson no matter what, and of my two stepchildren, he was the one I'd always liked—being so forthcoming.

"I'm sorry about all this, Jeppe," I finally said. "I don't know if your father and I are ever going to be friends again. I wasn't very good to him toward the end."

There was no point in lying to Jesper. He was fifteen; he wasn't a child who needed to be protected from the truth.

"He told my mom that you had a new boyfriend already."

"I do. I met someone this summer, right after your father and I came back from the US. And... I need some time away from your dad to see if this is what I want."

"Siri's trying to convince Dad you brought your new... boyfriend... into the apartment."

"That never happened, Jesper. I may not have been very nice to your dad at the end, but I never brought Mads to the apartment. I kept everything outside of our home."

"I think my dad still loves you, Laney," Jeppe told me. "Heck, I love you, too. I know I never told you before. But you're a pretty cool stepmom."

By the end of our conversation, my guilty feelings had flourished at an uncontrollable rate.

It wasn't just Jesper who called that day. Just when I was walking into the apartment, Ida called. She was terse, businesslike, with me as she informed me that she was very disappointed I'd started a relationship with Mads.

"It's against the rules, Laney," Ida explained in a cold, businesslike voice. "Any contact of this nature is expressly forbidden. It was outlined in the information packet I gave you."

"I'm not exactly a client, though," I said quickly. "I never signed any contract. I was still trying to decide what to do."

"Yes, well, now suddenly Mads has pulled out of the donations he was scheduled to make and it's a loss of income for the clinic."

"I don't believe you. You must surely have his... 'donations' in a freezer somewhere, just waiting to be used."

"We could file a loss of income suit against both of you, if we were so inclined," Ida continued, without addressing a word of what I'd said. "You two have put us in a terrible bind."

"I don't really see how terrible this could be." I was pacing, trying to figure out what to say to make her see that I didn't feel any obligation or guilt towards her or her company. "Mads isn't some superhero who has the sole responsibility for repopulating the planet or anything."

Just then, Mads opened the door and kissed me quickly before heading to the kitchen with shopping bags. "I'm making some Danish specialties for you," he said over his shoulder. "I think you'll like them."

I gestured at the phone and mouthed "Ida" at him. He stopped.

"I'd like to speak with Mads, if I may," Ida said curtly. "He hasn't answered any of my calls."

I held the phone out to him. "Ida wants to talk to you."

His shoulders tensed. "What does she want?"

"She'll tell you."

He took the phone and went back to the kitchen. I didn't want to listen anymore. I retreated to my bedroom. A little quiet, no drama from Ida, no bullshit from her about me or Mads. I changed into my loungewear of yoga pants and a T-shirt. I pulled my hair out of the tight bun I'd trapped it in this morning. And then I waited. Mads's voice carried. He was speaking Danish with Ida, so I couldn't understand everything but his tone of voice let me know he wasn't happy with anything Ida was saying.

I couldn't simply hide in the bedroom, but I was worn out emotionally after my conversation with Jesper. It had taken a lot for him to call me. And the stepson whom I'd thought had no feelings for me—who sometimes treated me like a thorn in his side and other times stuck to me like glue—told me he loved me. Why did he wait so long? Why did he wait until I'd already left his father?

A tiny part of me, the part that missed my life in Stockholm, whispered, "You would have stayed if you'd known your step-kids liked you. You would have stayed because you'd have felt like you had a family."

And I wasn't sure I dared admit it to myself. As much as I loved being here with Mads, if I'd met him, and Niklas's children had been more loving towards me, I would have stayed. I would have made do with being the extra mom. But there was also a part of me that would have struggled to come to the surface. And that was the part that practically screamed, "What about me? I want to have my own family, not just one on loan from his ex-wife! And Niklas didn't really love you enough to even fight for you. If he did, he wouldn't have just walked out and given up so easily."

When it was finally quiet in the living room, I emerged from the bedroom. Mads was at the stove, making dinner for us. Tense vibes rolled off him. I wasn't sure if I should go over to him, or just sit at the table and wait for him to open up. We were still so new to one another that I couldn't always read his signals. I hesitated. He sensed me behind him and said without looking at me, "The clinic is saying I have to return money to them or they're going to take me to court."

"How much money are we talking about?"

"Around 75,000 kroner." He drummed his knuckles on the countertop. "I don't understand, though. There was nothing in my contract that said I couldn't date someone I met at the mingle. It just says I can't date anyone I've provided with a donation."

"So why is she trying to make you pay?"

He finally turned around. "She claims I was scheduled to make another donation this week and it's a loss of income for them. It's bullshit. I checked. I wasn't due to do anything. I'd already gone inactive."

"We'll figure something out."

"Yeah, we probably will." I didn't like how resigned and uncertain he sounded as he returned to preparing our dinner. I took over peeling potatoes while he made beef patties.

After a while, he said, "She made it sound like if we broke up, and went back to 'normal,' then all was forgiven."

"Is that what you want?"

"No. Fucking hell, we've only just started, haven't we?"

"I just wanted to make sure you weren't having second thoughts."

"I'm not. Are you?"

"No. This is where I want to be."

"It's the same for me. I want to be here with you right now."

But later, when we were in bed together, our lovemaking felt awkward and strained. I couldn't concentrate, and Mads seemed less enthusiastic than usual. We gave up after a while, both of us agreeing we were too tired to continue. I was thinking about Jesper and whether I should tell Mads about the phone call, and about the money he was going to have to pay to get the clinic to leave us alone.

*   *   *

"I'm sorry, but your card has been cancelled."

"I don't understand. I haven't missed a payment," I said quickly into my phone. I was standing at the sales counter in Illum Department Store on Strøget, hoping to buy a new pair of running shoes, but the cashier had

just informed me my card was being rejected for payment.

"Ms. Halliwell, your ex-husband called and cancelled
the card last week." The customer service representative
informed me. "It's all in the file. I'm sorry."

The words sank in slowly. I should have expected this.
I snatched another credit card from my wallet—one that
was in my name only—and handed it to the waiting sales
assistant. She'd been watching, listening with interest to
my call with American Express customer services. I
wished she would look away. I wanted to slap her, but I
tried to keep my expression friendly, effusive. Inside my
embarrassment was taunting me, poking at my own stu-
pidity for blindly assuming he'd let me keep the card if I
just paid the bill myself. I should have known better.
That wasn't Niklas's style at all. He liked finality, and he
was serving it to me on a platter.

When my father first left my mother, he cancelled all
of their credit cards without telling her. She'd tried to
buy back-to-school clothes for me with her John
Wanamaker's card, but the card ended up being cut in
half by the sales assistant while other waiting customers
watched and tittered. My mother barely shuddered. She
was too proud for that. She put on her game face, impassive and calm, and pulled out cash instead from her
wallet. I glared at the other shoppers, hoping the anger
and shame emanating from me would be withering
enough that they'd stop treating us like we were afternoon entertainment. But they continued to whisper. One

woman even had the nerve to say, "That's what you get for not saving your pennies, hon."

"You don't know anything about us!" I lashed out.

My mother shushed me and said, "It doesn't matter. We've paid already."

On the subway ride home, though, she couldn't keep her cool. Tears streamed down her face. I held her hand and thought, I will never let any man do this to me.

And yet, here I was.

"You could have told me you were going to cancel my Amex card," I said tersely when he finally returned my call.

"Hello to you, too, Laney."

"Why didn't you warn me?"

"I did. I told you there was no going back. I should have thought that was warning enough."

"Why did you do it?"

"I've got no intention of funding your life while you're fucking someone else."

"I paid that bill with my own money, so you weren't funding me."

"What happened? Did you try to buy your boy toy a present and your card was denied?"

"I was trying to buy a pair of running shoes for me with the card that was in my name." I tried to stay calm, but the beginnings of a tension headache were creeping along the back of my neck. My scalp prickled. "I've never used that card to buy anything for Mads."

"You left me, Laney. You don't get to keep the privileges of being with me when we are no longer together."

"Niklas..."

"No, you don't get it, do you?" His words came out hard and fast. "You're not my responsibility anymore. You wanted out, so you don't get to have me topping up your account or making life easy for you. So, yes, I canceled your card because it was still connected to my account. If we're over, we're over."

"You should have told me, Niklas." But I didn't have the right to complain. He was right. I was the one being unfair. I made my choice. I walked away from that gilded cage of life with him. I gave it up.

"Likewise. But all I did was cut you off financially. I didn't lie to you, I didn't sneak around behind your back."

"What do you call that little fling you had with your ex-wife? That wasn't lying? That wasn't 'sneaking around'? At least I told you I was in love with someone else. You let me stay with you for five years while you kept on flirting with Karolina, comparing me to her, dishing out advice to me that she thought of! You may as well still be married to her. I was just your sexy piece of ass. Your good time girl. You didn't want a real future with me."

I waited for his response. I could hear him breathing and imagined him in our... his apartment, standing in the sterile kitchen, one hand gripping the edge of the granite countertop as he tried to think of a worthy response.

"I hope he's worth it, Laney. You wanted your freedom, and you got it. So I hope he's worth it."

*   *   *

The next few days weren't easy. I was so busy at work
that I didn't have much time left over for meeting Mads.
He was also swamped—he was still helping Anton finish
his table, and he had a delivery of kitchen cabinets to
make and he was behind schedule. Every day we texted
or had quick coffee dates that took no more than thirty
minutes. My colleagues teased me and said I was testy,
when really I was just tired of sleeping alone. I shrugged
away their teasing, but they were right. I was testier
than usual. I wanted to curl up in Mads's lap and absorb
a little of his strength. I wanted more than just a quick
brush of our lips or a Post-It note in the morning with a
few hastily scrawled words.

But there wasn't much to be done. Marius, Johan, and
I had been called into a meeting and informed that our
clients wanted major changes to the print and film campaign we'd pitched, the one they swore they loved, and
they wanted the changes done before the first of November. Their request hadn't really come as a surprise; as far
as I was concerned, this was standard practice. It happened with nearly every project. But Marius was furious.
He was so in love with the original idea that Johan and I
had to cajole him into making any changes. And it was
hard going. It meant we were still in the office when
everyone else went home. It meant we were often there

before everyone else arrived. And it ate away at our weekends.

So when we finally finished making the changes and the constant merry-go-round of status meetings and update meetings and debriefings—a moment that finally commenced on a Friday afternoon—the only thing on my mind was going home to Mads, to his apartment in Østerbrø and making love without any work pressure looming over me. I called him, but there was no answer. I skipped out of work early and rode my bike—yes, I was turning into a true Copenhagener and I was biking everywhere—to his apartment in Østerbrø. It was one of those afternoons when you realize that winter will soon arrive, with a perpetual layer of gray in the sky that feels dense and impenetrable, and already the sky was going dark. I hated days like this, but I kept telling myself things would be better by First Advent, when there would be Christmas lights everywhere brightening the darkness. I tried not to think about having to wait another month before any of that would happen.

Instead, I reveled in the freedom of moving across the city on my bike. And the only thing going through my mind was that soon I'd be able to focus on Mads and we could reconnect.

His workshop was covered in a sheen of pale sawdust. I waved my hand in front of me, hoping to prevent any of the dust from getting in my mouth and nose. But it didn't help. My lips tasted of sawdust; my hands already were dusted with it. I walked through the labyrinth of the cavernous workshop.

One of the carpenters was blasting Led Zeppelin and playing air guitar in between sanding a table leg. Another was staining a set of bookcases. I nodded at both men and continued weaving my way towards the corner studio area Mads called his. He was bent over a piece of fine cherry wood, planing it by hand. I watched as he worked, admiring how his T-shirt clung to his back, and the sheen of perspiration on his arms and the nape of his neck, despite the chill in the air. He'd cut his hair so it was closely cropped along the back of his head. Now, when it was shorter, the red-gold shone even more against his still-tan skin. He reached back and scratched his neck. My mouth went dry as I imagined him stripping for me. I said his name.

He looked over his shoulder and grinned at me. "What are you doing here?" He set down the plane and came over to me.

I shrugged and threw my arms around him. I was as giddy as a teenage girl hanging out with her boyfriend. "Can you escape from here for a little while?"

We kissed like silly teenagers—deep, long kisses as we groped at one another, not caring if anyone saw.

"Anton's coming in soon," he said and then sucked my lower lip. A little moan slipped from me. "We're nearly done with his table. I could call him, ask him to come tomorrow instead."

Anton would be annoyed. He hated changing already agreed upon plans, unless it was absolutely necessary. I didn't think he'd accept my wanting to get laid as necessary enough to cancel his woodworking lesson, so I told Mads I'd keep myself busy at his place until he and Anton were done. So we made plans to have dinner at home and watch a movie, though we both knew we'd abandon the movie before it even started properly. Mads gave me the keys to his place and said he'd call as soon as he and Anton were done.

I went back into the darkness, this time knowing that I would see Mads in a few hours and we would finally have some time together. It had started raining again, and the thin trench coat I was wearing did nothing to protect me against the elements. By the time I locked my bike in the courtyard of Mads's building, I looked more like something the cat had dragged in. I was certain my mascara was running down my face. My trench coat was dripping wet and sagging around me, and my favorite pair of loafers was waterlogged. I climbed the stairs to his apartment, collecting his mail on my way up. Inside his flat the air was chilly. He hated having the heat on, and didn't seem bothered by the chill. For me though his apartment was too cold, so whenever I came over I either turned the heat up, or lit a fire in his fireplace. Today I opted for both. I hung my wet clothes on the drying rack in his bathroom and made sure the floor heating was on. Then I put on one of his T-shirts and a pair of his pajama pants and rag socks.

A cup of tea was the next thing on my list. I searched his kitchen cabinets for the white peony tea I'd bought the last time I'd come by, then turned on his electric kettle. I was just getting a jumbo mug from the cabinet when I saw the letter from Copenhagen Cryo. The letter was terminating his association with the clinic, claiming he'd violated the contract he had with the fertility center and could be liable for a lawsuit. I read it again to make sure I understood. Some of the Danish words were completely different from Swedish, and it took me awhile to get a grasp of every sentence. But I understood--they were threatening to take him to court for violation of his contract. They insinuated that we'd knowingly engaged in an improper relationship that was damaging to the clinic's reputation. I put the letter back where I found it—on top of the glass jars where Mads kept his sugar, flour, and salt.

I tried not to think about our Copenhagen Cryo situation, but it was difficult not to. It didn't make sense that they were harassing us so much. They were behaving like Mads was their one and only cash cow, which was impossible. Ida had said he was a very popular donor. I wasn't surprised. His video was compelling enough that I'd viewed it too many times before the mingle. I'd already felt drawn to him from it. I could imagine other women watching it and reacting to his sexy half-smile and the timbre of his voice. He exuded a sensuality that was unstudied and arousing without being too overt.

And then I thought about how Ida had reacted when I'd asked her to suggest a popular donor. She hadn't needed to think very long. She chose Mads immediately. She even made sure we met. But one thing stuck out most in my mind—she'd said that sometimes women came to the mingles looking for relationships, not babies. And she hadn't seemed so adverse to it. She'd been very blasé about it and had simply said, "It happens sometimes." So if it happened sometimes, why was she trying to prevent Mads and me from having a relationship, especially when I had never signed any agreement to purchase sperm from their clinic?

*   *   *

Mads finally arrived a few hours later. By that time, the apartment was cozy and filled with the aroma of the lasagna I'd thrown together. I'd ask him about the letter later. For now, I wanted to focus on us. Mads, still covered with sawdust, was too beautiful. I kissed him and said, "I hope you're hungry."

He grinned at me, a sexy, promising grin, and countered, "I'm always hungry." He slid his hands inside my T-shirt and massaged my nipples until they were taut and sensitive. "Maybe we could wait a little while with dinner."

We ended up making love on the sofa. I sat in Mads's lap, riding and torturing him with the slow rocking motion of my hips. He cupped my ass with one hand and used the other to cup one of my breasts. Sometimes he tried to urge me on, but I wouldn't let him dictate the tempo. I wanted to savor the delicious swelling of his cock throbbing inside me. Even when his moans vibrated against my swollen nipples, I wouldn't give up. My limbs melted with each shiver he sent through me. My breath caught in my throat as my own moans escaped from deep inside me.

Afterwards, we lay together on the sofa, breathing heavily, completely sated. A languid drowsiness was seeping through me. We were both beginning to fall asleep when Niklas's ringtone startled us out of our stupor. I didn't want to move but Mads murmured, "Maybe you should answer it. It might be an emergency."

I scrambled for my T-shirt again and then found my phone under a sofa cushion.

"Did I catch you at a bad time?" Niklas's voice was even, but there was a hint of sarcasm to his tone.

"No, not really." I said. "How are you?"

Niklas ignored my question. "I received a very strange letter from that clinic of yours."

"Yes, they've been on the phone with me."

"Looks like you and Mads really stepped into the shit with this affair of yours."

"Is that why you called? To gloat?"

"No, I called because I wanted to know if they have a legal leg to stand on."

"Not as far as I know. I never signed a contract. Nothing was decided."

"And what does Mads say?" Niklas asked. Mads had hauled himself off the sofa and was in the kitchen now, naked. He set a bottle of red wine on the table, and then set out two plates.

"He's just as confused as I am. He went inactive once we decided to get together, but the clinic suddenly says he's causing them a loss of income."

"Should I get my lawyer involved?" Niklas offered. "We may not be together, but the only reason you went there was because we were supposed to be looking into alternatives."

"I really appreciate that, Niklas." The edge in my voice softened. Niklas was a good person; he always had been.

"I just don't want this dragging out." He cleared his throat, one of his nervous habits that I'd once found endearing but towards the end of our relationship it had become akin to the sound of nails scratching a chalkboard. "We both need to move on, and having this ludicrous business with the clinic between us isn't going to help matters."

"I know. I'm sorry about all of this." I glanced at Mads. He was leaning against the counters, still naked, watching me as he drank his wine. "Is Jesper all right?"

"Why are you asking about him? He's not your responsibility anymore."

"He was never really my responsibility, but I always cared what happened to him. And he called me a few days ago. He sounded down."

A dry rustling came through the phone. "I'll talk to him."

And then, just as quickly, Niklas rang off.

But the call left a strange pall over me. I wasn't used to Niklas sounding so cold. The control, the measured words—those didn't surprise me. Sometimes I'd over-heard his sessions with his patients, and his voice had taken on that same calm measuredness. But the chill to his voice, that was new. Even in his angriest moments with me, Niklas had never spoken to me like I was an annoyance or a stranger. But I had to face facts: cheating on him hadn't raised his opinion of me, and why would it? I'd put my own needs before the needs of our rela-tionship, and I'd done it willingly.

"What did he want?" Mads's voice shook me out of my thoughts.

"The clinic sent him a letter. He's getting his lawyer involved."

"Aw, hell, Laney. I don't understand what kind of game they're playing with us." Mads abandoned his glass of wine and returned to the living room. The fire was dying and a palatable chill began to seep in again. I shiv-ered and curled into him.

"I saw the letter the clinic sent you."

"*Fanden*...I should have told you about it." Mads tensed. "I didn't want you to worry."

"We're both in this," I reminded him gently. "I wish you'd told me instead of hiding the letter in the cup-board." Then I asked him the question that had been niggling inside me for a while. "Did you and Ida ever date?"

"What? No, it was nothing like that. I knew her before she started working at the clinic. She's the one who told me about the sperm donor program."

"How did you know her, though?"

"She's Adam's cousin, and we all grew up together in Humlebæk."

"And she was never interested in you? And you never slept with her?"

"I slept with her a couple of times in college, before I met Karin and moved to Stockholm." Then the dime dropped for Mads as well. "You think she's doing this because she's jealous? But that's all ancient history."

"It's got to be something like that. Otherwise, it doesn't make any sense. That first time I was at the clinic, the only time I was ever there, she told me that some women came to those mingle sessions just looking to hook up or meet partners."

"Yeah, that's true. It does. I've had women and men proposition me during those mingles. A couple of times, married couples have even approached me and tried to suggest having threesomes. It's like they think I'm some kind of gigolo just because I've donated some sperm."

"Did you tell Ida we were dating?"

"No, I just told her I was in a relationship now, and I didn't want to be active. She acted like this was fine."

"So either Adam told her," I speculated. "Or Trine."

Mads shook his head. "*For fanden...* goddamn Trine..."

Goddamn Trine, indeed.

The worst part of all of this was trying to pretend that Mads's past didn't touch me. Finding out about his past relationship with Ida only highlighted how little we knew of one another, and how we were both treading in unknown territory. I kept telling myself this was normal. No matter how connected we were, there would always be something new that we'd discover about one another. But that night, as we lay in bed and I waited for sleep to come, I couldn't purge thoughts of what he was like with Ida... and even how he'd been with his ex-wife. I didn't know anything about either of those relationships.

Niklas used to say that was the difference between Scandinavians and Americans—Americans wanted to examine every detail of their lovers' pasts; Scandinavians didn't care about the past, it was all about the future you were creating together. I guess my years of living in Sweden hadn't made me sufficiently Scandinavian. I didn't want to be a stranger in Mads's life.

But nobody came with a clean slate.

I was scared. Not of him. Just the intensity of how I felt about him. All those years I spent going from one man to another, hoping I'd find someone who'd kindle a flame inside me, who'd make me feel like anything was possible. And now I had it. So why couldn't we just be happy? I tried to close my eyes and practice yoga breathing, anything that would pull me into the land of dreams. But all I saw was a parade of women who'd all been in Mads's life before me. The women he'd dated, the women who bought his sperm so they could have babies, the women he'd had one-night-stands with. And now they were all streaming past, reminding me that life with Mads wasn't going to be orderly.

*　　*　　*

"You have to come out with us tonight." Johan perched on the edge of my desk. "Shut down your computer. Chop, chop! And text your hunk, tell him you've got a date with your GBF."

"So you're my GBF now?" I laughed as I did what was ordered. "This is such an honor. I thought you were here just to torture me with always being late with brainstormings and creative ideas."

"You are such a bitch sometimes," he said in mock horror. "Come on, Marius and I want beer, and we want to ogle some of these hot Danes. And we want to hear about what's going on with you."

"Wait. I'm supposed to meet Ingrid. Is it okay if she joins us?"

"Yes, yes. Just hurry up," Marius grumbled from the door. He was shrugging into an expensive-looking black overcoat. I was sure I'd seen it in the New Designers section at Illum. "Is she single?"

"No, she's very married."

"Fuck it, she can come. I can flirt with her until a singleton comes along."

"You are so chivalrous," I teased. I sent two texts very quickly, one to Mads, the other to Ingrid. Ingrid answered in record time. She would meet us there. Mads was slower to answer, but he texted that he had to run an errand and that I should have fun with my workmates.

"Is your hottie coming?" Johan asked.

"No, he said he had something to do."

"Cryptic," Marius mused. "I like it."

I rolled my eyes at both of them and put on my coat.

We ended up at a bar near Nyhavn. Marius ushered us in and said, "Trust me, this isn't a tourist trap. I've been here a few times."

"It's my round," I said as soon as Johan drained his glass. Marius and I had been waiting patiently for him to finish his beer. I scooted out of the banquette, and then gathered our now empty glasses. "The same, or you want to try something different?"

"Same for me," Marius said. He tapped his pocket. "I need a smoke. You coming with me?"

I shook my head. "I'm trying to quit."

Which was difficult. I loved everything about smoking, but Mads didn't smoke inside and I hated standing outside in the cold, shivering for the sake of a cigarette. And it was one of those wet, frigid nights. My feet were still cold from walking in the rain in ballerina flats. Niklas was right. I wasn't the most practical person. I ought to have a pair of stylish Ilse Jacobsen wellies, like all the other women here.

"Johan? You coming?" Marius asked.

"I could murder for a fag." He chuckled, and then the two of them headed for the door.

I went over to the bar and placed our order. The bartender was an Australian girl who didn't speak much Danish. I switched to English and she smiled in relief. "Thank God—are you a Yank? You don't sound like you're from around here."

"I'm American," I told her as I watched her pull our pints. "I'm just working here. Well, working and living here."

"Cool! Are you a love refugee too?"

"A love refugee?"

"Yeah, you know. You came here for love?" She set the first of my pints on the bar. "That's what I did. Came here for a Danish guy I met on my gap year, and I'm still here."

"Something like that." I grinned at her. "I was in Sweden first, with a Swede. Then I met a Dane."

"They know how to get us, yeah?"

I nodded and laughed. She set my other pints on the bar and asked if I needed help carrying them. I was about to answer no when the door to the bar opened and Mads walked in. I lifted my hand to wave, but his eyes swept past me and then he nodded at someone I couldn't see and waited. The bartender asked me again if I needed help. I shook my head and straightened my shoulders. "I'm fine. I've got this."

I managed to get the pints to my table without spilling and set them down. Johan had just returned and was hanging up his coat. "Fucking cold out," he muttered.

He rubbed his hands together and then looked around. "Where's your guy? I saw him outside."

"He's here somewhere. I don't think he was looking for me, though." I nudged his beer toward him.

Johan caught the sharpness in my tone. "Laney, don't jump to conclusions. Maybe he's meeting a client."

That jarred me even more. Johan didn't know Mads had been a sperm donor. "I'm not jumping to any conclusions. I'm just stating the obvious."

"No, you're jumping to conclusions. Just like you did that time with Niklas."

"Stop, Johan." I warned. "You're treading on thin ice now."

"Well, you did."

"No, I didn't. He was fucking his ex-wife," I reminded him tersely. "I didn't imagine it. He confessed, remember?"

"That doesn't mean Mads is fooling around." He tried a different tactic. "Now, did I tell you I found a great new flat?"

I shook my head, but I'd stopped listening. Too many worst-case scenarios were taking shape in my head. I wanted to trust Mads. I knew I should. But seeing him sitting there with another woman, watching him laugh at the things she said, the sudden smile he directed at her, it all unnerved me.

"You're right. He's probably here with some his friends. I'll just go and say hi, and then I'll be back." And

I stalked across the pub, ignoring the curious looks cast at me. I just knew I needed to confront him.

"Fancy meeting you here." I smiled a little too brightly.

Mads nearly knocked over his pint. He managed to right it before it toppled over. "Laney... *hej.* Yeah, what a surprise."

He stood up quickly and touched my arm, but I stepped away. "I'm sitting over there if you want to join me."

"I'm here with—"

"Yeah, I saw you were here with someone else." I folded my arms. My fingers clenched. "Interesting. I really hope she's commissioning you for some furniture."

"No." His jaw twitched as he glanced over my shoulder. I turned to see who he was looking at. The woman coming towards us was plain, almost mousy, but she had that Scandinavian poise that helped even the ugliest woman exude confidence. She was so focused on Mads, she didn't notice me. But there was something in the look he gave her that made her pause.

"I helped her... a while ago."

"Right." Everything pulled tight inside me. I tried to push it away, this awful tightness, but it burned. He promised there would be no more of these women asking for his help. Fuck. FUCK! It was the only word filling my head.

The woman inched forward. A nervous smile flickered over her lips. "*Hej! Er du Laney?*"

"I don't speak Danish." It was my standard defense when I didn't want to make contact with someone. She blinked at me nervously. Then I glared at Mads. I couldn't think of anything to say to him. My pulse throbbed. Mads tried to take my hand but I shook him off. "No, you... help your friend. I'm leaving."

I didn't explain anything to Marius and Johan as I snatched my coat and scarf from the coat rack. Mads was right behind me, trying to get me to slow down, but I shook him off. I pushed my way out of the bar and, once I was out in the night again, I picked up my pace, not caring that cold water was seeping in through the thin leather soles of my shoes. Just another mistake.

Mads called out my name. His voice hit the base of my spine, touching all the right buttons that made me want to melt, but that red-hot ember of anger was still glowing inside me. I shook my head and kept walking. But there was no point trying to run from a very fit Dane. Sooner or later, they'll catch up with you. He caught my arm and forced me to stop.

"Why are you running away from me?"

"You said you weren't going to help them anymore. You said it made you feel dirty."

"It wasn't that this time. She needed my help—"

"What were you going to do, Mads? Build her a crib? You know she wants to fuck you and you lie to me and tell me you have an errand?"

"She doesn't want that, Laney. And I did have to run an errand, and then I bumped into her. And now you're jumping to the wrong conclusion."

"Newsflash: if I catch you out having drinks with another woman, I'm going to jump to the wrong conclusion."

"Laney, just listen to me."

"I don't even know if I want to hear any of this."

"You think I fucked her?"

I glared at him as an answer. I didn't want to say it aloud but I was afraid that he'd given in to another one of these desperate women. I stalked away from him, craving a little distance.

"I'm not Niklas!" he shouted after me. He was still behind me, keeping pace. Damn his long legs! I started walking even faster, not caring that my shoes were officially ruined. I didn't want to hear his excuses; I just wanted to be away from him. "I'm not going to let you walk away, Laney. You need to hear me out."

I don't know why I started running. I saw the bus to Husum stopping at the traffic light. All I could think was going to Ingrid and Anton. I waved down the bus and jumped on right before the doors slammed closed. The driver asked me if he should wait for my friend, but I shook my head, paid my fare and moved through the bus until I found an empty seat. I didn't look out the window until we were pulling away from the bus stop. Mads stood there, shaking his head. He raked his hair back and then raised his hand in a reluctant goodbye. And the look on his face broke my heart. Hot tears were already streaming down my cheeks. My hands were shaking. I tucked them under my thighs, but it didn't help. The other passengers pretended not to stare, but I could feel the weight of their curiosity. I didn't want to look at them.

Oh God... what was I doing?

"What are you doing here?" Anton closed the door behind me, shutting out the raw winter air. "Ingrid's on her way to meet you..."

"Mads and I had a fight," I said before he could say anything else. "Or...no, shit, I don't know what happened. I just needed to be around people who felt like home for me."

"You look like hell."

"Thanks, Anton. I really needed to hear that."

"Look, go in the living room and warm up by the fire. I'll call Ingrid and tell her to catch the next train back, then we'll sort out some dry clothes for you."

I did as Anton suggested and went into the warmth of the living room. Anton must have been looking forward to an evening alone. A bottle of his favorite beer from Nørrebrø Brygghus stood on the coffee table along with a bowl of potato chips and a *Battlestar Galactica* DVD box set.

I sank to the floor in front of the fireplace and stared into the flames. Why had I run from him? I shrugged off my wet coat. I could hear Anton speaking in Danish to

Ingrid. He sounded more confused than annoyed with my appearance on their doorstep, and for that I was grateful. I should have stayed. I should have stayed and let Mads tell me what was going on.

"I caught Ingrid just before the train pulled into Nørreport," Anton said when he returned with some of Ingrid's clothes. "She should be back in a few minutes."

"I'm sorry I ruined your night-in."

"You didn't ruin it. You interrupted it--I was getting ready to see what Adama and the gang could offer." He handed the bundle of clothing to me. "Go and change into these. Ingrid will have my head if you get sick."

I retreated to their guest powder room and changed into the clothes Anton had found--one of Ingrid's cozy sweaters, a thick pair of leggings and wool socks. When I looked in the mirror, I grimaced. The rain had washed away most of my make-up and my mascara had left black rivulets on my face. I scrubbed it away until the face in the mirror looked like a younger, less certain version of me. Mads always said he liked it when I didn't wear makeup. He said my makeup was like a mask I put on to keep people from knowing the real me.

Mads.

Sooner or later I was going to have to call him and tell him where I was. I'd have to hear him out. I tried not remember the pained look on his face when the bus doors slammed shut. What a fool I was. The tears came again , hot and furious.

"Laney, you were supposed to meet me in town—" Ingrid stopped short as soon as she realized I was crying. She stepped into the bathroom with me and pulled the door closed. She took me in her arms and rocked me the way she used to comfort her daughters when they were younger, the way my mother used to soothe me when I cried too many times over my dad.

I tried to speak but the words stuck in my throat. All I could say was his name.

"We'll fix it," Ingrid assured me. "We'll sort everything out."

The next morning, my anger gave way to doubt. I lay in the guest bedroom at Anton and Ingrid's, acutely aware that I couldn't hide there forever. I could hear Anton asking Ingrid if I was going to be okay. She shushed him and said, "I'll talk to her."

I pulled the quilt tighter around me. I missed waking up with Mads. I missed how his long legs always took a little too much space in the bed we shared. If I were at home with him, we'd still be entwined around one another, waking a little, making love, falling asleep again in our cocoon of love and satisfaction. I wanted that now. Damn it! Why did I walk away from him? I should have listened to him. I shouldn't have jumped on that bus. I squeezed my eyes closed and muttered to myself, "You are a stupid woman, Laney Halliwell. A stupid, stupid woman."

I felt around the bed for my phone, but came up empty. Maybe it was in my bag. I wasn't even sure where my bag was. When I'd arrived last night in a blind huff, I'd blathered at Ingrid about how I hated men, all men, and how I hated myself even more. And the more I recounted how overdramatic I'd been, the more I cringed. The strained look on Mads's face when he realized I was not going to turn around and cross the distance between us haunted me. I covered my face with my hands and swore.

"Laney, are you awake?" Ingrid called from the other side of the door.

"I just woke up," I said, and swiped away my tears with the back of my hand. "Come in."

Ingrid crept in and closed the door. "Feeling better today?"

I nodded. "Though I feel a bit stupid, Inge. Can't believe I ran away from him. What's the matter with me?"

She climbed into bed and lay down beside me. It was almost like the old days, when we shared a house in Richmond. On Saturdays, she'd come into my room and we'd whisper about everything and nothing while Anton snored in the next room. "You're just scared, Laney. But you can't keep running. Sooner or later, you have to stop running away and let people in."

"I know." I snuggled down into the comforter. "I was afraid he'd tell me he was going to help her again."

"That's not what was happening, you know."

"Did you speak to him?"

She nodded. "He's downstairs."

"He's here?" My heart lifted. But just as quickly a tiny kernel of doubt opened inside me. "I don't know if that is a good thing."

"You won't know if you don't talk to him," Ingrid reminded me. She tweaked my nose and smiled. "Sweetie, you can't avoid him forever. You need to talk to him. He's just as torn up about last night as you are."

"How long has he been here?"

"He's been downstairs with Anton since last night." She stretched her long, slender arms over her head and then yawned. "He fell asleep on the sofa. I told him to come up to you, but he was pretty sure you wouldn't want to see him."

"I do want to see him," I said softly. I sat up now.

"You know, this is how normal relationships work," Ingrid teased. "You fight, you make up, you misunderstand each other. It's not like how it was with you and Niklas."

"I feel like such a fool."

"We all do sometimes, honey." She brushed my unruly hair away from my face. "And just remember, he's not your father."

"I know that."

"He's not going to abandon you the way your dad did. And he's not Niklas."

"I know."

"And you can run here whenever you want, because you know we adore you." Ingrid grinned at me. "But you have a man down there who loves you, and who's afraid you're going to leave him."

"I'm not going to leave him."

"Then tell him. He needs to hear it." Ingrid planted a kiss on the crown of my head and then scooted off the bed. "I'm sending him up here. So be prepared."

"Okay," I said, and then added, "thank you, Inge. You're the best."

"Of course I am!" She laughed and then winked at me as she left the room.

By the time Mads came upstairs, I'd rehearsed in my head everything I wanted to say to him but when he pushed open the door and stood there, looking for all the world like he was afraid I was walking away, I shoved off the covers and threw myself out of the bed.

He grabbed me in a tight hug and murmured, "I'm sorry. I'm so sorry," in my ear just as I was saying the same to him.

"It wasn't what you thought, *elskede*. She's a law-yer—when I bumped into her, I asked her if she would help me deal with the threats from the clinic. That's it. She's going to help me fight them."

We held onto each other.

It was all we could do. All we needed to do.

CHAPTER TWELVE

Closure

That weekend, I had to go to Stockholm to finish moving my belongings out of Niklas's apartment. Mads wasn't so pleased, but he understood there was no point in putting it off. There was unfinished business between Niklas and me, and there was no point in putting it off anymore. Eddy had moved out of her sublet and was together with Andreas again. She asked me if I wanted to stay with them, but I decided to stay in a hotel. It was easier that way. Besides, she said things were still tense between them, and I didn't know if it was a good idea to be caught in the middle. I'd already gone through enough of her numerous break-ups and make-ups with Colin to not want to be in the uncomfortable role of the innocent bystander.

I booked a room at the Clarion Sign. It was downtown and within walking distance of my old apartment on Dalagatan. Stockholm had been blessed (or cursed, de-

272 · KIM GOLDEN

pending on how you looked at it) with an early snowfall. In a few days it would be Halloween, and already the sidewalks were white with snow. Before I walked to the apartment, I met Eddy at Primafila for coffee. When I arrived, she'd already ordered mugs of black coffee and a small pitcher of warm milk for us. We greeted each other with hugs, and then she teased me for losing weight.

"Having a new boyfriend must be good for you." She winked at me and laughed.

"Yeah, it's definitely a good thing," I told her with a grin. "I don't get much sleep, but I'm not complaining."

"When do I get to meet him?"

"Soon," I told her. "He's a good fit for me."

We caught up, laughing about the men in our lives, about the crazy things that had recently happened to us. Then Eddy told me the story of how she won Andreas back from the teenage model. At first, there was a lightness to her tone that made me smile, but as she talked she sounded introspective. The story unfolded about how she'd bumped into him at a friend's fortieth birthday dinner and how Andreas, a little drunk and very despondent, confessed he missed her, and that he was ashamed of himself for leaving her.

"I didn't know what to say," she admitted. "I wanted him back, he wanted me back... it just seemed like we were supposed to be together again."

"And you're okay?"

She nodded, and I realized I hadn't seen Eddy so calm and happy in a long time. I'd missed her so much. I wasn't used to being away from her for so long. Not when she been a sister to me for so much of my life.

"So no more trying to reconnect with Colin?"

She shook her head. "That was a moment of madness. There's nothing left to revive there." Eddy rolled her eyes dramatically. "Whatever there was with Colin... it's gone. And we both know it now."

"Sometimes it's hard to let go."

"Tell me about it." Eddy sighed. "You know, when we were kids, we used to say we'd never go crazy over men like our mothers. And it happened anyway."

"At least we know a good thing when we see it," I said and grinned. "You figured out you don't want to go back to what you had. I figured out who I want to be with."

"I was worried about you. When you traipsed off to Copenhagen to be with your furniture guy. I was really worried. I just wanted you to be secure."

"I know. I thought I wanted that too, but I just couldn't stay with Niklas. Not after I met Mads."

"Andreas and I are a good fit. I think we both had to do a lot of stupid things to realize it, but we're good together."

"Good, I'm glad," I told her, and squeezed her hand. I hoped I would be able to say this about Mads and me once this craziness with Ida and Copenhagen Cryo was resolved.

I recounted the story for her—how Mads was being asked to compensate the clinic for loss of income when he'd already registered himself as inactive. I told her about his past involvement with Ida, and how both Mads and I were convinced Trine had told Ida about us. The more I divulged, the more Eddy's eyes widened. By the time I came to the end of the story, she swore and said, "Neither of us can ever have a normal day, can we?"

Later, I walked to the apartment and let myself in. I called out to Niklas. He'd said he would be there and that we needed to talk, but there was no sign of him. I stood in the foyer, waiting for something to happen, for some pang of longing to overwhelm me as I let my fingers trace the dado rail. I had expected some nostalgia, or a pang of longing to return to my old life. But I couldn't feel any trace of me left in the walls of this place. I went into what had been my office. Niklas had left some moving boxes there for me. He'd already packed all of my books. The vintage travel posters I'd hung were now propped against the boxes of books and protected in bubble wrap. My desk had been emptied of all my detritus. The uncoiled paperclips, the scribbled-upon Post-It notes, the packs of Big Red gum and hidden bags of Peanut M&M's—all of it was gone. My office was no longer mine. Niklas had boxed up my life with him, and erased me from this room. I wiped at my tearing eyes with the back of my hand and abandoned the room. In the bedroom, things were much the same. Whatever Eddy hadn't already picked up was in moving boxes and labeled with my name, and the address of my company apartment in Copenhagen.

The only trace of me left in the bedroom was a framed photograph of Niklas and me. The photograph had been taken two summers ago. We were on Gotland, outside Fröjel Kyrka, a medieval church not far from the village of Klintehamn. We'd gone there for his younger brother's wedding. In the photograph, we were standing in front of the ruins of the old cloisters. Niklas was wearing a dove-gray suit and, at first, he seemed younger and more relaxed. The tightness I'd noticed in photos later in our relationship was nowhere to be seen. I was wearing a silk sundress in a pale shade of rose that reminded me of a dress Mia Farrow wore in The Great Gatsby.

On the surface, we looked content, but my smile didn't reach my eyes, and Niklas wasn't quite smiling. I'd looked at that picture every day since we'd framed it and seen it as a barometer of our relationship. Whenever I'd felt lost or confused about my life with Niklas, I'd picked up that photo and told myself that I could be that happy again if I just tried harder. But now I saw that even then, we weren't really in a good place. Neither of us had wanted to admit it.

I checked the closets and drawers. All of my clothes were gone. My jewelry box was packed away in one of the boxes. I should have been relieved that this was the end. But it was difficult closing a chapter on your life when in some ways the ending hadn't really been written. It didn't matter anymore, though. I'd made my choice. And I was certain it was the right one, even if in the long run it didn't end with Mads. So I pushed the boxes into the hall and then walked into the living room.

"So you're really not coming back?"

Jesper was standing in the doorway, his hands shoved in the pockets of his KTH hoodie. He scrunched his eyebrows together.

"Jesper, you know it's better this way. Your dad and I... well, I don't know if we will ever be friends after this, but this is what's best for us."

"I made coffee," Jesper said. "Do you want some?"

I nodded and followed him into the kitchen. How odd it was to be a guest in what had once been my home. And Jesper, who'd always seemed so hopeless at taking care of anything, was actually a whiz at the espresso machine Niklas bought, but never learned how to use. He'd already set two cups on the granite kitchen island.

"It feels weird to be here now," I said to Jesper. "It feels like I never really lived here."

"Siri said the same thing." Jesper poured the coffee into the cobalt blue coffee cups I'd convinced Niklas to buy during our last vacation in Italy. "She's over the moon you aren't here anymore."

"How are you, though?"

Jesper shrugged. He ducked his head and his fringe of dark hair shaded his eyes. "I'm okay. It's... you know Mom is trying to convince Dad to get back together with her, right?"

"I figured that's what she wanted all along. I think your dad wants that, too."

"Laney, he said no to her. He said it was wrong."
Jesper shook his hair away from his eyes. "I think he still
wants you to come back, even if he's being a jerk."

Jesper sounded hopeful, but I couldn't let him think it
would change my mind. I didn't want to go back to that
limbo my life had become with Niklas, the perpetual
girlfriend playing second fiddle to the ex-wife, waiting
for some sign that I was more than just a good lay.
"Jesper, I'm not coming back to your father. I'm in love
with someone else. And he loves me."

"He misses you, though, Laney. I miss you, too."

"I miss you too, Jesper, but your dad... I think he
misses the idea of me. He doesn't miss me. Not really."

We finished our coffee, and then Jesper carried my
boxes downstairs, and he didn't groan or complain or
any of the other typical spoiled teenager things he used
to do whenever I asked for his help. And when the taxi
arrived, he loaded the boxes into the car, then he hugged
me and said, "You were a pretty good stepmom, even if
you don't want to be my stepmom anymore."

And that felt good.

Really good.

The first stop with the taxi was to a DHL service center.
I arranged for the boxes to be shipped before any mis-
placed sentimentality and curiosity could persuade me to
open them and rummage through whatever memories
they might contain. Then I made a quick stop at Urban
Deli in Södermalm and had an after-work drink with my

boss. Jens was relieved I was in Stockholm. He needed to talk to me about extending my stay in Copenhagen, he informed me.

"We like the results we're seeing, so we thought you might consider staying there another six months, possibly longer, to see this launch—and another one for the same client—to completion." He fiddled with his glasses as he relayed the information. I'd known Jens long enough to recognize this as a case of nerves.

"What else is going on, Jens?" I kept my voice casual; there was no point in pushing him too much.

"Well, let's put it this way..." Jens took a quick sip of his beer. "We're merging with the Danes, and they want half of us to move to the Copenhagen office. Marius and Johan have already said yes. So that leaves you. And the guys say they don't want to work with another copywriter."

I didn't need to think about it. "I'm in. I think Copenhagen is beginning to grow on me. Besides, I don't really have a reason to stay in Stockholm anymore."

Jens nodded and flagged down the waitress for a refill. "I heard about that through the office grapevine."

"Word does travel, doesn't it?" I laughed. "It's fine. It would have happened sooner or later. I think we'd already pretty much come to the end of the road, but we just weren't admitting it."

Jens grinned at me. "So... does that mean we can go back to our friends with benefits status? I miss hanging out with you."

"Jens, you have a girlfriend, so no, we aren't going back to the way things are. And... I met someone else already."

"Ah... you fell for one of those lug heads in Denmark, then. Happens to everyone. Must be something in the water." Jens stretched and then shrugged. "Anyway, I was just kidding. I already heard about your guy in Copenhagen from Marius and Johan. I knew it was only a matter of time before you outgrew Niklas."

"Now how could you tell that?"

"The two of you at our Christmas party last year. You didn't sit together, you barely looked at one another. And he treated you like an afterthought."

"I never knew you were so observant, Jens."

"You and I messed around long enough before he came in the picture. I think I know you pretty well. Or at least, I know the old you."

"We had fun together," I said lightly as the waitress plonked down a fresh glass of Chardonnay for me. "I think you'd like Mads, though. He's more... down to the earth than Niklas."

"Bring him to the Christmas party this year, and we'll see."

Later, I returned to my hotel, tired and wanting to soak in the bath with a good book before crawling into bed. Before I could make it to the elevators, I heard someone call my name. Niklas was standing by the reception desk. He lifted his hand in greeting. Though he was dressed impeccably, as he always did, his attire didn't impart the confidence he usually exuded. Instead, he looked uncertain. His smile wavered as I approached. Maybe he was rethinking his decision to show up. Maybe he was trying to figure out what to say. Neither of us really knew what the protocol for former lovers and greetings was. We ended up doing that awkward nod I'd always scoffed at when I saw others do it.

"I've already picked up the rest of my things from the apartment," I said and held out the keys to him. "So I should return these to you now."

"Laney, wait, couldn't we sit down and talk?"

I wasn't sure what we could say to one another but at least we would be able to end things properly. But the lobby bar felt too public and the restaurant was too crowded. "Let's go around the corner," I suggested. "There's a restaurant there called Cloud Nine."

"I know it," Niklas replied. "You and I, we ate there once."

I'd forgotten about that. But now he'd mentioned it, I remembered us going there after seeing a modern ballet performance at Dansens Hus. "All right, let's head there, then."

We walked out into the cold air and proceeded to Cloud Nine. It was a slow night, so we were able to get a table without waiting. And then it happened: we fell back into our usual routine. I annoyed him by reading the menu aloud and musing over which entree suited me best. He annoyed me by sitting in silence, not lifting his eyes from the menu, barely reacting when I asked him if he thought one dish was better than the other.

After we'd ordered, Niklas finally said, "I miss you, Laney. I know it's too late to say it, but it's true."

I drew back my hand. I didn't know what to do with his confession. "Niklas, we can't go there."

"I can't tell you I miss you?"

"No. It doesn't feel right. I'm with Mads."

"I know that, I can't help but know it. Doesn't change how I feel about you, though."

Our glasses of wine arrived, along with our escargot starter. Now that the escargot was in front of me, it felt wrong to eat it. It was too sensual, the gorgeous blend of butter and garlic and snail with toasted bread... but I ate because it distracted me from considering Niklas's words.

"If things don't work out with him, would you come back to me?"

I shook my head but there was a part of me that wanted to cling to Niklas's security. "I don't think it would work. I cheated on you. I lied to you."

"And I still love you. I'm still angry about what happened, but I still love you."

"It's no good, Niklas. Please, don't do this."

"Can I ask you something?"

I nodded. How many times had I started every uncomfortable question with those same words?

"When you went to Copenhagen, to that clinic, were you hoping you would meet someone else?"

"No, I just wanted to find a way for us to have a family. And I didn't think I could have that with you any other way."

He nodded slowly. "I should have never been so adamant about reversing the vasectomy. Now, I think I would have done it for you. I know I would have done it. I just didn't think you really wanted a baby."

I shook my head. "Don't say it now, Niklas. It's hindsight. And now it's too late."

"It being hindsight doesn't mean it's any less true."

"I don't think we should talk about this anymore."

"Is Mads here with you?"

"No, he's at home, in Copenhagen."

"Why didn't he come with you?"

"Neither of us thought it was a good idea. It felt too soon, too raw for him to come here again."

"Ah, yes. That's right, he was here that weekend."

I took another sip of my wine and tried to relax. But I couldn't help bracing myself for a confrontation. Since that night in Copenhagen, Niklas hadn't pressured me for information, for every gory detail of how and when I betrayed him, but I sensed he wanted to know. I think it was only his pride that prevented him from asking, and I didn't want to go through it again. I didn't want to relive that moment of watching him fall apart, watching our fractured life together crumble so easily.

"I have another confession for you." He bowed his head, his sharp features accentuated by the dimmed lighting. His lips twitched then he smirked and shook his head.

"I don't know if I want to hear it." I stared down into my wine glass. This was too much. I should have said no to meeting him. We didn't need to do this. It would do us no good.

"When we were in New York, I bought an engagement ring for you," he said softly. "I had this grand plan that I'd propose to you when we were in the business class lounge at Heathrow. And in my mind, I thought we could get married next summer, or sooner if you wanted. But it never felt like the right time."

That trip to New York seemed so long ago. I sipped my wine and stared at the plate of escargot. Neither of us ate very many of them, and they'd grown cold. And as I stared at those snail shells, I asked myself if I would have still cheated if I'd been engaged. A diamond ring wouldn't have killed the instant attraction I'd felt for Mads. It might have made me keep my distance for a while but, given a chance to be alone with him, I would have still strayed.

"Are you trying to have a baby with him?" he asked, bridging the awkward moment with another one.

"Not yet. It's too soon." But the irony wasn't lost on me. I'd left the man I was convinced I had to have a baby with immediately to be with the man who could give me a baby... and now I wasn't in such a rush. "But I know I want to have a baby with him. He feels... right."

"Did I ever feel right?"

"Niklas, I did love you. I still love you, too, but it's not the same. And it wouldn't be right for me to pretend I could come back if things don't work out with Mads. You wouldn't be happy, I wouldn't be happy. There'd be no trust between us."

"I forgive you. I know it doesn't change anything, but I forgive you."

The escargot disappeared. Our entrees replaced them.

"Does Mads ever worry you'll cheat on him?"

"I don't know. It's not something we talk about."

"Do you think you ever will?"

"No. I don't know. I hope not. I never thought I would cheat on you... but it happened."

"We never pictured growing old together, did we?"

I didn't say anything. I didn't want to admit that I'd never been able to imagine a future with us as pensioners, living in some cottage in southern Sweden or in an apartment in Spain like so many other Swedish pensioners.

"We just weren't meant to be one of those couples," I said softly. "I don't know if Mads and I are, either, but I want to explore the possibilities."

Niklas nodded and turned his face away from me. He was still so handsome. I noticed how women in the restaurant cast looks his way. He wouldn't be on the market too long.

After dinner, Niklas walked me back to my hotel. We embraced, and there was something comforting in being hugged by him. The vibe was distinctly platonic, just as I'd thought it would be. I didn't think we would ever find that spark again.

Niklas kissed me—it was the briefest of kisses—but it aroused nothing in me. I touched his cheek and we said our goodbyes. "By the way, my lawyer sent an email to the clinic, warning them off threatening you or me with a lawsuit. He blind-copied you as well so you can read it later."

"Thank you, Niklas."

"I'll always help you, if I can."

We embraced again, and then I watched him walk away.

This was the end of something.

* * *

I was soaking in the tub when Mads called. Hearing his voice filled me with an intense longing. I imagined him in bed naked though he was probably at his workshop finishing the final touches on the kitchen cabinets he was making.

"How did it go?" he asked cautiously. "No arguments?"

"It was good. Everything's fine." I assured him. "Niklas was fine. His lawyer is trying to get the clinic off my back."

"That's good," he agreed. "I called a lawyer, too. He says they can't force me to do anything. He says it amounts to blackmail, what they're asking."

"It is blackmail."

"So I think everything is going to be okay." He sounded so relieved. Then tension that had coiled inside him had finally released. "We don't have to worry about Ida trying to cause problems."

"What about Trine?"

"I gave her hell already. So did Adam."

"Good."

"When are you coming home?"

I liked it when he said "home." "I was going to come back on Sunday, but I think I'll change my ticket and come home tomorrow. I miss you."

"I miss you, too. Come home tomorrow and I'll do anything you want."

That sounded like the perfect offer to me.

CHAPTER THIRTEEN

Thanksgiving

A round the second week of November, I noticed two things: the winter darkness in Copenhagen sometimes weighed even heavier on me than it had in Stockholm, and my period was late. I didn't want to think about either of these situations. Scandinavian winters were notoriously dark, but we'd been lucky so far since the autumn had been mild and uncharacteristically sunny. As for the missed period, I blamed it on stress. I didn't want to consider any other possibility—not yet. It was too soon. Mads and I were still in that precious honeymoon phase every relationship has, when you're so loved-up that everything feels brighter, better, and more gloriously intense. But the more time went by, the more I realized I couldn't simply ignore it.

I'd moved out of the company apartment and into Mads's place, but it was too impractical for both of us. He hardly had any closet space, so three clothing racks from IKEA were doubling as wardrobes and clothes valets. We both knew we needed more space, but we couldn't really agree on what sort of apartment we wanted. We loved the neighborhood where he lived. It was multicultural enough for me that I felt at home and within walking distance of his workshop. And we both were a little shy of taking that next step—buying property together—when we were still so new to one another.

I almost didn't want anything to change. The newness of us, this slow process of learning how to be together and how to love one another was so exhilarating. I loved finding out his likes and dislikes. Mads was a map I was learning to read, and with each new road I found something wonderful or mystifying. Sometimes I let myself think about the baby I thought I'd wanted with Niklas and how happy and fulfilled I was now. I didn't want to jinx this moment.

We weren't ready for anything else yet.

All we needed was each other.

"*Elskede*, are you okay?" Mads touched my forehead, letting his palm rest there for a few seconds before he pressed his cheek to mine. "You feel warm."

I slid my hands into the back pockets of his jeans and held on to him. My limbs felt too heavy. I was too nauseous to think straight, but I didn't want Mads to worry. He had a commission to finish, and he'd been putting it off to spend his evenings with me.

"I'm okay," I told him, and rested against him long enough to let his arms slide around me. "I think I just need to sleep."

"You have a fever. You should drink some water." Mads stepped back and nudged me towards the bedroom. "Go back to bed. I'll take care of you."

I willingly climbed back into our bed. Mads lay down next to me and held me close.

"Close your eyes," he said in a husky whisper.

I didn't want to close my eyes. I wanted to tell him I felt like something was quickening inside me, but it seemed so silly. It had to be the flu. Everyone in my office was ill. Marius had spent the better part of the week at home. He'd probably given it to me with all his coughing. And that thought, the possibility of being ill and having Mads take care of me and make me feel better, that was enough. I finally closed my eyes and snuggled into him.

But then, one morning, I tried to go for a jog. And it ended before it had even properly began, with me throwing up in a wastebasket near Strøget. I almost fainted, but luckily another jogger, a woman who'd been following nearly the same route, came to my rescue. She helped me over to a bench and then ran to a nearby café to get a cup of water for me. I was still shivering and embarrassed that I'd puked in public. At least I'd made it to a wastebasket.

The woman patted my back as I leaned forward and she said in Danish, "This happened to me all the time

during my first trimester. You should bring some crack-
ers with you to keep your stomach settled."

"I'm not pregnant," I said in English. "It's too soon."

And I had too much to do--it was Thanksgiving, I
had to pick up the organic turkey I'd ordered from the
butcher in Torvehallerne. Mads's grandmother and Ingrid, Anton and their daughters were coming over for
dinner. I didn't have time to be sick.

"I can't be pregnant—it's Thanksgiving and I have to
make a turkey."

But she didn't pay any attention to what I'd said.
"And try not to run so fast. That will just make it happen
faster—the puking, I mean."

I tried to tell her again that I wasn't pregnant, but
saying it felt so ridiculous. I needed to find out. I could-
n't keep pretending that it wasn't a possibility. I was one
of those women with an irregular cycle. I could never
boast that my menstrual cycle was like clockwork. If it
was, it certainly wasn't one with the precision of a Swiss-
made clock; it was more like a third-rate clock that sput-
tered and stopped, then ran too fast, then stopped all
together. But one thing was certain: I needed to buy a
pregnancy test from the pharmacy, or go to a health
clinic and ask them to help me. I managed to stand without feeling like another wave of nausea would hit me.

"Are you going to be okay getting home?" she asked
me.

I nodded and thanked her for her help. As I headed back up the street, she called out to me, "It'll ease your mind if you find out now."

I took her advice.

I stopped in the next pharmacy I passed and bought a home pregnancy test.

I couldn't take the test at home; our water was off since our upstairs neighbor was having some plumbing work done, so I walked to Mads's workshop and made a beeline for the bathroom there. It was grungy and in desperate need of a good cleaning session. I never understood how men could ignore grime in their own bathrooms, but would complain about dirty public bathrooms. But right now, I didn't care how filthy the bathroom was—hell, I'd clean it later myself—but right now I needed to find out what was going on with my body. So I followed the instructions, peed on the stick and waited the requisite two minutes. Then the result came—two pink lines in the little display window.

I was pregnant.

I didn't think, I just walked through the workshop to Mads's space, still clutching the test in my hand. He was pouring himself a cup of coffee. Grayish morning light shone through the dusty window and made his reddish-blond hair glow. I said his name, and held up the test stick.

"Really?" he grinned at me, looking more like a little boy than an incredibly beautiful grown man.

I nodded. "Really."

He put down his cup and came over to me. One muscular arm looped around my shoulders while he peered down at the pink plastic stick. "I'm going to be a dad," he mused. "We're going to have a baby. This is amazing—when? How far along are you?"

"I don't know... maybe three months?" I hadn't had my period in a while. I hadn't even thought about it. I'd told myself it was stress that was making it late, but maybe I'd known all along.

We were both doing mental calculations, trying to think back to how many times we'd forgone condoms. We were careless. Neither of us ever thought about that precaution. I'd stopped taking the pill when I first went to Copenhagen Cryo.

"Are you ready?" I asked him, a little nervous he might panic. I wouldn't blame him if he was—I was already panicking. I'd wanted a baby, wanted to start, but now there was a tiny bit of fear bubbling inside of me. What if I was just as bad at parenting as Karolina had been? What if I turned into one of those awful latte mammas Eddy and I hated so much? I didn't want to be the woman in the café who barreled in with her baby sedan and behaved as though all public spaces were an extension of her living room.

But then Mads smiled at me, and the joy in his eyes and the nervous excitement rolling off him let me know we would be okay. We could do this together, and we'd

be all right. We'd be better than all right. We'd be happy, we'd be fine.

"Eddy's going to freak out when I tell her." I laughed.
"We used to joke around about how she was always first
doing everything in our family."

"My grandmother is going to be tickled pink when we
tell her."

"I don't think my dad will care," I admitted. "He's got
his other family now. We've got your grandmother,
we've got my Aunt Cecily. We don't need anyone else."

We kissed, and laughed. Then Mads suggested we go
home and let the news really sink in. I should have been
at work, he needed to finish those cabinets. But today,
neither of us cared about those responsibilities. I sent a
text to my team and told them I was sick. Mads called
the couple who were waiting for their cabinets and said
told them he had a family emergency today, but that he'd
deliver the cabinets at the weekend, and he'd even install
them for free since he was inconveniencing them. His
offer must have sounded good to them, because they
readily agreed.

Then we went home to our messy apartment. And we
celebrated with lovemaking and an open fire. I imagined
having a houseful of babies with Mads. I didn't think
about the other children out there—the ones who might
look a little like him, the little boys who might have his
wild hair, the little girls who might have those same pale
eyes that flashed from leaf green to hazel to amber. He'd
helped so many couples find their own happiness. I was-

n't going to begrudge any of them for being the first to have his child. This time it was our baby, and it would be ours to keep. We had something, someone, we were thankful for.

We'd tell everyone else soon enough.

This is just the end for now. There is more to come of Laney & Mads's story...

About The Author

Kim Golden is a native of Philadelphia, PA. She is the author of *The Melanie Chronicles*, *Linger: a short story*, *Choose Me* and *Snowbound*. She lives and works in Stockholm, Sweden. Find out more about Kim, her writing, and her latest NaNoWrimo at **kim-golden.com**. And check out what she's reading at **kimtalksbooks.com**.

If you enjoyed reading *Maybe Baby*, please drop Kim a line at kimtalksbooks@gmail.com , tell all your friends, or write a review on Goodreads, Kobo, BN.com or Amazon.

Acknowledgements

There are so many people I need to thank who helped *Maybe Baby* become a reality.

First of all, I'd like to thank my ever patient husband, who puts up with my general moodiness and my ramblings about plot, characterization and annoying hypothetical questions. You know you're my muse. You always will be.

To Kim Kane, thank you for listening to me ramble about Laney, Mads and Niklas for close to a year and never getting bored with it. And thanks for letting me read the naughty bits to you in public—do you think we shocked those Swedish ladies who were eavesdropping? You are the best writing buddy a girl could have!

To the Matera Brainstormers, I don't know what I would do without all of you. You've helped me so many times when I was stuck, when I was muddled. I am so glad to have you all in my life. It's amazing what intensive brainstorming sessions fueled by Italian coffee and long lunches with lots of wine and plenty of fabulous food can bring forth.

To Sussi Lindebjerg Malek, I am so grateful for you help with the Danish phrases. Thank you for making sure Mads didn't sound like an old-fashioned fuddy-duddy. You are a lifesaver, sweetie! Mange tak!

To the chicas of the NaNoWriMo Chick Lit group, thanks so much for cheering me on during NaNoWriMo 2012. Even when I fell behind by 15,000 words due to a bad case of the flu, you kept encouraging me to write on. Somehow, I finished a day early and the result is this novel. You are brilliant!

To Lesley, Dean, Grace & Marley at Caserma Carina, thank you for being such splendid hosts! I revised many scenes for Maybe Baby while sitting in your lovely garden and enjoying a glass or two of Verdicchio di Matelica. Looking forward to writing another book while staying at your lovely country house.

To the staff at the Hotel Kong Arthur in Copenhagen, the idea for Maybe Baby came to me while sitting in the hotel courtyard one summer evening. It was the perfect locale for the start of Laney and Mads's love affair. Thanks for making every stay so comfortable and so inspiring. And yes, you do serve the world's best gin & tonics. Tord swears by them.

To Christina Plöen, thank you so much for being such a wonderful friend, for our evening chats at Tegnérs Gömstället and now Knut, and for inviting Tord and me to Yngsjö every year. Whenever I stay there, I end up feeling so inspired—it must be the great company and that wonderful view.

 To the fantastic team at Black Firefly Production, I think it was serendipity that brought us together. There I was trying to figure out just how the heck I was going to find beta readers, a cover designer, an editor, a proof-reader and someone who could whip the formatting into shape and then Facebook made sure our paths crossed. You made the entire process so easy and the help you've given me has been absolutely amazing.

And finally, to my mom, Barbara Golden, who will prob-ably shake her head when she reads this book and wonder why her middle child writes about women doing naughty things. I know it's not really your type of book, Mom, but you were the one who kept encouraging me even when you wished I was doing something more prac-tical. Love you! :)

www.ingramcontent.com/pod-product-compliance
Lightning Source LLC
Chambersburg PA
CBHW031250170626
46807CB00001B/80